Forgetting Andrew

A Novel

Tia Finn

Printed in the United States of America
First Printing, February 2017
tiafinnauthor.com

ISBN-10: 1543035132
ISBN-13: 978-1543035131

Cover design: Jordan Finn | Phoenix, Arizona
Author Photo: Connie Stonebraker

This novel is based on the true experience of the author and has
been set within a fictional framework to protect the
identities of anyone bearing any resemblance to
the characters within.

With the exception, of course, of Andrew.

For Tess and Jor

'I am, because you are'

And for my 'Annie' who taught me

everything important about life and love

"Keep some room in your heart for the unimaginable"

Mary Oliver

1 ~ Don't Get Your Hopes Up

It's funny how the faces that stay with you forever either belong to people you love or, well, *don't* love. As age and time take their toll, so much detail slips away. So many small things forgotten. Here's the good news: Most of the things you forget really never mattered. They just seemed important right when you were smack in the middle of them. Funny. At least now it seems funny.

When I close my eyes, all these thirty odd years later, I can still see Andrew's face as clear as my own reflection in the window glass. More than that, I can see his expressions. How he looked when he was happy, or angry, frustrated- even lost. It doesn't seem right that I can't remember the other boys that way, the ones we all knew just as well. But that's how it is. I had no idea how one boy I met in the sixth grade could color all the pages of my life, but that's what happened. And I guess maybe you'd like to know why. And how.

I'm not sure I really want to tell this story, because that would mean remembering a lot of things that hurt. I'm not even sure I can do it. I've spent the last 32 years trying to forget Andrew--but it's kind of impossible. As you'll see.

I could call this chapter "New School." But then you'd get optimistic about sensible chapters and a chronological tale of my life. Somehow before I even get going here I know it's not going to work out that way. It's hard enough to let myself remember all this stuff, let alone in the order it happened. So, I'm asking for a little patience here. It's a pretty good story; you'll laugh, you'll cry, you'll want to shout at me. You *will* shout at me. What more could you ask for in a book?

Ok, so here goes.

I really didn't much care for the new school. My mother needed a dose of drama in her all too Catholic life, so when the town we lived in suddenly became too big for one Catholic school, she yanked us all out of the old comfortable place and deposited us squarely in Our Lady of Saints catholic school in the sixties was a unique and solitary institution, build firmly on myth and miracles, where all questions were met with disapproval and a ruler across your knuckles. Ask any Irish or Italian kid and without fail you can get novels full of anecdotal proof. I was no different.

Ok, that's not entirely true. There apparently always was a Buddhist locked inside me, trying desperately to get out. Out of Pittsburgh, out of my mother's sight and out of confession. My father, who converted at some point from his farmhouse Methodist childhood (I think to appease my mother's folks who wanted a big white wedding), tried hard to do the right things, as conveyed by the monsignor each Sunday morning. It's kind of telling that my two major memories of that experience were the parking lot road rage after the morning mass, and my father threatening me with no social life if I did not "get in there and tell my sins." When I once ventured a heartfelt argument that I didn't have any to tell, the poor man whispered through clenched teeth, "then make some up."

My brothers spent a good deal of their Sunday afternoons on their knees in the living room, trying hard to look penitent before it got too dark to ride their bikes. We'd moved into the new house and new neighborhood the year before, complete with beautiful suburban trails and lots of places for kids to wander and play. So here we were. A little bit about us. I was a young-for-third-grade eight-year old, with three brothers hell bent on killing each other and a kid sister who'd almost died at two, but instead became frighteningly adept at manipulating all of us.

Looking back, I see now my mother must have been terrified of her. She really couldn't win… if the kid had died, she'd have gone to hell; if she didn't baby her and bend to her every whim, the kid would make *her* life hell. But to me, she was just a spoiled rotten pain with a nasty penchant for terrorizing me.

My father had parlayed a door-to-door job selling sewing machines into a buyer's position for a major department store where he would plug away for the next 35 years, until the board had stolen enough of his and the other employees hard-earned pension to bankrupt the place. Ah, the age of non-regulation. But I digress. So, the fruit of his labor was this house. To our family, who'd shared a one-bedroom (plus basement) apartment half a block from the streetcars' whine, it was like a TV house: As nice as the one from *Father Knows Best*, but with better appliances. And a pretty street with a playground at the bottom of the hill and trees and everyone had two cars and a bunch of kids. It was everything a kid from Indiana thought he'd never have and rarely got to enjoy, since he had to work pretty much seven days a week to pay for it.

My mother.

I suppose I'd better introduce her now before we get too far into the story. Maria Theresa Capelli-Evans was the quintessential product of the 50s. Raised by first-generation Italian immigrants, she was groomed to be wife and mother and absolutely nothing else, except maybe cook. But she wasn't genetically predisposed to the lifestyle. No, Maria longed for smoky nightclubs, Lana Turner wardrobes, and a passion that in those days was reserved for the Lana's of the world. My mother said, on more than one occasion, "That Johnny Stompanato, what a guy." If you aren't as old as me, or don't know the story, Mr. Stompanato was Lana's lover, who was shot by her daughter during a mysterious domestic incident. He was gorgeous in that Hollywood leading man kind of way, but overall nothing but a glamorous thug, known only for petty crimes and his very pretty girlfriend. But my mother thought he was the bee's knees. Cat's meow. Get the picture? I didn't know it then, but I realize now that all she really wanted was any kind of escape. Since that didn't appear to be an option, she settled at first for fantasies about movie stars, then moved to more local, and available, men. Problem number one.

However, the more difficult problem was this: She hated children. Someone should have picked up on this, at least by number two. She hated the suburbs, and she hated my father. She hated her father too, because when she made the one escape attempt while pregnant with the oldest of what would be five children, he shut the door in her face after firmly telling her to go back to her husband where she belonged. I still don't know why she listened to him that time. She certainly never listened up till then. Or since.

Maria made a pact with herself (or at least one of her personalities) to make diamonds out of dust. Lemonade from lemons. Hell, she determined she would spend money as fast as my father could make it, and though she'd never stepped foot in the south, she could put on the perfect Southern belle rendition of "Well, I just didn't know that ol' bank wouldn't cash the check. I still HAD checks, didn't that mean I still had money?" You get the general theme here. It's hard to think that her husband explaining it for the thousandth time would really make a difference. In the end, my father just had two banking systems: One for her, and one for real life. Come to think of it, he had dual systems for just about anything involving my mother.

More on that later. Back to the daily rituals that went along with Our Lady and the Saints. Considering this was the age of Motown, James Brown, and the Beatles, Catholic school was just a bad idea. Every human in the world old enough to articulate was rebelling against something, and that just isn't permitted in any institution that incorporates daily scripture readings and large iconic statues of blessed things. In other words, I was destined for disaster from an early age, due to my nearly incessant use of the word *why*.

I met Andrew Cosentino on the fourth day of my first week in our fifth-grade homeroom at OLS. He kicked Bill Higgins when he stuck a pencil in my braid and basically glared him into removing it. I saw none of this, but got the detailed play by play from my best friend to be, Pally Miller. She sat behind Andrew and was one of those really pretty, but terribly shy girls who ends up taking care of the universe and waiting a long time to remember to take care of themselves. She'd gotten her nickname in grade school. Her real name was Patsy, but she was so friendly to absolutely everyone, including the kids whose name no one ever knew, that everyone called her Pally. She is still Pally all these years later, and she is still my best friend.

When I passed Andrew the next day, I mumbled a quiet "thanks" up through my protective hair shield, and he smiled. He didn't shrug it off, or walk away, or pretend he didn't hear me. He smiled and held my gaze for at least five seconds. Those moments, the ones where someone looks at you and really sees you... they stay with you, like the faces I was talking about before. And I know it sounds crazy, but I kind of loved him from that moment on.

For the next year or so, we'd say hello in hallways, and I watched him play football, or baseball, whatever the season, and he'd wave at me on the sidelines in the stands with the other cheerleaders. (In Catholic grade school, anyone who could afford the white sweater and the sew-on tiger patch was a cheerleader.) We rarely spoke, but there was something between us that didn't need words. Indefinable but strong. When the day in sixth grade came that we had an actual conversation, it happened as easily as if we'd been having those talks forever.

The thing about Andrew is that he's been dead for 32 years now, but our conversations never really stopped. For a while, it was really weird, and I didn't tell anyone because they all thought I kind of lost it when he died anyway, and, well, you just don't want to fuel that fire. But through the years, I've gotten used to him being around. And since my life has been so far from normal, it's been a big help having someone who gets the whole story. But I should probably explain this.

Ok. Where should I begin? I know, I know, I was just at the beginning and now here we are like 30 some years later, you don't know me much, you don't know him at all, and he's dead. But here's the thing. To understand all of it, you kind of have to know the ending before I tell the whole story. Trust me, you'll get what I mean soon enough.

Somehow, though he's "technically" been gone for all these years, Andrew has found a way to be there for me when I really need someone to keep me from… you name it. From losing my mind, from being so afraid I can't breathe, from sheer madness. And often, as it turns out, from ending up dead. Like him.

Let me give you an example. There was the time ex-number-two decided the suit I put on to go to a wedding was a little too sexy for his taste. So he basically beat the shit out of it—while I was wearing it.

Andrew showed up. I was curled up in the corner of my kid's bedroom in the dark, watching blood trickle down onto the suit and thinking hard about how close the color of blood is to cinnamon in just the right light, and maybe I would have said the exactly wrong thing as my ex stood there staring down at me, and I wouldn't even have been here to write all of this. But Andrew whispered all the right words in my ear. He helped me get up off the floor, washed me off, and somehow kept me sane and safe that night. He talked to me afterward and tried to get me to stop taking the blame. He knew me, he knows me, he knows all of it. And he still shows up.

If you keep reading, if all of this isn't too out of the blue for you, then in time you'll come to understand why. At least as much as I do.

Maybe you're thinking, *poor thing, she's hallucinating.* But it's not like that. He's real, when I see him. He's solid, not some ectoplasmic ghostly thing. If he sits on the couch, the cushion sinks. Get it? I feel the air change in the room and I hear his voice clear as a bell. I don't know what it is, but I don't want it to stop. I don't call him, I don't conjure him, and a lot of the time I wish he'd be quiet. But I know that won't happen. It's just how he was. I mean is. Always.

By middle school, Andrew was Drew to all of us. He was a dedicated athlete, even though at 5'9" and 160lbs. his choices were limited. I became the wrestling groupie since it was an easy excuse to get out of the house four mornings a week. I walked the three miles to the gym, paying my way with donuts, cookies, you name it. The coach didn't mind it either because his boys definitely worked harder in practice with any kind of female audience, even a quiet one. And most of the guys dated my girlfriends or hung with my brothers so they all kind of tolerated me. I wasn't the cute girl. I was awkward, not sexy, and at barely five-foot-tall I reminded them of their little sister. I wasn't a threat or much of a distraction. "Plain." That's the word they used back then. "Plain Jane Elaine."

2 ~ Back to The Future

Ok fast forward to now. Summer, 2005.

Yes, it's going to be like this. One minute you are hanging out in my high school with me, and the next--who knows? For now, it's here in my 49-year-old life in the Arizona desert. I've been here for a while now, and the only part I really like is the distance it put between me and a lot of difficult history. Oh, and I like the fact that my kids are here. At the moment, I'm struggling to get my almost ten-year old to focus on the math homework and not the video game he'd rather be playing. My other child, Rosie, the college student, has moved out and on with her life and I'm here with my boy Riley, and my friend, Andrew. The house would probably seem too big for Riley and me and a part time ghost, but Rosie is in and out since she opted for a school only twenty minutes away. I wonder if she knows how glad I am about that. I'd miss her too much if she lived in some faraway place and only came home for school holidays and summer.

The thing about Rosie is that even though she's always been the one with it all figured out, everyone sees it but her. I know in time she'll realize how good she is at life; she's like me that way. All the neon signs in the world couldn't convince her, but one day she'll see her reflection in a store window and she'll just get it. Riley, on the other hand, is convinced no one has anything figured out *but* him. He has adopted an air of resigned acceptance to the fact that without him to keep us informed and on track, well, he just doesn't know how we women would manage. So, all in all this is us, a 'normal -in the modern-day sense of the word, a family. Unless, that is, you count Andrew.

Speaking of… Andrew is here just now, in the middle of my day. In the beginning, he seemed to save his appearances for the dark times, the scary parts. But over the last nine years, I've come to realize he just likes it here, and even though there is almost zero drama anymore, he's comfortable and he wants to be around us. At the moment, he's laughing because I'm such a procrastinator, just like I always have been. I need to go to the grocery store but I hate that part of the mom job, so I put it off until we are down to brown rice and dried beans in the pantry.

And then there's this book I've been trying to write. Or lately, trying not to write. Or at least trying not to think about writing. But we'll get to that in a while. The funny thing is, I don't just do it with the hard things. The procrastinating I mean. I do it with the good things too. Reading a great book, for example. I' get almost to the end and then I hide it from myself because I just don't want the story to end. And like it was with Drew. He figured out we had something special a long time before I did. And when I did know how I felt about him, it – well – it terrified me. I was the girl who hid in my books and journals, talked to almost no one and basically floated in my own space. I barely existed in my mother's orbit, and my siblings were just a lot of noise at the dinner table. Looking back, I can't remember a single emotion before Drew, except for what I felt for my dad, and that was mostly a kind of mixed salad of fear, respect, and awe.

With Andrew, it was nothing short and-Juliet, I'm going- to -die-if-I-don't-have-him forever, knock-down, drag-out, SHUT-the-front-door love. And I had no idea what to do with all that emotion.

I'll bet you've figured out what I did. Nothing. Oh- we were friends. Best friends. We hung out, but mostly just the two of us, and definitely not when he was with the wrestling guys, or the "in crowd" that he ruled without even trying. We talked at school and on the phone almost every night. We talked about our families and our dreams, and though we didn't talk about the bad stuff, it was there, like an unspoken undercurrent that hummed along under all the other parts of life. And that's how it was with us all through junior high and into high school. Andrew's dad was one of those glamorous but mysterious guys who did something indefinable but made a ton of money. And being Italian, well, folks just made assumptions. To be honest, I'm not sure to this day what he did to make that money, but there was plenty. Later I heard that not too long after Drew died, he just walked out the front door one day and never came back. Didn't take a dollar, or a jacket even. At that point, everything he ever cared about and worked for was buried with his only son. The money just didn't matter anymore.

I guess we didn't realize back then how much he loved Andrew. He was so hard on him. It was so much pressure for a young kid, sometimes I thought he'd crack. But instead he'd crack me up. He'd smile that crooked squinty green-eyed grin, and make some stupid mafia joke, or talk about his mom's "imitation Italian" cooking till I couldn't breathe, I'd be laughing so hard. I knew even then that those conversations, that feeling of someone knowing you from the inside out, was one of the few things that made him happy. That, and winning. At wrestling, or at winning an audience, a scholarship, the top of the class spot – that kind of winning was what made him feel like a worthy person. Or at least worthwhile in the eyes of his dad. To Andrew, it felt like the only way he could earn his father's affection, which meant so much to him. So he focused, and fought, and suffered for each win. But he never really felt like any of it was ever enough. I'm guessing realizing all the missed opportunities he'd had to tell his son what a great kid he was, or how just trying made him proud – or even just that he loved him must have played a part in pushing him out that door. I'm just guessing though.

After a while in high school, we'd sort of become part of a crowd. By now we were all sixteen or seventeen. Drew and his pals were heading into their senior year, and me and most of the girls who hung around were either sophomores or juniors that fall. We spent the summer driving around in Stan Poranski's old VW van that had only one seat, and it was great. We drove down to the Point and the guys dared each other to jump off the unfinished bridge that went across the river to the unfinished football stadium. We'd been warned our whole lives that the river water was so polluted from the steel mills that a splash could give you the plague, but this had become the thing to mark the end of boyhood, so they jumped the 30 feet anyway. And somehow, except for a few bruises, and a bit of chastising from their parents later- they all survived to become part of the local legend. Rites of passage are usually that fearless and full of daring and risk, if you think about it. That's what makes them the kind of moments you mark time with. And it's those moments you remember, far past what comes later.

As a group, we sort of drifted in and out of casual romance that summer, mixing up couples till pretty much every girl had kissed every guy at least once. Including me. There wasn't much jealousy and I don't remember even one fight. At that point, we felt like life would go on forever and nothing was so fragile that we had to try too hard to hold on to, so we just flowed on in the moments enjoying each other. By the end of the summer, we'd exhausted all the possible combinations and were all just friends. If anyone was sleeping together back then, I was too naïve to notice. I had suddenly become one of the cute girls, my hair shiny and long, and my body finally figuring out I wasn't a little kid anymore. My aunt Annie had helped me get contacts, so the old coke bottle wire rim glasses were history. I felt pretty for the first time, even though Maria did her best to remind me I wasn't even close. But when I was with my small group of pals, the girls fussed and the boys stared as though I was someone they'd never seen. This attention was something so foreign to me I had no idea what to do with it. But I loved every minute.

Andrew pipes up…from his stool at the kitchen counter, which I can see from my little writing space-slash-studio that I've carved out of the family room. "You drove me crazy." I watched you going off with this one or that one, and I had to just let it happen. But you made me nuts. You never figured that out, did you?" He spits this all out in a burst of uncharacteristic frustration. I roll my eyes at him and say "Right. 'Mr. Prom King' was jealous?" But he doesn't laugh. He just looks at me in a way that I know it must be true.

Ok. Where was I going with this? Hey- I did warn you I might ramble. But that's how memory is; you are on one road full of bright sunshine and smiles and suddenly you don't know how but you are deep in the dark woods, alone and lost. I hope you can be patient, because every little bit of it will make sense, eventually. Promise. Scout's honor. Pinky swear.

Now that *that's* out of the way, I remember. The whole "putting off till I can't put it off anymore what I should be doing now" thing. What I SHOULD be doing is re-writing the outline for this book, and getting in touch with the agent who works with a lot of our authors. I should let you know that I work for a VERY big publisher, but I'm about 400,000 leagues removed from anybody who would ever look at this stuff. HOWEVER, as my friend here (you know who) keeps reminding me... I WORK FOR A PUBLISHER. (For future reference: Capital letters do not mean I'm shouting at you. Just at myself.)

I've finished outlines for two other stories, five chapters of another book, and an entire collection of poetry. But really, if I'm honest (and I do want to be honest with you), the only one that really matters is this one, this story that I am trying to get down on paper for you, and in truth, mostly for myself. However, I have a list of excuses for not finishing these things that could wallpaper Montana. Twice. Andrew is chuckling from his perch on the kitchen counter, though I don't hear him arguing the point. We both know it's true.

So, are you wondering at this point if I'm a little... well... *off*? Or if my drugs are just very, very good? I wonder too, so don't feel bad. But no. It's just that for the last 32 years, I 've sort of lived with a real, live ghost. He shows up when I'm lonely, when I'm sad, when life is too sweet to describe and when it's worse than when he died. I've been to therapists, hypnotists, mediums and psychic healers. Once I tried to tell Rosie. She just gave me that little dog- tilted head thing and said, "*okay*" really quietly and I said, "Never mind honey." But no matter what, doctors or drugs, he just doesn't go away.

And you know what? I don't really want him to.

Ok, what next… I guess I should finish up the early stuff, because the rest of it starts to get confusing unless you have that part. It was my junior year in high school, around early October. The last part of Indian summer in Pittsburgh, when the mornings have that unmistakable chill and the trees start to turn all kinds of red and orange. The smell of autumn is unmistakable, sort of damp leaves and smoke. It was my very favorite season and I couldn't stay focused on anything for wanting to be in the woods that surrounded our neighborhood, walking and breathing it all in.

My mother at this point had begun to find solutions to her boredom that were, shall we say, a little bit outside the lines drawn for married women and mothers in those days. My dad worked long hours as a department store buyer, so from November till April we rarely saw him, so much so that he'd taken an apartment in town to avoid the ridiculous commute at midnight back to the burbs, just to turn around and go back at five in the morning. If I'm honest, I think he'd also long since decided that he and Maria were just biding time till we were out of the house and one of them could file the papers.

But Maria wasn't going to let life pass her by, no sir. Consider her many forays into "career land", that fictional place for ladies of a certain age in the 1960s. She'd taken a stab at Sunday School teacher (didn't work due to the 'Martinis before Mass' ritual to which she was more faithful than any man), then practical nursing (asked to leave the program because she kept sneaking cigarettes around the oxygen tanks and face it, no one has enough insurance for that little habit), when she finally landed on the perfect path of study. For *her* needs, that is.

Beautician. In those days, hairdresser, beauty operator, whatever you felt like calling it. This job had it all for mom. A private space where she could hang out with the girls away from us kids, plenty of gossip and close to the local businessmen's lunch and happy-hour haunts, which made a stop on the way home pretty damn convenient. And being ultra glamourous was a requirement for this job. When you needed to sport the newest hairdo and makeup for your clients, well it just didn't work without the latest in cocktail attire and accessories. She felt certain that these were all bona fide business expenses. Thanks to Dad's credit cards and double-discount days at his store for employees and their families, she had access to a seemingly endless supply of all of the aforementioned essentials. It would have all worked out fine if any of those items had made her happy for more than the time it took to remove the price tags.

She went to school for about a year, taking great care to doll up her pretty little polyester smocks with a black pencil skirt, smoke stockings and stilettos, full makeup, some form of rhinestone earrings, and a pin. She looked like something from a Doris Day movie--just not Doris. More like one of the girls Doris was always trying to fight for her man. She smoked nonstop. In the morning with coffee and at the end of the day with her ubiquitous martini. But my Dad had figured out she was a lot easier to deal with when he let her have her way, so he paid the rent on a two-chair beauty shop in the next little town and let the rest go on without watching. I guess we all learned to do that with Maria. It was just easier to tell her she looked really pretty and see you later than to ask questions and risk her wrath.

See, now, in the age of Oprah, Dr. Phil and enlightenment, I understand that my mother was more than a frustrated housewife. She probably suffered from a severe hormonal imbalance at best, but most likely some form of psychosis. We're talking bipolar manic-depressive stuff. Her moods swung wildly, and not just when she was drinking. She was balanced on a terrible tightrope all the time: Dressed for cocktails by four, or locked in her dark bedroom for days with one of her "headaches." I didn't realize till college that whatever her ailment, her doctors hadn't helped with the fifties combo of Valium and Percodan, prescribed to bored housewives and accident victims alike. Maybe that makes sense after all, since so many women of her generations ended up wives and mothers by accident or pretty much a complete lack of any other options. And just like the little girl with the curl, when she was good... well, she wasn't around. But when she was bad, she was, indeed, horrid.

As the oldest girl, and a true child of the sixties who embraced everything fashionable, I struggled to find my look among bell bottoms and miniskirts. The problem is I never made it past five feet, and I inherited a couple generations of Italian curves. Too many curves to embrace the other wave of hippie design, the braless look. I did my best to pull together something nice every day, but never managed to pass the judges' table in the kitchen without some withering look. "Are you going out like that?" She'd snarl from behind her magazine and coffee, a thin swirl of smoke the only evidence there was a body connected to the disdainful voice. "Um, yeah," would be my feeble attempt at an exit line.

"I really don't think so," she'd say, in her version of amused maternal guidance. "Try again." A glance at the kitchen clock usually revealed less than five minutes to get out of the door and down the hill to the bus stop, so this meant running upstairs, putting on the navy blue wool slacks and cashmere pullover she deemed appropriately dull and sexless, stuffing the skirt into my book bag, then dashing out before she could stop me for another inspection. I wasn't the only girl to ever pull a mini up over her slacks to change on the bus, but I'm pretty sure I was the only one to do it almost every day. And then there was my hair, and the question of makeup. I wore my hair in the style of the day, which is to say, no style. Parted down the middle, and halfway down my back. But it was black coffee brown, with glints of red in the sunlight. My son Riley has my hair -- like it was back then -- thick and shiny and grows like a weed. But no matter what, all I ever got from her was, "Really? That's the best you can come up with?" or, "Jesus, you look like a witch."

Later, after Maria entered beauty school, I would long for these days. Because who better to use as a practice model than the ready-made head of hair right there in your own house! I just wish at some point in the unarguable parade of ridiculous attempts at creating the next exotic "as seen on the pages of Vogue" do, she'd also managed to pluck my uni-brow. Or teach me to use eyeliner or allowed me to wear any makeup other than Bonne Bell lip gloss. But any attempt I made to find a more grown-up version of myself just made her angry. And I had learned early on that it was simply not worth it.

I know. You're thinking this is just about the litany of every girl growing up in the sixties when styles and morals were as changeable as the weather and everything was about breaking the rules. True enough. The difference was I've only described the good parts so far. I could handle this, and my unflappable Pollyanna personality would bounce back from any negative commentary she could dish out before the screen door slammed behind me. The part that I still have trouble with I've yet to mention.

See, my brothers were all in love with her and she loved men in all shapes and sizes so they were free to come and go as they pleased. She ruled their long hair cool, their enormous bell bottom jeans groovy, and their early smoking and drinking outta-sight. Kevin, Kelly, and Evan (yes, I know, Evan Evans, I'm sure you know who thought that was funny by now) were her golden boys, and each had a talent for keeping her enthralled. Kevin, a year younger than me, was the athlete. He spent as much time as he could away from the house. Between basketball and football practice and games, and lifeguarding at the local pool during the summers, it worked out well for him. Still, she was front and center at any game that didn't get in the way of her social life, dressed to the nines and managing to alienate all the other moms.

Evan (who later changed his name to Jesse – who could blame him?) had rock and roll in his blood and took off at 14 after my dad dropped him off at school one day, determined to assure his actual arrival. Evan had a penchant for missing the bus and finding his way back home after everyone else was gone, just hanging out watching soaps or jamming with his other potential drop-out buddies. When my father figured that out, he decided to drive him every morning. The first day he did that, Evan walked right in the front door of the school, and right out the back. He waited an hour, walked home, packed a bag, grabbed his guitar and disappeared for the next eight months. He didn't leave a note, but did abandon a half-smoked joint on the edge of the bathroom sink as a farewell.

Kelly was the one who had my heart. No obvious talents except a great sense of fashion, an unending supply of charm and wit, and the ability to lose every job he ever got within a week. Oh, and he could make a death row inmate on his way to the chair laugh. He would instigate, provoke, and tease without prejudice. Mom, me, the quarterback, his brothers, the nuns, the pastor, the local police. I asked him once how he managed not to get the crap beat out of him, and he looked at me with dead gravity and said, "Easy. Right before they hit me I make them laugh." He turned 46 this year and it's still working for him.

By the time Lana came along, Maria had decided how mothering was going to work for her. And by then one thing was certain: She was no June Cleaver, Donna Reed or Harriet Nelson. Let's just say if we'd all seen "Mommy Dearest" back then, we'd have known exactly which role Maria had chosen as hers.

The boys and Lana don't understand why mom and I aren't close. Or to be honest, why I find it difficult to be in a room with her beyond twenty minutes. And despite having plenty of reasons that I could have given it was too hard for me to explain to them. Maybe that's part of what this book is really about. As the oldest, it was fairly easy for her to target me if things weren't going her way. Whenever she ran out of the drug of choice for the day, Maria became quite another person. To be fair, being stuck in a one-bedroom-plus-basement, pre-war apartment with four small children and one on the way would test the best of characters. It was also abundantly clear that Maria had not figured out how to stop having babies, a fact that made her even angrier. To be fair, birth control in those days wasn't exactly easy to find or figure out.

I get the incredible frustration she must have felt, the overwhelming and unending tiredness of it all. But we had neighbors and friends on the block, all in the same boat; she had lots of options for help. My dad had hired at least three different babysitters to help out, but Maria abused them without exception so they never stuck around for long. After a while, she decided that she'd just pocket the money he gave her for sitters. Her reasoning? I was by then almost seven, certainly old enough to help out.

And I wanted to, believe me. Anything I thought would get a smile or even a nod of approval out of my mother, I would do willingly. But as you can imagine, leaving a seven-year old in charge of three smaller brothers didn't usually go so well.

The first time I recall, I was home from school with a cold. Evan was five and sick with a worse version of the same cold. Kevin was six and at the neighbors', and Kelly was still in diapers. Maria was pregnant again, this time with a girl she would call – can you guess? Yes. Lana. And not at all pleased. No one told women not to drink during pregnancy back then and she basically thought it was the only way to get through nine months of hell. She stuck to fancy liquors, like crème de menthe, Kahlua, and brandy she could slip into her coffee. I guess she'd run out of all the above and she emerged from her room with Kelly. Evan was stretched out on the living room floor watching TV and I was sitting at the kitchen table coloring. I remember staring at her for way too long because I'd never seen my mother with so much as a hair out of place and she was, at this moment, a mess. Her shoulder length black hair, normally worn in an impeccable French twist or curled and shellacked into a flip, was wild and dirty. She was wearing a cashmere twin-set she was two months too pregnant for, and a skirt that fit because the zipper was only halfway done up. She had bare legs and penny loafers and she grabbed one of my dad's topcoats and the car keys and her purse all in one swoop.

"Watch your brothers," she mumbled as she headed for the door. "Mommy," I started to say before she turned and lunged at me. I'll never forget her eyes. They were huge, bloodshot and wild. Her teeth were clenched and she held me by the shoulders really hard. She shook me over and over and kept repeating, "I never asked for any of this. I can't do this and I don't want to be here. Just watch your brothers and keep your stupid little mouth shut, ok? And Do. Not. Tell. Your Father."

The phone rang a lot that afternoon, but I was afraid it would be my father, and I would not be able to lie to him, so I didn't answer it. Maria had called our neighbor Mitzi before she left to ask if she could keep Kevin for the afternoon and said she was running out to get some groceries. I don't know how long she was gone. But to a scared seven year- old it felt like forever. It was almost dark and I'd tried to feed the baby but he had finally cried himself to sleep. I gave Evan cookies and a banana which he had pretty much occupied himself with by squeezing it over and over again   till there was banana everywhere. The day had turned into evening and the radiator hadn't kicked in and I didn't know how to turn it on, so on top of everything else it was getting cold. I found blankets for all of us and turned on all the lights because I thought that might help. I pretended I was a mommy the best I could and tried really hard not to be scared of being alone in the house. If I have known what was coming I would have saved up all my bravery for later.

Around seven, she turned up. She called Mitzi and said she had fallen asleep with a terrible headache and just woken up, and asked if she could send me next door to pick up Kelly in a bit. It was clear she'd found a fix somewhere, and by the look of her smudged lipstick, I guessed she didn't find it alone. She smelled of alcohol and cigarettes and perfume that reminded me of my dad's aftershave. She was slurry and sleepy and not at all pleased that the baby started to cry when she walked in the door. Still wearing her coat, she warmed a bottle for him, which she handed to me. "Here, that ought to shut him up." Evan started to cry as well, probably because he hadn't eaten much all day and he was sick as well. The chorus of sobbing children combined with a dark cold house suddenly became overwhelming. She looked at me like everything wrong in her life was all my fault and didn't take a breath before she hit me. Clean in the face. I was so shocked I didn't make a sound.

"Can't you do ANYTHING?" she snarled as she turned and went to pick up the baby who was crying again. I don't remember the rest of that day, or night or whatever time it was. I just knew, in some unfathomable moment of wisdom and understanding, that my childhood was over. And that I was living with someone who saw me as the enemy. And always would.

Andrew is here, of course, he always shows up when I'm trying to avoid the emotions this type of memory calls up. "You know, it wasn't really about you, E," he says from somewhere behind me.

I turn to see him watching Namaste Yoga on the TV with no sound and trying to assume the pose. I laugh despite myself and he says, "Hey, I'm a wrestler, remember? This stuff is cake,", slightly insulted at the look on my face.

"I know," I say, feigning an imitation of my teenage awe, "almost state champion." That gets him and he drops to the floor laughing, and holding out his hand, motioning me to come closer. Caught in the moment I start to cross the room to where he sits on the rug when Riley's voice breaks the silence.

"MOM, can Anthony and Michael and Daniel and Shadow and Kyle and Jeremy come over and swim right now please can they please it's really hot and the pool is actually clean" (I wince as I realize this is true for once this summer) "and please we'll be really good please can we can we can we…"

I turn to share the moment with Andrew but of course he's not there. Riley mistakes the look of disappointment on my face and his smile drops.

"Ok, never mind," he says, before I grab him by the shoulders and tilt his head up for a quick kiss. "Sure honey, I was just thinking about something else and that's why I was frowning," I say, as I squeeze this boy who has all of his father's wonderful qualities and not one of the bad ones. "Go make sure their moms know and make them bring their own towels. Oh, and don't leave the towels or t-shirts on the ground this time. The dogs will chew them all up again and I'll have to take a second mortgage to replace them."

My son heads out the door and I stand staring at the space he leaves Behind whenever he goes. I just can't explain what that boy means to me. I savor the air still full of his smile and decide I've written enough for now. It's another day like the day I started to describe, a kind of Indian summer day almost unheard of for August in Arizona, and I want to take a walk. We'll pick this up later and I'll tell you more. I promise.

Ok, what I meant to be a few hours' break, turned into a few days away from writing. My sister had another crisis and needed some money, Maria is here for an extended visit with Lana, and I'm not sure who is driving whom more crazy… but because my mother seems to feed off anyone else's drama, she decided she was maybe going to have another stroke right now and we had to do another round of emergency rooms and pharmacies. Oh, and Riley decided to change his name. Just life, as usual. For now, I'm back at the computer and trying to remember the important things I want to tell you. I guess I have to take you back to high school again. June 1971. Eleventh grade had been good for me. Drew went to the State wrestling championships and came in second, which he is still explaining to me to this day.   "I had a really bad cold," I hear from the other room, where my very old friend has taken up residence for the morning, determined to "supervise" my writing efforts.

He's trying to figure out how to work the new DVD player we just bought. If he does, I've told him he can watch whatever he wants, because no one else here has figured it out. "I know," I respond respectfully. "Otherwise we would have to refer to you in all things as Pennsylvania State Champ, Lightweight division of 1971." "That's correct," I hear him say, happy that I've acknowledged this obvious fact. This is followed by mumbling I have come to recognize as the normal response of any male who is in the process of assembling or operating electronic equipment. I decide he will be busy for a while, so I turn back to my screen.

Junior year, aside from a few ill-fated prom decisions, which I
will describe in detail later, had been filled with picnics, parties, football games,
and lots of friends. I had a life, or at least the beginnings of one. Maria was
occupied with extracurricular activities, and almost never home. That left me
free to plan my summer and I couldn't wait.

But summer had barely begun when there was a falling out in our small
crowd of friends. We were all just getting to the age when gossiping about
stuff was almost more fun than doing stuff, but suddenly there was a rumor
going around that quickly got out of hand. Drew had been away at wrestling
camp for a couple weeks, and when he got home one of the guys told him
that he heard I'd said some pretty mean stuff about his best friend's
girlfriend. In actual fact, I'd only met the girl once and it's true, I didn't like her
one bit. She was one of those girls we all knew in high school; one look at her
and you just knew someone was going to get hurt. Funny, I can't remember
her name, but I can see her long reddish auburn hair and green eyes clear
as day. Her look and her name both seemed exotic for Pittsburgh at the
time… Monique or Daria, something like that.

Anyway, our friend Cal was head over heels for the beauty, and
oblivious to her manipulations. Apparently her real target was Andrew, and
her plan was to first to get me out of the picture (apparently, the girl was
smarter than me, seeing as I didn't even know I was IN the picture back

then), then to get Cal gone, and then to zero in on the object of her affections. It almost worked.

She went crying to Cal, saying I'd talked a mess of nonsense to all the other girls when we had all gone for an end of the year party at the skating rink, and she'd overheard in the lady's room. Cal stopped me in the hall the next day at school and pretty much told me to shut up and stay away. Cal and I had been friends since third grade and had commiserated plenty over the years. He was one of those people who would never hurt anyone intentionally, and it hurt to have him think I would be that kind of girl.

But what was worse was that everyone believed her story (delivered with just the right amount of bewildered tears and drama) and in a matter of days, I had slowly drifted into my old isolation. I'd never learned how to fight back and I really didn't know how to deal with such an awful lie. Then school ended, and my lonely exile began in earnest. I got through the days in my usual silence, filling the time with chores, books and writing, but I was bewildered and hurt. Drew came back from camp and the call I expected never came. I had no idea what to do, no inkling how to fix things. I remember thinking that I hadn't really understood how lonely my house was till then. The ache was so violent I can still remember the feeling of crying inside myself.

To make it worse, mother Maria was right in the middle of what would turn out to be the "worst" years. It's all relative. I mean, when you are six and your mother starts slapping you around like you are a grown man, that's bad. But when you are sixteen, and she adds the verbal self-esteem bashing ingredient (because she never figured out how to hit me without leaving a bruise), and she threatens every freedom you have - the fear factor just goes off the charts.

My father Francis was living downtown at this point pretty much all the time (we would later discover that he and his future wife Deborah had already begun a relationship), my brothers were never home, and Lana was the devil. By early August I'd pretty much given up hope and stopped going out at all. Instead I stayed in my room and slowly curled back into myself. I wrote. I slept, and cried. But alone, in that room, I was able to remember who I was, even if I'd never been that lonely before. And I wasn't someone who would do what that girl said I did.

Everyone but Pally just turned away from me. Pal worked on them, because she knew it wasn't at all true, but it was no use. Andrew was sort of the unofficial (unknown to him) leader and the rest of the crowd followed his lead. And this girl had laid it on thick, adding just enough invented detail to inspire doubt. Drew just couldn't understand why I'd do something that would hurt Cal, or anyone. But since neither of us were fond of or much experienced at confrontation, the rest of the summer sort of melted away in silence. I just withdrew deeper inside myself and I'm not sure what would have happened if the Monique-Daria girl hadn't screwed up.

Yes, she was determined and clever, but like all manipulative creatures, she had a fatal flaw: She was impatient. She tried flirting with Cal's buddies, but he was in deep and he ignored it. She was petulant and demanding and he bent over backwards to make her happy. Finally, she turned mean and told him she had met someone else. And then far too quickly, she made a move for Drew.

She more or less played her ace, and he saw right through her. Drew went right to Cal, and then rounded up the rest of the group and got the answers no one else had taken the time to figure out. That's when he showed up at my door.

6 ~ Falling

I remember the day so clearly, it's like a movie I can play in my head anytime I want to. It was a Friday, late afternoon. The sun was warm against my back, counterpoint to the cool breeze from the open window in front of me. I was standing at the kitchen sink washing up the leftover dishes, enjoying the quiet. My mother was already out for the evening, dad was at work, and the rest of the kids were off on their own. Such a rare thing, to be alone in that house.

The front door was open with just the screen door letting in the scent of an early autumn. He walked in quietly when he saw me straight ahead of him, the path from the hallway directly to the kitchen sink lit by the afternoon light. The sound of the water running masked his soft steps. He slipped his arms around my waist gently and pressed his face into my hair, and I nearly fainted. Funny how he didn't startle me at all. I had just missed him so deeply, that the relief that flooded over me was overwhelming.

He whispered, "I'm so sorry, E." I don't remember how long we stood there, but I know I was crying for a long time. I couldn't put into words how much I'd been hurt, but he knew somehow that I'd barely survived the last month. He couldn't stop telling me how sorry he was, how wrong he had been, how much he'd missed me. He kept asking for forgiveness until I turned around and looked him straight in the eye. Then he kissed me for the first time in a way I can't describe, and in that moment, everything changed for me. For us. For always. That night I wrote the words *Elaine Cosentino* in the back of my journal over and over and over till I couldn't smile anymore, and fell peacefully asleep for the first time in weeks.

Even though that was hardly the beginning of us, it was a new start. That whole year we spent lots of time together with the group and talked every night for hours on the phone. Sometimes I'd almost be asleep when a shower of small stones would tap against my window and he'd be there, outside under the maple. I'd check the hallway for signs of life before sneaking out the back door. We'd sit on the porch and whisper about everything and nothing and just lean on each other. But we never really took "us" public. No one would have said, "He's her boyfriend." I was never thought of as "Drew's girl."

Still, we went everywhere as a couple. There was a kind of connection that kept us together and at a safe distance at the same time. I can't explain it. "THE CATHOLIC CHURCH AND OUR PARENTS," pipes Drew from the corner. "Stop reading over my shoulder," I say, without looking back. "Don't have to, I can read your mind," he laughs.

Anyway, the whole sex thing hadn't really happened for me yet, and we have the rest of this story (pages and pages) to tell that part of it. About midway through the spring, I started to get excited, because Prom was just around the corner, and finally being a Junior, my dad had said I could go. IF someone asked me, that is. I never thought it would be anyone but Drew… but we ended up in some silly argument and though I waited and waited, he didn't ask. Funny, I can't remember a single thing about that fight. Isn't it always that way?

In a burst of totally uncharacteristic confidence and "I'll show HIM," I asked a sophomore friend to take me. To complicate things, this guy Rick, had just broken up with one of my best girlfriends and I naively believed her when she'd sworn she was glad to be rid of him. I saw him as the "make Drew jealous" guy, and she saw me as the girl who couldn't wait to step in and make Rick forget her. Everyone around me except Rick was more than a little upset with me. Have I mentioned that sometimes I could be more than a little bit clueless?

"Do you remember what happened next?" I ask our friend. He's got that look on his face again, where I've caught him unguarded and exposed. He just stares at me and shakes his head.

"We wasted so much time," he says. "I wish…" And then he's gone. I'm left there at my desk, in a room that's gone past twilight to the dark, and I'm alone and I don't want to talk about this anymore. I close the laptop lid and my eyes, and suddenly I'm so very tired.

I head back to my room, light a couple candles and run myself a bath. It's coming on to fall and there is an early chill in the air. Or maybe it's just my old bones. My head is swimming with all this remembering, and I need to distract myself with the business of right now. The need to and the have to and the should do. Funny how we can fill ourselves up with all the busy work of life that is so meaningless in the long run.

But the truth is, I love to clean my house. Do the laundry, really anything that makes me lose myself in the task. My best friend tells me all the time would find a reason to clean up heaven rather than just sit and be still. I laugh and agree, but what I can't tell him is that it's so hard to be still when there are all these memories waiting for the quiet, when they will jump out and all over me. It's not the clean I'm so much after, as the noise and distraction from what is inside my head. The truth is, the smell of bleach can pretty much clear out any other thought you might want to have, and that's one thing they don't put on the label.

7~ Reinvention

I turn off the tub before it overflows, and take a moment to check on the now-sleeping Riley, aka "Jack" these days. Yes, after his hero of the moment – and yes, I'll explain in a bit. I pick up the blanket that has slid onto the floor and try to tuck it back around this ever-growing boy. When I realized that all the things that didn't feel right at his school weren't about him, but about that school, I decided to try to find a better fit. Somewhere where the teachers would appreciate a kid who always had music playing in his head and pictures dancing across his brain. I found the perfect place in the little main street area of our town. Full of kids just like Riley. As we filled out the annual registration forms, he stood and watched me for a few minutes. It was obvious there was something on his mind, but he was struggling to find the words. Finally, I put down my pen. "Riley, what is it?"

"I uh, um, I uh…" He tried to get it out but it wasn't working. So instead, he shouted, "I want to change my name!" Then he stopped, as if he had no idea how the words had actually escaped his mouth. "Ah. Ok, well," I stalled. "Do you, um, not LIKE your name?"

He looked at me with surprise. "Oh, no that's not it. I'm doing the inventing thing," he followed up (clearly expecting me to understand).

"Oh. Well. Ok…" I said. But it was clear from the look on my face that I really had no idea at all. He came over and sat on the arm of the chair beside me to explain. "Remember this summer when you were talking to the lady from your work who got the new job? YOU said when you go to a new place and nobody knows you and you can be anybody you want and nobody knows you so you can be a NEW kid and nobody will say you are doing stuff wrong just because you are that other kid who kind of got in trouble all the time. THAT invention thing?"

I will admit that for a minute time sort of stood still and I felt that deep kind of mom guilt that I had missed it. That whole time I struggled with him through fourth grade's seventh layer of hell, all the while cursing new math and the silly rules we impose on kids trying to learn, I failed to understand that he was right there too. In hell, I mean. And I never once acknowledged that. For that year, I was essentially the devil, or at least her assistant. And all that time I spent helping one of my colleagues figure out how to manage her life, my own son was so desperate to be in a different place in his world that he was grabbing on to every word he heard. Oh, the things we miss when we are so wrapped up in what we think we need to do.

So, we discussed the fact that yes, you can change your name and reinvent yourself when it's something you've really thought about. But since your life might present many opportunities over the years to change, and grow, and yes, even reinvent yourself, you wouldn't be able to change your name more than – well – probably once. He agreed to this and told me he had picked the name. We locked eyes. I nodded and wrote the new name on the forms.

And here we are, with the newly reinvented Riley. Now known to all and sundry as Jack. Which kills me, because I had no idea where that came from until the other day, when he patiently explained to his pal AJ that it was after Jack Black from the MOVIE, that one they watched over and over again all summer ("School of Rock").

At any given time, you'll hear us shout for Jack, Riley, and even the occasional "Sparky." For that one, I blame our friend Zodie, and she is happy to take credit for the moniker she leveled on the two-year-old, sparkplug version of this boy. Of course, it didn't help that she'd found the only way to settle him down was by agreeing to an endless viewing session of "Tarzan" (that girl has the patience of a saint). But then again, my son has been in love with Princess Zodie from the day they met. I guess we all have a little patience for anyone who thinks we are a goddess. At least that makes sense to me.

It's weird, but Riley has always reminded me of Andrew (NO, do the math, there is a more than 30-year gap here, and there's no trick to this part of the story). I see it in his build, his coloring, and his endless mischief. It's the tilt of his grin and the sweetness of his eyes. This is a child I almost didn't have and wouldn't trade the world for, even though you will wonder how he ever came to be as you read on. Still, it's eerie how he can use an expression in such a way, or wrinkle up his face when he doesn't like something, and I almost do a double take. For now, I stop staring at his sleeping smiley face in the light from the TV cartoons, and turn back to my bath, flipping off the show as I go.

I catch a glimpse of myself in the mirror as I turn to slide into the tub. I've gone a bit blonde over the last year just for fun, and ok, to cover up the hint of gray that threatens now and then. Sometimes it still takes me a minute to recognize myself. My olive skin has turned a few shades darker from the summer sun, and the time in the gym this last year has paid off. I may feel 70 some days, but it still surprises me that I'm about to hit 49. I laugh that I even think this and sink into the near-scalding water.

You know how that feels? The water so hot it takes your whole consciousness away for a second, and then sends a rush to your brain that lasts for another few minutes. How for those few minutes you forget everything – the good, the bad, the ugly, the beautiful. It's that Zen nothingness the Buddhists are forever touting. And for those brief minutes, you understand why.

I'm in that blissful fog when the cell phone rings and snap damn I'm back in the mom business.

"Hey Rosie", I say while smiling into the phone. "Mom."

"Yep, that's me."

"No. Mom."

"What?"

"I'm so stressed." (Uh-huh, I recognize this voice.) "What's up?"

"Mom. JESUS. Just listen."

"Uh-huh. Listening."

"OK. So me and Elle are like going to the 'Shut Up' concert tomorrow and Tara wants to go too but every time we take her she finds some guy and leaves us and then I worry about her all night and how she is going to get home and I don't want to say no and be mean but like SERIOUSLY she needs to get a life or another friend and I don't know what to do, what should I do?"

I struggle for the right response, trying desperately to remain in my blissful Zen zone. But what I come up with isn't rocket science. "Well, tell her you can't take her because you definitely don't want to be responsible for her and you're sorry, but she should find a different ride." I can feel, if not hear, my child's disdain for this offering.

"Great. Then she'll hate me and tell everyone I'm a bitch. No, thanks. You

don't understand. You don't get it at all. JESUS. Mom. SERIOUSLY."

Uh huh. I say this to myself. I am not silly.

"I'm hanging up".

Uh huh. (Again, to myself.)

Click.

"Yes dear, I love you too." I say this last part aloud, to my bubbles. I need more

hot water. And maybe some wine.

Turns out I fell asleep pretty easily last night. Probably the combination of just plain tired and one tiny glass of wine, but no dreams, no nightmares, no crying and lots of the sleeping. I do love the sleeping part, but when I crash like this it usually goes on for a while- and so around 7:00 this morning, Andrew sat on the end of the bed and basically stared at me till I woke up. Or at least I'm guessing he did, because I WAS sleeping so who really knows.

It was lucky, though, since I had to get the other boy who lives in my house (you know, the real one?) ready for school. Anyway, I lift one eyelid and there he is and he's wearing a tux.

"Huh?" I yawn and stretch at once. "Got a hot date Romeo?"

"UH-HUH," he says. "Remember?"

I give him a look while I unfold myself from the warm cocoon I've made in my bed and pull on a robe, and head to turn on the coffeepot. I suddenly realize what he is talking about, but when I turn to look at him, nothing. He's gone. But I get it. I sigh, make Riley some breakfast which he eats in front of SpongeBob and Patrick and the gang, while I pack his lunch and get him ready for the ride to school. All through the drive I am thinking how quickly these little-boy days are passing, and know I have to be here for these moments. All of them. *Not* in my head tripping over memories I want to forget. So I focus, and we chat about the day ahead and what he thinks about the new teacher he's just met and I kind of float along in the moment, just loving this kid. Here and now.

Back at home I grab another coffee to shake off the fog, and settle in with the laptop to remember where I left off. Oh yeah. Right. The tuxedo was Andrew's not so subtle reminder.

Ok, so flash WAY back to the prom. May, 1971. High waisted jeans, halter tops, platform shoes. Disco. You with me? Back then there was only one prom in our small town, for both juniors and seniors. Andrew was a senior, so this was a big deal to him, the last hurrah and all before graduation. He'd won a wrestling scholarship to Pitt, where he'd get a chance to study architecture at one of the best programs – and not on his father's dime. He had his freedom in a bigger way than he'd hoped for and everything was falling into place. But I had really thrown a wrench into the dream boy's dream date fantasy when I'd hastily invited Ricky after Andrew and I had our little spat.

In his usual fashion, Drew figured he wouldn't get mad, he'd get even. He did just that by asking some girl, I can't even remember who except I do recall thinking "WHAT?" right before I had the moment where I realized I'd put myself in a corner this time. I figured we'd just get through it, make up, and look back someday and laugh about it. Actually, I acted like I didn't care at all, which of course made him kind of crazy.

But then he comes up with what I can only refer to as a SINISTER plan. I'd forgotten that Drew was pretty much Rick's high school hero; they were both on the wrestling team and Rick thought Drew walked on water. When Drew suggested we double date for the prom, Ricky thought he'd died and gone straight to hero heaven.

No one asked me if I thought it was a good idea. The karmic irony does not stop there. Ah no, I'd made sure I'd set myself up for some pretty good paybacks by what I'd done so thoughtlessly and over nothing. I wasn't really surprised when the iodine and baby oil tan I tried for turned into a raging sunburn that peeled the day before the prom. Maria was stuck at home with a sprained ankle, which had resulted in a burst of maternal enthusiasm. While downing her usual Friday night round of gin and vermouth, she set my hair in a thousand tiny pin curls, assuring me I'd have the glorious mane of curls a la Marisa Berenson, the 70s lion-haired icon of teenage girls everywhere.

What I got instead was a frizzed and wiry mess, so out of control we had to slick it back into a barrette and Aqua Net it out of its misery. Plus, the goo she'd put on my hair caused my eyes to tear up so badly, I had to wear my giant round wire-rimmed coke-bottle-thick glasses instead of my contacts. My brother Kelly made some remark about the small animal trapped on my head as I ran down the hall to try to disguise the leprosy peeling from my face. He caught my backward glare and hid in his room for the rest of the pre-prom drama. Smart kid, that one. But the worst part of all, was the dress. Now to get the entire meaning here, you need a little history. "Oh, that dress," Andrew says, from his perch on the kitchen counter. "Yeah, that was, uh, well um… "

"Go ahead," I say. "I looked like a birthday present."

"Yeah! That's it," he says.

But one look at my expression and he smiles apologetically, makes the "zipping my lips" face, and heads back to wherever it is he goes when he's not here helping me remember.

Ok, here's the history. My dad, Michael Francis Evans (known to most of those who loved him as Francis), although a fairly successful corporate business man for his day, had grown up the child of poor soybean farmers in Indiana. He'd seen the Depression and watched his family struggle. He never really moved past the thriftiness that had allowed them to survive, even though he now had enough money to buy back that farm ten times over. He believed strongly in a frugal lifestyle, and while not cheap exactly, he was far from generous. So, when my mother asked if we could go shopping for a prom dress, he suggested we try to borrow one. Since it didn't involve HER wardrobe, and would in fact leave more room on the charge card for her next cocktail ensemble, she chose this opportunity to be an agreeable wife and concurred this was a brilliant solution!

If you could see me, even now, you'd understand the issue with this plan. I barely clear five feet. Back then I weighed around 87 pounds soaking wet and they didn't really make a ton of options in the size zero range in those days. But my mom, being the resourceful person she could be when she set her mind to it, found the one girl in the county who was as tiny as me, had gone to a prom, and hadn't given away the dress. And what a dress it was: A Catholic dream of a long white matte satin column, with a high cowl neck, and sleeves that came midway down my arms. Under the empire waist, a three-inch satin sash of lemon yellow wrapped obi style and came to a sort of bow in the back. I looked vaguely like one of the church candles with the yellow ribbons tied in the middle. Whatever the word for beyond hatred is, that how I felt about the dress. My mother thought that the white patent petite heels she bought (without me, so they were about a half-size too big) were perfection, and it was those or my tennis shoes, so I wore them. But the elbow length white gloves I refused. Ok, I wore them till we got in the car, but seriously. WHAT WAS she thinking?

Do you have the total picture now? The peeling lobster-like skin? The round, coke-bottle, wire-rim glasses, framed by dark-brown frizz? The candle dress? OH yes, VERY pretty. I wanted to come down with the plague and be confined to quarantine until it was all over. Or die. It was that bad.

And you know what? The rest of the night just about made that wish come true.

I stop my little stroll down memory lane because it's time to pick up Riley from his school to take him to band practice at the local high school, then take care of some mom errands before I return to write more of this down so you can enjoy the debacle that was to come. We aren't in the car ten minutes when I catch Andrew's reflection in my rearview mirror. I hate it when he does that. I obviously can't talk to him, but let's face it, even a person who's not real who just appears in your back seat is a… well… a distraction. To make it worse, he's smiling that 'I know what you're thinking' smile. And he usually does.

I ignore him and drop Riley at practice with the giant bass he has insisted is his "instrument of choice." It barely fits in the car and is almost as big as him, but I'll give the boy credit, he's devoted. He lugs the thing across the parking lot and I smile to myself. He's such an individual, this kid. Fearless, determined, sweet-natured and funny as all get out. His imagination goes in twenty-seven directions at once, and the questions never end. Like the time he decided that I really should teach him Italian. Since, you know, he is Italian, and I'm Italian, and well, he just really thought he should understand the language. He was about seven at the time. We were watching SpongeBob when a commercial for "la Vita è Bella" came on, which instigated his questions and the whole discussion. Naturally, I agreed to a short, introductory lesson.

So we'd sit and watch Patrick and Squidward and their antics, and during the commercials I'd give him a word or phrase, and he'd patiently repeat it. It went something like this…

"Ok Riley, let's try *hello*. Say *ciao*."

"CHOOWWW."

"Good. Now, *faccia bella.*"

"FACHA BELLLLA."

"Excellent. That means, 'beautiful face', like mommy.'"

"HA HA HA HA HA."

"This is easy," he says, clearly unimpressed by my vocabulary lesson.

"Fine. Try this one," I offer, upping the ante.

"Buongiorno, Principessa."

"Huh?"

"You heard me… sound it out. Bon – Jor- no – Prin- Chi- Pessa."

He's listening, but even after I repeat it one more time, even more slowly, he turns and looks at me with complete confusion and says, very clearly,

"VIRGINIA, TAKE YOUR PANTS OFF?" before we both collapse with laughter.

End of lesson. God I love this kid.

So, like my friend Zodie always says… why on EARTH would I expect to have children any less, shall we say, INTERESTING, then myself? Indeed. I am blessed with two completely unique and challenging children. But they keep me on my toes. That's important, right? Especially for a woman who has regular conversations with a dead guy.

I drive home, alone it seems as I glance in my rearview to check. I make the stops at the drugstore and the market and consider a trip to the nursery for some new tomato plants, when I remember my promise to finish the prom story. So, I head home, pick up the mail on the way in to the house and grab a bagel before I start. I'm staring out the kitchen window watching the dogs chase the birds when I hear him.

"Where were we?" he chirps. I pretend not to hear.

"Ahem." Let's just say he's persistent. "Oh, you're back," I say, feigning surprise and turning to grin at him. Andrew is sitting at my kitchen counter spinning one of those annoying fast food toys that only work for the first five minutes and the rest of your life you spend explaining why to your child.

"Cool," he says. "I don't remember these."

"Well DUH," I respond. Drew looks up and me and smiles that famous crooked smile. "   "Yeah, right. Huh? Who is this guy again?"

"SpongeBob," I tell him. "Lives in a pineapple under the sea."

"Huh?"

"Never mind." We can spend hours on this. The funny part is that sometimes the only time I feel like I really know what I'm talking about is when I'm

explaining it to Andrew.

And there's a lot that's happened in 32 years to explain. Just think about it. VCRs. MTV. DVDs. And CD's for that matter. Blockbuster... the ENTIRE concept of Blockbuster. THE INTERNET. Right, you get the idea of the scope of our conversations. We never run out of things to talk about. But then, we never did.

Back to the prom: Let's just say it was one of those nights you never forget, but for all the wrong reasons. Despite my peeling, itchy skin and disastrous hairdo, my date was enthralled. Go figure, but he wouldn't keep his hands off me. This, for some very annoying reason, delighted Andrew, who took every opportunity to encourage Ricky as well as to nuzzle up to his own date -- all purely for my benefit. I was miserable.

To make matters worse, when the prom ended, Drew had the bright idea for all of us to go to the local pancake house and have breakfast. I wanted nothing more than to go home and crawl under the blankets and pretend the whole evening was a bad dream, but since we had come in Drew's car, that was out of the question. Rick, of course, was thrilled. More time with me, more time with his idol... he was king of the hill.   That's when I had the bright idea. Can you guess? Oh come on, haven't you ever been to a prom? I knew all I had to do was ask one of the football players in the room and a flask would be produced. So, I decided I might as well numb my pain, proceeded to drink all the vodka and orange juice the team could provide.

"Oh right, I'd forgotten that part," Andrew pipes up.

Really? Which part? Me trying to sing in Spanish while the waitress attempted to take our order? Me trying to fling pancakes across the restaurant in hopes of hitting your date? Or just the ME that YOU and RICK decided to LEAVE ON THE BENCH ON MY FRONT PORCH after you rang the bell and ran so my mother didn't KILL YOUR SORRY ASSES???? WHICH PART ANDREW? WHICH part?

He has the good sense to stay, but it's a struggle for him not to laugh. He's trying so hard to look remorseful, but he's failing miserably. I look at him a long minute trying to stay mad, and it's useless. We smile and I shake my head and close my eyes for a minute remembering again, but when I open them, I'm alone. When you think about it, it's like that with most folks and their memories. They're alone with them most of the time.

I'm really nothing special.

Rosie is yelling at me from the hall, "Mom, do you have any waterproof mascara?" "Why?" I yell back.

"MOM, do you?" I'm realizing more and more no matter how I ask a question,
I rarely get the answers with this child. Just more questions. Since Rosie moved out of the house, I see her only when there is a crisis, an occasion, or she is out of something critical AND money at the same time. I'm so proud of her metamorphosis into this girl-woman-college student -professional that sometimes I just cry thinking about it. She doesn't think she's good at anything and I can't think of anything she's not good at. Why does it always seem to be like that?

Anyway, she's on her way to some concert again and she's stopped by on her way to finish the makeup ritual.

"Rosie, it's not raining, and you aren't planning on swimming tonight, are you? So why do you need waterproof mascara anyway?"

"Oh Lourd-es MOM. Because the hot boy is going to be like --- she holds her hands about two feet apart --- THIS far away from me and I'll probably cry because he is like SO PRECIOUS, so um DO You? I have to go."
I sigh, shake my head and point at the drawer in my bathroom and head towards the blasting Nintendo action coming from Riley's room.
"Hey buddy, turn it down, ok?" He doesn't hear me of course. I stand in the

doorway and try to block out the dirty socks and bath towels that landscape his room. "Riley." Nothing. "RILEEEEEEEEY!!!!"

"GEEZ MOM, you scared me. Why are you yelling??" I don't even try to explain.

"Just turn it down, babe." "Oh. Ok." He does. His eyes haven't once left the screen in the whole three minutes of this magical mother-son moment. The joys of parenting are NOT underrated, despite appearances in this house.

I head to the bathroom to see how Rosie's search is progressing just as I hear her "Bye mom" echo as the front door slams. Sometimes it just all goes too fast.

"You can say that again." I look at Andrew leaning in the doorway of the living room. And suddenly, I can't speak for remembering how much I have always loved this man. Or, more accurately, this boy. I've wondered a million or more times what kind of man he would have been, what kind of father. But it isn't hard to imagine. He was a wonderful boy and the best kind of friend. I just wish I'd got to watch it all evolve. I wonder if he really can read my mind, because even though I haven't said a word, he's looking at me as though he knows exactly what I'm thinking. It's crazy, in all the years we were together, when he was alive I mean, there were so many moments that engraved themselves on my heart. The time he ran past me by the lockers in eighth grade and kissed me on the way out, right in front of Sister Mary Sara. The night he snuck over to the Fishers' house where I spent half my life babysitting and we stood in the dark on the front porch and both struggled to find the words to say what we felt for each other, but ended up just holding on to each other for what wasn't long enough.

The time he drove me up to a hill high over the city and showed me his "spot," where he would go to worry and think and try to decide about life. Where he kissed me while Stevie Wonder sang "If You Really Loved Me" on the car radio. The kind of memories that are so deeply carved into your brain that you can feel the way the air felt at that very moment. You know what I mean? The kind of memories that feel so good they hurt.

As much as I've come to believe he is real when he is around, I can't make myself test it by reaching out for more than a rare hug that I swear is real but two seconds later convince myself I've just imagined. It's the wanting it that's real. In the back of my mind I guess I'm afraid there is some line there, and if I cross it, he will disappear forever. But I ache for it, in ways I can't describe. And there is no drug for that kind of pain, that I can tell you. As the end of the school year drew near, life with Maria continued to remain interesting. Years later I would find out that her stay in the hospital a few weeks after the prom, which resulted in a much longer recovery at home than she liked, was not exactly the result of "female troubles," as she'd told everyone. What she'd said was something along the lines of, "Something was wrong, you know, *down there*?" And that they had to "take it out." I had no idea what she was talking about, but the whole unspoken story seemed to garner heartfelt sympathy from all her girlfriends, who now came to our house for their afternoon cocktails, since Maria couldn't drive quite yet.

In honor of their daily presence, she decided to play the "good mother." What that really meant was that now I couldn't go anywhere without the third degree. By the time I turned fifteen, I strong enough for her to realize that hitting me was out of the question. But I had no defense against her verbal assaults, and they were endless. I got quieter and quieter and that drove her nuts. And my dad, who had all but moved out to the apartment in the city, suddenly was home every night.

There was a miserable sort of tension in the house and it wore me out. Drew was working that summer at yet another wrestling camp at Penn State, so life at my house was pretty dismal. He called almost every night, but the four-hour distance made it nearly impossible to see each other. I spent the summer writing, babysitting for neighbors, and taking care of

I kept waiting to feel like things were somehow different, but I don't know, it just felt weird. Suddenly boys were everywhere and they were interested. I don't remember how it came up, but Andrew noticed too. And paying attention.

One Friday afternoon he showed up without warning. He was at Pitt by then, and living in the dorms. Between his busy class schedule, work, and wrestling, I hardly saw him. We still talked every night on the phone but I was missing him badly.

My life wasn't any easier. My mother the movie star (if only in her own mind) was now fully healed. Sporting a new "frosted" bob and a fresh tan from week in Florida spent "recovering," she stayed busy entertaining absolutely everyone at her friend Liz's new bar. She was never home and suddenly I was responsible for taking care of the four other maniacal siblings, cooking dinner for the household, and managing the endless laundry. Oh, and my senior year at school. *That.*

Just like every 18 year- old, all I could think about was what would come next. After high school. All I wanted was to go to college and move out and away from Maria. But there just wasn't enough money to get me anywhere without divine intervention. Since writing was what came naturally to me, my only hope was to try for a local foundation scholarship that required a series of essays, short stories, and free writes over a four-week period. And that meant every night that fall I either walked to the library at the high school, or hid in my room, or worked at the kitchen table if Maria was out. The days melted into nights and I found little time to sleep. It got to where I'd grab a catnap anywhere, anytime, any way I could. I slept on the bus, in study hall. Jesus, I even slept at a football game once. Took a long time to live that down.

That's how Drew found me, that Friday afternoon in late October: Asleep at the kitchen table.

"Eeeeeeee." Someone in my dream was whispering in my ear.

"EEEEEEE." My head shot up and I cracked him right in the nose.

"JEESSSSUUUUUSSSSS!"

"Well, what the hell did you expect, sneaking up on me like that!"

"Why are you sleeping in the middle of the day, E?" He asked, while checking his nose in the mirror/ Then he looked at my reflection next to his and shook his head. "Dang it girl, you look done in."

I smiled. "Yeah, kinda." He said he came to take me for a ride in the Grand Prix. He'd just gotten it back from the repair shop after his sister Lucy had wrecked it (for the third time) and he'd really missed his baby (the car, not me). I conceded. "Ok, but I have to wash my hair or it'll never dry before I have to go to the library later."

I knew I'd have to spend three or four hours to get the week's work behind me. I'd had a weakness in my lungs since childhood, and could end up with pneumonia at the drop of a hat.

It was so cold in the big halls of the city library, so I knew going down there with a wet head couldn't be a good idea. Drew responded smoothly. "Cool. I'll wash it for you." I just laughed. "Yeah, right. How are you going to do that?"

"Get the shampoo and a towel and come here." I did, and he took me down to the laundry room where there was a huge sink. "Stick your head under there," he instructed.

He took his time, gently washing and carefully rinsing my hair, wrapped a towel around my head, and took me by the hand to the backyard. It was a beautiful fall afternoon and the sun had warmed the concrete steps where we sat, with him one step above me. He gently dried my hair with the towel and began to comb through it. I don't know how long we sat there, but it seemed like hours, and I don't think either one of us said a word. It was like a kind of music, the rhythmic stroking of the comb through my hair and his body leaned up against mine.

There it is, one of those memories I was talking about. The kind that never fade.

In the middle of writing this, I just saw a commercial about a show about writing sitcoms. I thought of Drew right away, and of course my 32-season Emmy hit of a life history and bingo! Visions of fame and fortune danced in my head. But then I thought about it. There was so much more to it than a sitcom. Too many situations, not enough comedy. So back to the keyboard, and the remembering.

See, when I decided to call this book "Forgetting Andrew," it's not because I ever did. It's because it is the one thing I can't imagine ever doing.

Fast forward, real time. It is spring of 2006 and it's been a bad beginning to the first half of this year. One of those stretches of month after month bad news, after more bad news, and things you never see coming. I've been to two funerals, and am dreading the email that is bound to arrive any day that will send me to a third. I let myself be talked into a minor flirtation with a much younger man, who decided to not tell me he was engaged. (I am not a hussy; I stopped that train right in its tracks.) Really. Don't you know me at all by now? Oh, and my dog died. Seriously. It was the worst part of everything, because that little dog loved the HELL out of me. Unconditionally, makeup or no makeup; even when I was too depressed and sad and worn out to walk her, she still loved me. We had rescued her a year before from a puppy mill when the poor thing was less than a year old, a scrawny little Yorkie who tried to bite me the first night. We settled that and then she was MY dog. Lola.

Like the Donovan song. L-O-LA, Lola. Sweet as cherry cola. Aka Lollapalooza, Lo and Lukie Loo. She was an amazing little thing and boy did she have me. No one else EVER got me out of bed on a freezing winter morning for a half-hour walk, and I doubt any two-legged variety of species ever will. My bones are old enough to know better.

So, where was I? Right. Bad year. You go through enough bad stuff and you start to really believe that it's Armageddon. Or that you won't live to see Armageddon. And that it won't be so bad if you miss it.

Anyway, after all of that it was Easter.

Have we discussed this holiday? You'd remember if we had. On a scale of one to ten, I'd rate Easter a negative 15,246. For various and sundry reasons, not the least of which it is the anniversary of the weekend ex #2 tried to seriously kill me. I don't use the word "seriously" half-heartedly either. You see, this man, whom you will come to know and loathe, had tried many times to "sort of" kill me. I'm not sure why he wasn't more focused in many of his efforts. He was, in all other ways, your classic overachiever: Boarding school education, scion of the moneyed family that adopted him, artist, musician, athlete, scholar. He was also thwarted in all these endeavors by a nasty flaw. His temper messed up everything he ever tried to do right. That happens with bipolar people. And I know you'll be mad at me, but it's really too soon to talk about all of this. There are things you should know and try to understand about what happened first, so that you'll be able to forgive me for what happened later.

"Right NOW," yells Riley. "RIGHTNOWRIGHTNOWRIGHTNOW MOM COME RIGHT NOW." I'm starting to almost laugh as I wipe my hands on a dishtowel and head towards the backyard when I hear the demand in his voice turn to tears. He's standing outside the door with both hands covering something on his leg which is absolutely pouring blood.

"Oh my god," I gasp, and in seconds I have him inside and up on the kitchen counter, where he is wailing at the top of his lungs. Rosie, who is home doing laundry, is by my side in a heartbeat (I'm surprised the neighbors aren't here too, as loud as this boy can yelp). I've almost forgotten that his pal Jeremy was here, but he's standing behind the counter now, white as a sheet.

"Rosie," I say quietly, nodding towards the other boy. She takes over there, so I can work on prying Riley's hand away from whatever is causing this bleeding. And there it is, a rusted screw, probably a half-inch into him at the meaty part of his upper thigh. He'd fallen off the old playhouse I'd been meaning to get rid of since he'd outgrown it years before, but where he and Jeremy had climbed in hopes of getting a glance at the girls in the neighbor's yard.

"Ok mister, we have a decision to make here." I speak calmly, looking him in the eye. He has that startled look that kids get when they're not sure if they are more scared of the pain or of being in trouble. I press gently around the wounded area; the bleeding has stopped and it is clear the puncture hasn't hit an artery.

"What?" he says. Now it's just the two of us, we're in that zone we've always had where no one else is there, even in a crowd of thousands.

Eye to eye, I give him the facts. "How deep does it feel?" I ask. "I don't know mom, it just HURTS," his calm fading and fear finding a voice.

"I know, babe, but do you think it will come out if you pull it quick? Or do we leave it in while we drive to Urgent Care?" He looks down, considers for a minute and then says "out" quietly. He pulls it out quick and clean.

"Ouch," I say, as I pull his head to my shoulder so he can cry it out without Jeremy seeing. He holds a compress on it, wrapped in a dishtowel around the leg till we get to the Urgent Care. The doc is impressed with the size of the screw, orders a tetanus, and packs the resultant hole with antibiotic. He also orders an x-ray to assure we "got the whole screw out" and we hang around for another thirty minutes till he's read it and is satisfied. Riley is by this time over the whole thing and fairly psyched he will have a big "hole" scar on his leg, "pretty much forever, huh mom?"

My adrenalin, however is gone and I'm left exhausted and wearing Jack's blood pretty much all over me. Jeremy's been waiting the whole time at home with Rosie, so I let the boys order pizza and put a movie in on the big screen in the living room, then lock myself in the bathroom for a hot soak and a good cry.

I'm up to my neck in bubbles holding on to a glass of wine when I hear Andrew, who is sitting on the floor of the shower across from me and chuckling.

"How is he?" he says, smiling at me softly.

"He's fine," I say.

"And you, mom?" he asks.

"I'm a basket case. But he's fine," I repeat, staring into Drew's eyes. "He's fine." And we just stay like that for a long time, with me missing the live version of my boyfriend more than I can explain.

I don't know where Andrew is buried. He died in the middle of a September midnight on a forlorn stretch of highway somewhere between his last cup of coffee and the Georgia-Florida state line.

We'd cooked up a pretty good plot the week after my high school graduation, a few days before I left for my summer trip to visit my godparents/aunt and uncle, Annie and Ed. It was their gift to me - a summer away from home, from my ever-stranger mother, from raising my brothers, and from the steel town summer of Pittsburgh. I was to spend all of June, July and August with them, only returning home in time to pack my bags for college.

Annie and Ed had always given me a safe place to go whenever I had a break, and that continued for years, even after I'd moved out of my parents' house. Ed got me my very first waitressing job for that summer at a local pancake house, and my first car. The baby-blue Bonneville sitting on his front lawn was mine for the whole summer after graduation. Whenever I was with them, I had a seat at the dinner table in a real family. For the first time, I had an idea of what that could be like, good times and bad, and a mom and dad who came together every night with a love that carries on to this day. When I think of it, I got most of my ideas about being a grown woman from the time I spent with Annie and Ed and their family. To be honest, I've spent the last twenty years or so looking for the kind of true love that they had and still have, after all the ups and downs, good times and disappointments. That kind of love and partnership are rare, and it's one thing I knew I really wanted for my own life after spending time with them.

Anyway, Andrew had come by one afternoon the beginning of my senior year, after his first few weeks away at school. The summer sun had faded and afternoons were starting to chill. He'd had to pick up some things from his parent's place and decided to surprise me at the house. My mom had gone out with her pals early, and the boys were all out hunting for the weekend. The house was quiet and the leaves had started to turn, making everything glow with that burnished gold light that is often the sole redeeming factor for living in that part of the country.

I was sitting on the front porch staring at the maples that grew in almost every front yard when he drove up. He stuck his head out the window and yelled "get a jacket and come ON." I laughed and ran inside, grabbing a random denim jacket that was a size or two too big and a house key, before locking the door and jumping in beside him. He kissed me noisily and never stopped grinning.

"*What?*" I laughed. He started rambling on and on about wrestling, the meets coming up, his father wanting him to stay at school on the weekends and train, and how he couldn't wait till this year was over. I was so mesmerized by his uncharacteristic conversation; I hadn't noticed where we were headed.

"E," he said. "Look." I looked ahead and gasped. The entire hillside in front of me was covered in a rainbow of autumn's finest work, in radiant gold, red and bittersweet. I looked to the side and behind and everywhere I turned the trees were in full regalia. We pulled over and got out of the car, following a path that led down to a large clearing, the floor of the woods covered with a mosaic of newly fallen leaves. A small creek moved fast enough nearby to drown out the sounds of all but the birds and the rustle of the trees, and we found a log and sat close together, eyes wide and silent.

"I love you, E," Andrew said, without looking at me. "I love you so much sometimes I think I'll go crazy if you don't hurry up and graduate and come live with me."

We'd never said these words. I mean, I never truly believed I was a long-term thing for him. I wanted it, I dreamed about it, but I'd resigned myself to just having whatever this was for as long as it lasted. I hadn't dared wish for more. And suddenly here it was. I couldn't speak. He turned to me and took my face in his hands, looked me in the eyes and said, "Don't say anything now. I just wanted you to know how I feel."

The year seemed to fly, as those magical times often do. We saw each other as much as we could manage between school and responsibilities, and never skipped our nightly phone calls. And as my graduation drew nearer, I felt lighter and lighter at the thought of finally getting away from my mother and being with Andrew. He'd found a small apartment in Oakland, near the university and the small college I was going to attend thanks to a scholarship that had come through.

Between our part-time jobs, scholarships, and a couple of student loans, we knew we could make it. The only catch was that we couldn't tell anyone. Maria had already threatened me enough to know she would do anything and everything to stop us if she found out. She'd seen us talking one day when she happened to be at home when he'd stopped by to drop off a book he'd found that he thought I would like. I knew she was home so I thought I'd been really careful and casual with him. But she'd seen it. The spark between us. And she warned me in one sentence when I walked back in the door. She looked at me as though she was seeing me for the first time, no longer a child. A woman, coming into her own. And she stopped me as I passed her, grabbing me by the arm. I didn't look at her so she came around so I could see her face as she spoke. And all she said, through a smug smile that didn't reflect in her gritty stare was "Oh that is NOT happening. Not in your wildest dreams". I didn't acknowledge her words, but shook her hand off my arm and walked away. But I knew then that this would be a journey I'd take on my own. And I'd have to be very careful.

When Andrew and I stood in the middle of those woods, and he turned to me and said, "I want it all with you, Elaine. Is that what you want?" I bet I don't have to tell you what my answer was.

Andrew Cosentino proposed to me on the night of my graduation on the monkey bars at the Saxon School playground at the bottom of the hill by my house. The same playground where we'd snuck away to swing late at night and tell each other our dreams. He had grabbed the large pan of lasagna from me as I carried it to the makeshift café Maria had created in the garage for the party she'd deemed non-negotiable. Then he pulled me over to the side of the house out of everyone's sight.

"I have to give you your present right now," he said, grinning. I looked behind me, and for a minute I was frozen, thinking of what Maria would do if she realized I'd cut out on her big to-do. But it was one of those moments when you just go for it. I figured whatever it cost, I'd have some time alone with Drew and it would all be worth it.

We cut down the hillside through the woods and out the other end of the path, then up the hill to the swings. Drew climbed onto the monkey bars, which were shining in the fading sunlight. It was a warm early evening, and the bars were still hot from the afternoon sun. I pulled my skirt under as he pulled me up to sit beside him, and kicked my ballet flats off so I could curl my toes against the warm metal.

He laughed at me, my hair all curled and pinned up per Maria's instructions, now loose and wild in the breeze.

"I love you, E," he said, and handed me a rose he pulled out of his back pocket. It was a little flattened and faded, but the color was the same as the sunset we were watching, and that one small flower smelled like a garden full of roses.

"I love you too, Drew," I said, twirling the rose and trying to keep the tears from coming. He was holding my hand and before I knew what he was doing, he'd slipped a small gold band with a tiny round diamond onto my finger.

"I want it all with you, E. Forever. And I want all of it to start now." When it all hit me I lost my balance from sheer emotion. And when I fell off the bars, I sort of kicked Drew in the head, and when we stopped holding each other, laughing, crying, kissing, and trying to brush the dirt off of my white dress, I realized we better get back to my house. Hopefully we'd get back before my mother, queen of the graduation party if not mother of the year, noticed I'd slipped out. I was lost in the moment when I noticed he was bleeding from a small cut just above his right eye.

When my grandmother handed me her hankie right before I left the house that night, she'd said, "Here, you shouldn't cry on this happiness, but if you have to, cry on this." I still had it in my pocket, so I wiped the small bit of blood from Andrew's face and kissed the spot again and again.

"You will be the best mom," he said at that moment. I thought of that folded handkerchief with the faded rose pressed in the pages of my yearbook, and wondered how something so perfect could end so sadly. I felt just like that rose. Old, faded and sad. I wondered if thirty more years from now I would still feel this pain so clearly, still see Drew's face in the fading sunlight, still feel the warm steel against my toes whenever I recalled that day. I know now that only living things fade, it's our emotions that never age at all. When I remembered Andrew's prediction, I thought of Rosie, and Riley and all the ways I thought I'd failed them.

All these long years later, I let myself look him in the eye, and say, "I've really tried Drew." "I know, E," he says. "I know."

So anyway, we had this plan all worked out. The idea was for Andrew and Freddie, his wrestling buddy, to drive down to Florida and pick me up. We'd drive back north and detour to Atlantic City, get married, then go home and break the news to our families. But the plan changed a week before the trip. Drew's parents had suddenly bought a winter place in St. Pete and needed one of their cars driven down. So Andrew drove his Grand Prix, and Freddie drove the folks' Cadillac.

They followed each other the whole way, planning to stop in St. Pete, drop off the Caddy, spend the night, and then head to Fort Lauderdale to pick me up. Andrew called me two days out. They were in South Carolina and they had just eaten so much barbeque they were about to burst. He was raving about the sauce, and said they'd found a motel in southern Georgia for the night. The next day they'd make the drive all the way to St. Pete.

"Two days, baby," he said, "and then we start our new life. Two days." I smiled so hard and forgot to speak. He laughed. "Ok, goodnight, E. I'll call you when we get to Florida." No cell phones back then, so you called people from pay phones at rest stops when you found them.

"Ok, be careful," I said. "Always," he smiled into the phone.

That was the last word he ever said to me when he was alive.

Rosie is on the phone. It's her third call in twenty minutes and she's driving me crazy. "Mom, I swear. I hate, I mean *really* hate my roommates."

She's the one who decided it would be fun to spend her first year in college living with four boys who love her like brothers, but are also as sloppy and loud and smelly as Riley. I'm wrestling with the big dogs outside while I try to pull weeds in the backyard since this spring Arizona thought it would be fun to try rain. Lots of rain. I actually don't mind it; I kind of get sick of waking up every day to sunshine. I know, that's weird, but remember, I grew up in the grey city. In the Pittsburgh of my childhood, the soot in the air was so thick my mother used to keep a dish towel by the front door, for wiping the thin mist of black off the glass milk bottles before she brought them inside from the milk box. Milk box. Oh geez. See? I really AM old. Where was I? Oh, right. Rosie and rain. And weeds. Funny, it all kind of goes together. God bless that girl, but sometimes she can find the black cloud in everything

"MOM!" She's yelling now. "What?"

"You aren't listening to me again," she says with that tone in her voice, the one that says if you hadn't given birth to me, I would never spend a minute with you. "WHAT?" I repeat.

Quieter, she asks, "Can I come over there and do laundry?"

"Sure," I say. "Of course."

"Ok, bye."

And with that, the girl is on her way over. Soon we will begin the "visiting" ritual: She will arrive, laundry baskets in tow, no detergent of course, and with a million stories and complaints from the week. My role, as defined by Rosie, is to sit patiently, offer food and drink, hand over the remote, and listen. Without interruption, or emotional response. Or opinion, or commentary of any kind. Oh, AND to stay up long beyond my normal bedtime, since SHE doesn't have to get up until ten the next morning and SHE needs company.

I love her. Someday I know I will look back on these days and be so grateful we had them. Right? But for now, sometimes the girl just plain wears me out. And because I love her so damn much, I let her.

Drew pipes up from Rosie's room, newly christened the "Buddha" room, where the plan is for me to meditate, workout, and hide. So far, it's just a plan. There is nothing in there but an old chest of drawers and a few baskets of good intentions. Rosie has forbidden us to change the color or "destroy any of her memories." I'm hoping that doesn't apply to the wax puddle by the window, the after-effects of a candle-making experiment, or the collection of garden gnomes that still graces the windowsill.

"You know you would go crazy without her," comes Mr. Logical's commentary. I don't answer. Hearing his voice while I am still soaked in the memory of that last phone call is almost too painful to let myself remember. I need to get through this next part, I know that in my brain, but in the rest of me - the part that bleeds every time I even start to think about what happened next, there is nothing but pain.

Riley and his three amigos suddenly fling open the front door and break the moment. I'm grateful, for once, because this will take a while. They are 11 going on 16 now, on the brink of bursting into taller, bigger, wilder boys. Like babies who can actually enact their wildest imaginings, they are unpredictable and a little scary. Wide-eyed and grinning, they are covered in mud and smart enough to hover in the front hall not touching anything. This last bit they feel they need to tell me really loudly.

"I KNOW WE KNOW WE AREN'T TOUCHING ANYTHING!"

Danny, with the freckled face of an angel and the soul of mischief, starts laughing so hard he gets everyone going. Even Andrew, who is now perched on the living room sofa observing the show, joins in.

"What the heck?" I say. "Where did you manage to find MUD in Arizona?" This starts off another round of giggles and guffaws, which quickly turns into back slaps and the beginnings of a dangerous wrestling match.

"Riley?" I warn, with the look that implies… NOW.
Riley tries to hush the other boys and regain the well-known and heavily relied-upon innocent face that he has come to know is often the best route for imparting unfortunate information.

"Well," he begins, "first of all it totally wasn't our fault."
I nod and gesture for him to continue, darting a look at Andrew that tells him to stop laughing now or leave the room. He sobers up instantly. He knows that look as well as my son does.

"See, Danny threw the football over the wall and so we walked around the long way LIKE WE'RE SUPPOSED TO and went to find it. But it was in the canal. And WE KNOW we aren't EVER supposed to go near there or in the water, but

Kevin got a long stick and was trying to make the ball come back so we could get it. Danny was holding onto the other end so Kevin wouldn't fall in, but then he like, did. And then Danny fell in trying to get Kevin. And then Kevin couldn't get out so I tried to help him and then he…"

He is talking ninety miles a minute and the other three are nodding (including Will, who by some miracle is still clean and dry) and I can picture the rest, so I put up a hand and cut him off.

"Side of the house. Hose. Now." I hand them three old towels and point back out the door. I know that it will be a mess, a water fight and most of the mud will still be on them when they are done, but I'm not having it in my shower.

They troop outside like defeated soldiers, and head for the makeshift shower, but it's not long before I hear whooping and hollering and we are all back to normal. I find their swimsuits in Riley's room and toss them over the fence.

"Leave your clothes in a pile and I'll get them. Then take a swim." Luckily, we've had an early spring and the water is just warm enough to send them in. I spend the next twenty minutes trying to get all the mud out before I take the clothes in. It's one of those mama Zen activities; you eventually just lose yourself in the act and don't exactly know where your mind goes. I'm usually grateful afterwards, and today is no different. In fact, today, I'm especially thankful for each and every distraction that comes along.

My old friend is waiting in the laundry room. "You should learn to do laundry, you know, then you could be helpful instead of just annoying," I mutter. He is laughing, but I think I have somehow hurt him. How is it, I find myself asking, that you can hurt a dead person's feelings? I wonder for the fifteen-thousandth time if I am really just crazy. But I look up and there he is, sitting on the dryer, trying to fold the towels, and smiling that lopsided grin that unlocks my heart every time. You do understand, right? I'm not crazy. I'm just still very much in love with the boy. And, enter Rosie. Drew smiles and disappears. Rosie has caught me more than once in the act of what appears to be me, talking animatedly, to myself. She has enough trouble being nice to me these days, I don't need to give her reasons to taunt me.

"I'm in here," I call, loud enough for her to hear but not loud enough to be accused of shouting. She drops her purse at the front door, I hear the familiar sounds as shoes come off by the couch, and the laundry basket hits the floor just missing my feet with a thud. "I brought detergent." She flashes a proud smile. And she thinks this is the reason I wrap my arms around her and hold her for a really long time.

"Ok mom, um, what the heck?" She squirms from my hug.   "Nothing, just missed you," I say, my back to her as I turn on the washer full of the boy's clothes. "Sorry, babe, the boys had a canal bath and they got here first." "Ohhh. Ooooookaaay. I bet that's a good story," she says, and heads for the kitchen. I follow her, make us both some iced tea, and lean against the counter. "Yeah," I answer, looking out the window at the boys in the pool, but I don't offer any more details and I'm grateful when she doesn't ask.

I'm suddenly exhausted and I don't object when Rosie asks if we can just sit and watch TV for a while.

I don't even mind that we have to watch all four episodes of "Gilmore Girls" that she has recorded. It's kind of nice to just forget about losing Andrew for a little bit. Just for a while.

I guess it's finally time to get to the punch line, eh? Ok. Enough with the procrastination, at least with this.

It was after that last night, when I'd smiled for hours after Drew and I hung up. That night, the one when everything changed. Well, Andrew and Freddie did get back on the road that night. They headed down the interstate for the next motel rest stop, the one the waitress at the diner told them always had room. But about ten miles later, Drew must have dozed off, because while Freddie watched in horror, the car lights in front of him slid off the road to the right and crashed into a bridge abutment. No explosion, no flames. Just a dull crash and then darkness.

The impact broke his neck, and Drew was dead. Just like that. Freddie told the police, when they finally found them, that he didn't know what to do except drag him from the car, in case it blew up. Long before cell phones, it took a passing motorist to stop, and then drive on to the nearest service station miles away. to call the highway patrol. The police couldn't figure out how Freddie managed to get Drew out of the car, which was pretty much a pile of twisted metal and stones from the bridge, but he did it. When the sun came up, they found him sitting on the side of the road, holding Drew like a baby.

It didn't take long for the news of the accident to reach Pittsburgh and our little town. The grapevine did its job and my mom, still working the graveyard shift at the diner where all the cops hung out, got the news pretty early. And she couldn't wait to call me. I guess Freddie told everyone why they were headed to Florida, so my mom was so overcome with information, she didn't know whether to be angry or delighted in the turn of events. But Maria played the part with all her friends, and managed a few shocked tears for the audience. No one saw her smile when she headed for the pay phone.

I'd spent the morning sunning and smiling by the pool. I was just headed for the shower when the phone rang. Ed was upstairs and he answered. I stopped in the kitchen for a glass of water and was walking with it towards my room when I heard him yell down the stairs for me.

"Elaine, it's for you." For a minute, Drew flashed across my brain, and I smiled just at the thought of him. I was still smiling when I heard my mother's voice. She didn't sound happy.

"I know all about your little plan, my dear," she said, in the voice I knew was sugared with at least one vodka and OJ by now. I didn't get a chance to respond, she was talking so fast. "But it's not going to work out for you, sorry to say."

"Mom, what are you talking about?" I was really confused and stopped to take a sip of water.

"Andrew Cosentino is dead. The cops told me this morning. His car hit a bridge wall somewhere in Georgia, and he died instantly. Do you hear me? Drew is dead".

My aunt told me later that I dropped the glass on the tile floor, then must have fainted. My uncle came running down the stairs to see what happened, and found me lying in the middle of broken glass with the phone still in my hand, and my mother's voice laughing. I don't remember him picking me up and laying me on the sofa. I don't remember coming to and not talking to anyone for three days. I don't remember going outside on the third day at dusk and throwing my ring into the canal. I don't remember packing up all my stuff and leaving for home a week later, and I don't remember flying there or who picked me up at the airport. I don't remember any of it. I've forgotten it all, and I think it's better that way.

Even now, I'm feeling that numb empty feeling that followed me for the next three months. I hadn't gone home for the funeral. I was still in shock and the doctor who'd come when I wouldn't speak told Annie and Ed he wasn't sure I could handle it. God bless that man, whoever he was. I know I'm still in one piece, even if that piece is a little damaged, because he kept me from that. Pally went, and called me after, and she said, "OH, E, I'm so glad you weren't here. It wasn't him, it didn't even look like him."

I told her, "I know," and thanked her for calling me. I didn't call her, or anyone else back for a long time. A really long time. I guess by now that's not much of a surprise to you.

When Andrew died, I was 17 and about to start college. I had only gotten a small scholarship and my dad was sure I wouldn't appreciate a higher education unless I worked my way through, so I needed to figure a lot of things out -- despite the fact that my mind was still in a pretty dense fog, and the rest of me was completely numb.

I knew only one thing for sure at that point. I couldn't go back to living

in my parent's house. Only partly because Maria had reached a whole

new stage of her "career" and was now considered a homewrecker since by

now everyone except me and my brothers knew the truth about the real

reason for her stay in the hospital the past summer.

They all knew she'd had an affair with the local High School football

coach, who happened to live down the street. When my dad had found out

Maria was pregnant, it was because her doctor called HIM to give him the bad

news that it was an ectopic pregnancy. In those days, wives weren't considered

able to make decisions as important as what to do about a serious condition

like this, so the doctor calling my dad made perfect sense -- except for one

tiny detail. My dad had all but moved out that summer and was living

downtown in an apartment. And he knew, and knew that my mother knew,

that it wasn't his baby. But god bless him, he did the right thing. Meaning, he

packed up and moved home, paid for my mother's hysterectomy, and beat the

shit out of the coach.

I came home just a few days before I was supposed to start college. She

couldn't even look at me. That much, I do remember. I was enrolled in a small

women's college near Pitt, but I needed to find somewhere to live since I

couldn't afford the apartment that Drew had lined up a month earlier. And I

needed a job.

I avoided everyone in the days leading up to the start of school by

taking the bus to Oakland and just walking around campus all day.

One day, I saw an ad on the outdoor bulletin board, looking for a "mother's helper" to live in this family's house and watch their kids at night, while the mother worked. I called the number and arranged to meet Maya that afternoon for coffee. She explained that her husband, the VP of a local steel company, was away getting

his MBA at Harvard, and she was a Dean at a local women's college -- ironically, the same school I was starting in a few days. She needed to go to her office for a few hours each evening, and sometimes on weekends.

Maya reminded me of a younger version of Annie, and the job felt like a perfect fit. I could live there, and would have my own room and bathroom on the top floor, all to myself. I could go to class all day, come home, and help her out. It didn't pay much, about $300 a month, but free room and board was more than I had hoped for. And it guaranteed the one thing I really needed: Every hour from waking to sleep would be full of responsibilities. I wouldn't have time to think about anything but school and work. She offered me the job if my references checked out, and promised to let me know soon. The next day when I called her just to check in, she asked when I could start. I moved in two days later and never lived at home again.

I would tell you more about those first three months if I could remember. But those first days of college, the days with Maya and her wonderful kids, Zeke and Katie, the fall that Drew and I always called our favorite season – it's all gone. I don't remember any of it, even when I see pictures from that time. It remained a faded blur, until the first time I saw him again.

It was snowing on December 9, 1972, the day before my 18th birthday. Not that light pretty snow where the lights of the city shine on the frost and the whole thing looks magical. No, more of the Pittsburgh special variety, grey, sludge, and sooty ice. And colder than you want to know. Maya had taken the kids to New Jersey to see their dad, and left me to mind the house. I was looking forward to a few days on my own, except for being just a little nervous about figuring out the radiator. I got home from my late class, shook the snow off my coat, and turned on the hall light. That's when I heard him.

"E."

I smiled, and almost turned to the sound, when I realized I was hearing things. I decided I'd have a glass of wine instead of the tea I'd been planning on my long walk home. I had a bottle in my room so I headed up the stairs. That's when I heard him again.

"You aren't hearing things, Elaine. It really is me." I turned around slowly. You know, like any heroine in any scary movie. And there he was. Wearing his letterman sweater, needing a haircut, smiling that loopy smile. I'm pretty sure I just stood there for a very long time. Then I sunk to the step and stared.

"I'm not a figment of your imagination either. See? Touch me." I couldn't though. I just couldn't touch him and then lose him all over again. I shook my head, but I still didn't speak.

Drew talked to me for a while, and tried to say a million things, but I wouldn't talk back. I wish now I could remember everything he told me, about the accident, and what it was like after that, how he felt really scared and how he wandered around for a long time before he figured out how to find me. But it's just bits and pieces. The only thing I really remember is what I said when I finally believed he was there. "Please stay."

I spent two years there and would have never left, but the family decided to move to New Jersey and they sold the house. It was harder saying goodbye to them than it had been to leave my own home.

I found a room in another house close to campus and finished school there, working nights and weekends in the college bookstore to pay my way and carrying as many credits as I can so that at the end of it, I'd at least have a bachelor's degree. I wrote and studied far into the wee hours to get my schoolwork done and keep a good average. It was brutal, and lonely, and mind-numbing. But I did it. I graduated in three years, and won a small scholarship to a Master's program in English Lit with a teaching emphasis, in what would turn out to be the coldest city in upstate New York. And because Andrew was there, I moved on with whatever my life would turn out to be.

My father had finally divorced Maria when Lana had sided with her and turned on him. God bless him -- he never stopped trying with that girl, but she was not letting anyone close in those days. So he left, and was happy starting a new life with Deborah, who I would find out later was just a few years older than I was. They were busy trying to have a child of their own while also raising Deb's two small daughters from her first marriage. They barely noticed anyone else those years, and understandably so. In all that had happened to me that last summer, my father never spoke a word about it. He took me to lunch now and again, mentioned boys from my crowd, girls who'd already gotten married, boys who might be a good catch for me. It was all I could do to keep from screaming.

Lana had proven that she was aptly named, and that the original Lana had nothing on her in the drama department. It's like that to this day. We were five years apart, so never close as kids, and I was gone before she turned fourteen. Not that I could have helped; the kid was born with a wild streak, and unlike my mother, had no rules and regimens set by society to hold her back. By her fifteenth birthday, she'd experimented with drugs, sex AND rock and roll, if you count all the musicians she'd slept with. By that time, Evan had toured the country with several iterations of what would become a semi-legendary band (ok, if only with the groupies) and was hanging out in Pennsylvania, trying to get a studio together with one of his bandmates who'd coincidentally married Dee, one of my best friends from school. Kevin had turned a moderately successful college football career into a coaching job after he blew out his knee, and moved his young wife and son to Minnesota. He's still there, with four boys now and the same job. Kevin is the only one who seemed to find that level, normal family life that the rest of us would have to hunt down for years. And Kelly? He'd decided there just weren't enough women in Pittsburgh so he moved to Vegas, where he'd work his way through several engagements and two marriages. But that, as they say, is another story entirely.

Lana found every excuse to hang out with Evan and his boys, more for the drugs than the sex. Or maybe because the sex bought plenty of drugs. When I'd moved out to work for Maya, I'd taken Lana to lunch and tried to talk to her, to let her know I was always going to be there. To try to give her the guidance that should have come from someone older and wiser than me. She smirked across the table and said, "Thanks for lunch, and fuck you." We didn't talk for close to ten years after that.

My mother drank more and more and was running up a record with the local police after a series of collisions with inanimate but very noticeable landmarks. By this time, she had driven the family station wagon into the stoplight in front of the fire station, the fountain in front of my dad's store, and the corner of our house several times. She just couldn't make that last curve as she attempted to pull out of the garage into the driveway. Personally, I'm just surprised the house is still standing after 20 odd years of dealing with her rage.

I was young to finish college, barely 21 and I'd accepted a scholarship for a year-long writer's workshop in a program in upstate NY, at a prestigious university. This would qualify me for a 2- year master's program and a job as a teacher's assistant which, as part of faculty, I would get for next to nothing. It sounded perfect and the answer to a prayer. But it turned out to be the coldest place I'd ever been. (I hadn't been to Minnesota at that point... but if you have... let's just say that Ithaca is colder.) I was struggling with being completely on my own, and frankly, with being so cold all the time. The only friend I had was Drew, and in those early days, he wasn't around that much. Or maybe I had shut down so deeply that he was there but I couldn't feel him. It was dark in my heart and everything was numb. What once would have been exciting and joyful, going to class and immersing myself in amazing books and thoughts, felt like someone nicking away at me daily with an icepick. After six months, I started looking for somewhere else to go, even though it meant I would leave without finishing the degree.

I found a job in Chicago through a classmate. It turned out to be part-time work in the research library of a big publisher. It would be work in a field I loved, reading and fact-checking, and I thought maybe I could try to make a little extra money writing for the local paper. Best of all, it was two states away from Pittsburgh, which meant I could stay clear of any drama and Maria. So I took a chance and accepted. I found a room in a shared apartment, but I was still barely making ends meet, even with two other roommates, so I started writing freelance for a small literary magazine. The city was so different from Pittsburgh, and I liked it. The cold was different. The light was different. And there was the lake to sit and stare at for hours while I imagined my life if things had turned out differently. Andrew seemed to like it and when I sat there by the lake shore with him beside me I felt something like hope. Almost.

Even so, it was hard. I struggled like we all do starting out, but I was away from Maria and I was on the verge of a life. Well, at least what felt like a life after the past two-and-a-half years I had spent without Drew, but getting to know his ghost. Life had not kept any of the promises it had made to me, at least the important ones. The happy girl I'd always been, despite the world around me, was now hibernating - cautious, unsure, and uncertain about what would come next.

16~ A Call for Help

I thought life would just go on and I'd settle into a comfortable, predictable routine. For the next 15 months, that's what happened. I was busy and I knew what to expect each day.

Then in late May, I got a call from Lana. She sounded uncharacteristically frantic because Maria had been rushed to the hospital... and it wasn't looking good. The call came as a quite a surprise. I'd stopped interacting with my mother when I left the house for college. I spoke to my Dad and Deb now and again, sent cards at holidays. My brothers had become a mystery. They were all out on their own, finding themselves, and once in a blue moon we'd connect. But I was mostly in the world navigating life alone.

Andrew was around then more or less like he is now, but both he and I were still adjusting to that fact. For the most part, if I was relatively happy and safe, he was happy too. Francis had been remarried for almost two years now, and had been promoted to a regional vice president at the store. As a perk, he and Deb had gone to Japan to check out what the new Sony folks were designing in the way of home electronics. Since they'd never had a real honeymoon, he had extended his trip with a few weeks of vacation and wouldn't be back for at least another week. Even after he'd left, the kids always knew he'd show up to help, or get Maria or any of them out of a jam. But without cell phones or email back then, there was simply no way to reach him on his tour.

For the first time in what would become a common scenario, my family seemed to think I was the only person who could help. Lana said my mother had asked her to call me and ask me to please come home. She said that if my mother managed to survive at all (though always prone to dramatics, Lana sounded genuinely scared), Maria would be in the hospital for a while, and there was no one there to take care of "things." I took "things" to mean "her." She was the only one left at home and although she'd lived a lot during her 17 years, she was still my little sister.

At that point, Kevin was at college on a football scholarship, Kelly was living with a buddy in town and working at the store with dad, and Evan... I mean Jessie... he was off doing his rock and roll thing. So even though I was overcome with anxiety at going back into the fray, I've always been driven by doing the right thing. Or what seemed like the right thing at the time. Even if it wasn't the right thing for me. It wouldn't be the last time I fell for one of Maria's schemes, because believe you me, she is a fine actress. I wish she would have chosen that as a career, instead of saving those skills for an audience of one.
And that one, being me.

I called my aunt, my mother's younger sister in Florida. Annie was the only woman who had ever "mothered" me in any way, and so it was logical to ask her what I should do. She too had spoken several times with Lana, and was convinced there was more to the story. She agreed I would have to go home to know what was really happening.

So I did. I packed a suitcase and left that day, leaving behind the what money I had saved for the rent, and a note for my roommates explaining where I'd gone. Then I made a quick call to work and the paper letting them know I had

a family emergency and would know more about when and if I would be back,

after I reached home. I spent the next 10 hours driving the 467 miles alone in

my beat-up Rambler, worrying what I would find. I wondered how I would

feel if Maria died before she could tell me she was sorry for everything. I

wondered if she *was* sorry. I wondered how my life would be if I had to go on

with so many unanswered questions. Without knowing if my mother had ever

loved me at all. By the time I pulled into the driveway, I was an emotional

wreck, fully prepared to go to my mother's hospital bed and make her talk to

me and find a way to make everything all right.

As it turned out, there was no need to go to the hospital. It was about

four o'clock on that late spring afternoon when I parked the car. As I ran up

the stairs from the back porch I heard a familiar deep-throated laugh coming

from the kitchen. I climbed the last step and I saw her sitting at the kitchen

table, a martini glass and the ever-present ashtray in front of her, hair perfectly

done up in a French twist, fully made up, eyeliner and red lipstick intact. She'd

had the grace to don a silk kimono, the only reference to her supposed illness.

Lana stood at the kitchen sink, pouring herself a Coke and sneaking in some

vodka while Maria wasn't looking. She had her back to me, unaware of my

entrance.

My mother took a long drag on her cigarette and exhaled slowly, smiling.

Her eyes glittered as she drawled, "Well, look what the cat dragged in." Lana

turned at the sound of her voice, and in that moment, forgot to hide her complete satisfaction at my confusion. And I suddenly understood that at this point, whatever this was, they were in it together.

Before I could ask the nine million questions racing through my brain, my mother gave me the only answers she was willing to give out. "Turns out it was an allergic reaction. I'm better now," and then she laughed. Lana turned away as she laughed along, although somewhat nervously. "Um, yeah, guess it wasn't as bad as we thought. Sorry."

I hadn't spoken a word. My brain was full of confusion and questions, but I just couldn't begin that conversation. I sat down on the top step and I really don't know how long I sat there. I felt a new emotion, worse than any of the wounds my mother had inflicted over the first 20 years of my life. Ah, I thought- this is what betrayal feels like. Even though I was in a kind of shock, I knew that I had to get out of there. I'd nearly run out of money on the way home, as I'd left most of what I'd saved for my share of the rent and other bills in my rush to get home. I didn't even have enough for gas to get back to Chicago. I didn't know what to do. Just the same, I turned to my mother and said, "I'm glad you're alright. And I'll be leaving tomorrow."

17~ A Way Out

I went upstairs to my old room and sat on the bed. I was so shaken by the whole farce that I couldn't even cry. To this day, I don't have a clue as to what the motive was in bringing me home that way. I wondered at what kind of people would take pleasure in such a charade. I felt like I was a hundred-years old or maybe just crazy. I threw my coat off and laid down on top of the covers and curled up into a ball and went to sleep.

I woke up with my coat draped over me like a blanket and Drew sitting on the floor by my bed. It took me a few minutes to figure out where I was, and when it all came flooding back to me, the tears came too. He smoothed back my hair.

"Don't cry, E. They don't even understand what they did." I just shook my head.

"I have to get out of here." He nodded and just kept holding my hand, looking nervous. Then he said, "I can't stay here, E. I mean, I haven't been here since…" He smiled a sad smile. "I can't stay. And you shouldn't, either." I looked at him and watched as he became nothing more than light shifting in the air. I sat for a while, then realized I had only two options: Dad or Annie. I went to the kitchen and dialed my father's office. Maria was pouring herself a cup of coffee when she heard me ask for him.

"He's not there, darling," she began, but before she could finish her sentence, my father's secretary told me he had a meeting to attend in France after his holiday in Japan, and now wouldn't be home for another week. I'd have to wait till Maria either went to sleep or leave the house to make my next call. I went to my room and counted what was left in my wallet, about twenty-three dollars and change, no credit cards to my name, and the new account I'd just opened in Chicago had about fifty bucks. I hadn't even thought to bring my checkbook, and my roommates were just that, not friends, certainly not the kind you could ask for a loan. My choices were now whittled down to calling Annie or finding some kind of job just long enough to get me back to Chicago.

I threw on my coat and walked down to the playground. I kept expecting Drew to show up, but he never came. I didn't realize till years later that it was still too painful for him to be there, and especially when he couldn't help me. There was too much of himself, his dreams and the life he'd wanted for us, still hanging in the familiar air.

I don't know why it took so long for me to think of the pay phone down at Morelli's Market. I walked the half-mile shortcut through the woods and exchanged greetings with Mr. Morelli, then excused myself and walked around back to the old phone booth. It was a leftover from when the store had been a gas station and no one ever bothered to take it down. I dialed the operator and gave the information to make the collect call to Annie. When she answered, I didn't have to explain much beyond what I'd seen when I got home. Annie sighed.

"I tried to reach you before you left, after I talked to the hospital. I'm so sorry. I wish I could have saved you the trip."

"What really happened?" I asked, wondering if the story my intuition had begun to weave would turn out to be accurate. Annie hesitated for just a minute.

"She overdosed. There were too many pill bottles in her bag and drugs in her system to tell what did the trick. They didn't think she meant to do it though. At least that's good news." Then she was quiet. I leaned my forehead against the glass of the phone booth.

"Annie, I can't stay here, and I don't have any money to leave. I don't know what I'm going to do," I said softly. I could hear her smile over that long-distance line.

"Elaine, what do you want to do?" she asked softly. My head was swimming from lack of sleep and the confusion of it all. I'd missed two days of work by now, and I hadn't even called them because I'd been so hellbent on getting home. I figured I'd lost my job. I'd only left a few bits and pieces behind, I hadn't even had time to accumulate much in the few months I'd been there. And, whatever life I'd begun there would be stained with this betrayal, or at least that's what it felt like then.

"Can I come there?" I asked her. "Can I come stay with you and Ed till I find a job? I promise it will just be for a couple of weeks." I figured Florida was far enough for a fresh start. I had so many good memories of being there, plus it was warm. Maybe even warm enough to melt the chill that had wrapped itself around my heart.

Annie said, "Of course, if you're sure that's what you want." I told her I was sure and she arranged a plane ticket the next day. I left without saying goodbye to my mother or Lana. I mailed a note to my roommate and told her I'd send money for her to mail my things. The rent was paid for the month and I wrote that I was sorry but I knew she'd find another roommate in a heartbeat. I called the bookstore and the paper and explained as best I could, and they were kind.

Four hours after that plane took off, I landed in Ft. Lauderdale and started my life over again. I'd spend the next eighteen years there. I'd get married, have my first child, and come close to dying. See, that's what's left of the story. Just keep reading. And trust me, though there appears to be no sense to this knotted-up sequence of events, in time it will all unravel in a sort of perfectly imperfect pattern. You'll see.

After my exodus from Pittsburgh to the safe harbor I'd come to count on with Annie and my Uncle Ed, I think I slept for most of the first few days. I'll admit there were a few years where I really tried to get lost and find myself at the same time. And because they loved me, they let me. I got a waitress job with Ed's help, seeing as he knew everyone in town and they all pretty much adored him. It's still like that, after 50 years of running a successful construction business, he still goes to the local children's museum in his town to see what needs fixing. And who he can help. And he was just like that with me.

Annie had always been his right hand at the business, and for more than 20 years she helped him try to make it work. But when the slump hit and his jobs got smaller, she got a job of her own at the private hospital nearby. She'd spend almost 30 years there, and she still tells me it went by like a flash. During those years, she raised two great boys, and tried to help me figure out life. Whenever I've stumbled, she's been there to tell me it will be ok. During the worst times, she let me keep my pride, but she never lied to me. She never pretended it was ok when it clearly wasn't.

Besides Francis, Annie is the one person in my life who helped me know what the right thing to do was in any given situation. And that is no small thing. They'd always been my anchor and when I needed them, a port in a storm. This time was no different.

The best part of moving to Florida, outside of my new proximity to the beach, was having Annie and Ed close by. For a while I worked at a steak place, evenings, and then when I knew it would take more than just one job to move out and into a place of my own, I took on a shift at a breakfast joint. Because those jobs filled up my bank account but not my brain, I decided to try to finish what I'd started in Ithaca.

I contacted my old advisor at the university and arranged to take a few courses in what they were calling "long distance" education at that point. Remember, this was long before the days of the personal computer, online learning, and hell… it was even a couple years before FedEx was born.

For the next few years, my days were something like this: waking up before sunrise to work the very early breakfast shift at the 'Ham N Egg', where I enjoyed a cast of regulars. Someday I swear I will write a book about that place. Walter "two eggs poached, dry toast, butter on the side" was my favorite. He growled, barked, and banged his three-pronged cane on the floor when he wanted more coffee. Marva, "the lady with the neon-orange lips" who left her lipstick stain on every coffee cup she touched. Bob, the wannabe rock star who manned the grill mornings so he could rehearse with the band in the afternoon and rock out in dive bars at night. All for basically no money except the feeling that it was worth getting up every day. The list goes on, but I'll save it for a different story. The very best part of this job, was that this place, which didn't hold more than twenty-five diners at a shot, was right across the street from my new 300-square-foot studio apartment, perched above a dry cleaner, real estate office, and orthopedic surgeon who happened to also own the building. I paid $125.00 a month for that place, and scraped to make it.

Anyway, after heading home from the Egg, I'd study and type my assignments on a typewriter. A manual typewriter. Once a week, I'd take a large manila envelope to the Post Office and mail it off to my professors. The school had agreed to honor my small scholarship so I only had to pay a nominal fee for tuition, and of course I had to cover my books. I never managed to get through to a Master's degree, but I got a lot of education and the help I received from kind and caring professors made me feel good. That was like water in the desert back then. By 3:00pm, I'd be in the shower, then donning yet another polyester uniform to head to the Pit-Stop, a well-known steak and chicken house, where I often waited on Annie and Ed and their friends, especially if they knew I'd be working. At night, my station would be empty and clean and I'd head home to grab a few hours of sleep before I started the whole routine over again. I did this for about two years, till a brutal case of exhaustion and pneumonia forced me out of the breakfast business. When I'd recovered, I found a better evening shift at a four-star restaurant on the water, and the tips more than covered my bills. Now that I could sleep past five in the morning, I took advantage of my new schedule and the offers my co-workers had been making to "show me the night life." And in the late 70s, south Florida certainly had plenty to offer in that area. I soon had a favorite hangout, a small club tucked behind the "strip" on Fort Lauderdale beach, just about a mile from my apartment. The Village Zoo was just as the name implied: A soft-rock, disco hangout with a bartender who made a

great Tequila Sunrise and a DJ who closed the place each night with

Stairway to Heaven. The crowd was a menagerie of old hippies, disco babies

village people and lost girls. So I fit right in. But the real lure was the guy who

took IDs at the door. His name was Keith, and he was a doppelganger for…

can you guess who? I quickly developed a crush. And he seemed to return my

feelings, but Andrew seemed to show up every time I got close to this guy..And

he wasn't at all happy about it.

Andrew pipes up." *That* guy." He's playing with Riley's video controller

and every time he accidentally kills poor Mario, I hear a loud "oops, sorry,"

which is often since the closest we got to video games when he was alive

was Pong. Let's just say the degree of difficulty in Riley's simplest game is

light years beyond what it took to chase that little white dot back and

forth, even under the influence of quite a few beers.

"Drew? You had something to say?" I ask. He just shakes his head

shakes his head and deliberately avoids my gaze, but I know what he's thinking.

In those days of 'free love' and you know, make love, not war and all of that liberation

a 22-year-old virgin was something rare. But then Keith came along, all smooth and

sweet and looking like my dead boyfriend. He didn't even have to ask. So it

happened.

And I felt mostly… sad.

Just another moment that I should have shared with someone I loved beyond

description, and there I was with… "*That* guy," says my friend in the corner.

"Yeah," I say softly. "That guy."

The thing with that guy, and any guy I'd tried to date over the years since Drew had been gone, was that I just couldn't let myself go. And while I liked the initial feeling of being with someone who could hold me, kiss me, and say all the things I wanted to hear, my brain would start whispering things I couldn't really hide from myself.

So before anyone got in too deep –since I couldn't really access any emotions of my own – I would end it. While it's hard to remember a lot of the feelings of those years, I do remember the way I put one foot in front of the other to try to build a life. A life without Drew. A life, I thought, without love.

I soon realized I'd gone as far as I could in school. I'd had enough of waitressing and the kind of manic life that came with working till the middle of the night, dancing till dawn, and waking up at noon to lay on the beach till it was time to do it all again. I was ready for a real life. And to have that, I needed a "real" job.

I had always felt best when I was in a library, a bookstore, or a museum. Those jobs were quiet, I could be around the things I loved – books and paintings - but have plenty of time to write. Basically, I could hide in plain sight. But Florida being so young culturally, there really weren't any museums or galleries like in the northern, bigger cities, or real publishers like in Chicago. I didn't have enough of a track record to approach a newspaper, nor was that what I really wanted to do anyway.

It was on to plan B. Except for one little detail: I didn't exactly have a

plan B. It was by pure accident that I wandered into a small bookstore one day,

in search of a book of Auden poems, and found a job. *The* job. It was in the

very funky part of town, the artsy part where I was in my element. I could also

be the quiet girl, because that's what people expect of a girl in a bookstore.

And since it was very quiet a lot of the time, I started to write. Not for school,

not for scholarships. For me.

I'd written poems, kept journals, and even tried my hand at a few short

stories since I was in my teens. Writing was always a way for me to sort things

out. Now, though, it took over. When I wrote, no matter what it was, I lost

myself in what I was doing and it felt like I couldn't think about anything

else. Writing became my surefire escape, a mental retreat. But suddenly,

as I started to let myself feel again, writing became something different.

Like breathing, I really had no choice but to write. Every day, if even for a few

moments. A few words. It was as if a sharp knife had been drawn against my

skin and all the poison of the past was slowly pouring out. Some days it was so

painful I would forget to breathe for pages. I know this because I'd put the pen

down and suddenly gasp for air.

I felt a kind of relief, the kind you feel when you realize you DO know the way

out of the woods. I learned that no matter what, I could deal with whatever the

road ahead would bring, as long as I could write it down.

I was wandering around the small art gallery three doors down from the bookstore on my lunch hour one day when I met Lo. She was up on a ladder and I didn't even see her at first.

"Hey, can you help me?" was all I heard. I looked up, trying to find the source of the voice, and after a few minutes I found her. A girl about my age was perched precariously at the very top of a ladder, trying to hang a complicated mobile from the ceiling.

"Hi," she said. "I've managed to get kind of stuck up here, and there is no one else due in for about an hour." We grinned at each other. "You work in the bookshop, right?" She leaned in for a closer look while she white-knuckled the ladder with the hand and the corner of the wall with the other.

"Yeah, that's me, the book wench. I'm Elaine." I extended my hand until the ridiculousness of that gesture made us both laugh at the same moment. She told me her name was Lilliana but her friends all called her Lo. I steadied the ladder and helped her down. She dusted herself off and offered me a cup of coffee. I checked my watch and happily accepted. And with that we began a friendship that has lasted more than 30 years.

Lo was just what I needed at that time, the right combination of fun and practical wisdom. She was married but pretty sure it had been a mistake. I loved being there to listen when she needed to talk.

Drew showed up every now and then to check on me and by now I'd figured out how to handle that when other people were around. I never told anyone about him. Not the live Drew, or the dead one. As long as I didn't share the story, he would stay all mine. Also, I thought it was my best chance at avoiding therapy.

I enjoyed Andrew's company when the store was slow, until he decided one

day it would be amusing to change the book covers on all the new arrivals.

He'd figured out by then that there were a multitude of things he could do

without being noticed.

Turns out the only people who could see him were me, animals, and

very small children. Other than that, he was invisible. He used that to his

weeks exchanging books and not speaking to him (which, by the way, really

annoys someone who has only you to talk to).

Despite his penchant for practical jokes, with Drew for company, my

new friend Lo, and Annie and Ed close by, I started to build a real life in

Florida. It felt right. It's where I had waited for Drew. It was where there was

family – Annie, Ed, and my grandparents too, who loved and supported me.

More importantly it was where my mother wasn't.

After about six months at the bookstore, I was promoted to assistant

manager. I upgraded to a one-bedroom apartment closer to the beach. Over

the next few years, I'd fill my life with writing, learning to surf, and the few

new friends I made, although mostly I hung out with Lo and Annie's gang. I'd

finally built the family I'd always wanted. I spent time with my grandparents,

learning their stories and how to cook. "Real Italian, not imitation," pipes up

my friend. I smile at him and we both remember so many things at once.

Instead of yearly visits and quick trips to the mall with Annie, we'd meet for

dinner, or catch a movie. We both acknowledged that in another life, she

would have been my real mother. In this one, we'd settle for just knowing we

loved each other as if she was.

Slowly, my smile, the one before that awful night in Georgia, returned. I felt surrounded by love. I had work I liked, friends and family, and time to heal. The only thing missing was the thing I could never have: Drew, alive and real and with me.

By the time I turned 26, I'd dated and danced and avoided commitment at all costs. I never got my heart broken because I never fell in love. In fact, I'd made a big decision about all that. I would try to find a new best friend, since the one I hung out with most was, shall we say, unavailable. And then I would marry THAT guy. So.

In the meantime, Pally had moved to Florida with her new husband, the doctor. Ron was really handsome and she was as beautiful as ever, but still Pally. She longed for quiet nights at home and kids, and Ron craved a constant social life. But somehow as a couple, they worked. I met Bill a year after she moved down the street from the house I was renting, and a year after that, I married him. He was nice looking, funny, and relentless in his pursuit of me. I liked his family. I liked him. I didn't love him, and I felt safe choosing someone I thought couldn't break my heart.

Even if he died. Great plan, right?

Right.

Bill was your average "average guy." He had that thing where he got attached and for him, this was it. He looked bewildered the first time he told me he loved me, and I laughed.   We'd been dating about six months and I was drifting between mild lust and like. I wasn't so much in a hurry to get married, but in those days if you didn't have kids by your early thirties, it was pretty much over, and I really wanted kids. Or at least "kid." What finally pushed me into the possibility of more was that Bill swore he wanted all those things, too. After a year of dating, when he   asked me for the fourth time, I consented. I'd started to believe he might be   my last

chance. Funny how you know in your heart when you've just agreed to give

up.

My friends all had the same reaction when they met him. "Um, really?"

was the general reaction. "I mean, he's cute, and he seems nice, but…" They

mostly let it drift off there. What they weren't saying, didn't want to come out

with, was, "Are you KIDDING?"

Everyone could see it but me. I had my eyes on something else. I

think they used to call it "the biological clock," and it was ticking like crazy.

It makes me sad that I didn't stop and think longer about what 1 was doing,

but at the time it felt like I needed to jump. I'd been avoiding love for so long

because I really believed I'd never find anything like what I'd felt before, so I

settled for what I thought I could control. Big mistake. Huge. Every step closer

to the wedding I felt more and more sure I shouldn't do it.

But I couldn't figure out how to make it all stop. I felt silly and I

couldn't find the words to explain to everyone that I was still in love with a

dead guy, who by the way I still got to hang out with. Drew wasn't any help

either. He was around a lot those days before the wedding, mostly making fun

of Bill's little idiosyncrasies. In some ways, I married Bill as a kind of revenge

against a universe that had seemed to punish me for no reason. The only

problem with that strategy was that the only person I hurt in the end was me.

In the end, I closed my eyes and let it all happen to me. The wedding, the honeymoon in the Bahamas, the making a little domestic life in the tiny apartment. It was ok for the first couple of weeks. I mean, seriously, weeks is all it took for things to start to slide downhill. Maybe that's why I don't make fun of celebrities (or anyone) who divorce after a month or several. Because I truly understand that you can be so blinded by what you think you want and what you think you've found, that you dive in on a wish and a prayer and maybe a lot of cocktails, and when the fog clears and you look at each other across the scrambled eggs one morning, the only clear thought is, "Oh holy crap!"

Bill quit his job at the bar two weeks after we got back from the honeymoon. It was the fourth or fifth job he'd had in the two years we'd been together. Clearly something was missing in his work ethic, because my suspicion always was that he hadn't exactly been the one to initiate the partings. He wasn't a big partier, didn't have some big dream of a career he'd rather be chasing, and didn't have a "master plan." He was just lazy. In a big way. I didn't know it then, but found out much later in our marriage that he'd never bothered to finish high school after he failed one class his senior year. All he had to do was complete it in summer school but he just couldn't be bothered. He wandered away from high school just as he wandered away from jobs, from opportunities, and later, from me and his child.

The weird part was that everything he left behind he would end up carrying in the large chip on his shoulder. He held his many failings against the world, and whomever was conveniently close enough to blame. But our life together had begun, so I put my head down and determined to find a way to make it as good as I could. Pally had her first baby that year. She, little Isabella and I spent the afternoons I got home from the bookstore early walking to the beach together. We were both happiest when our husbands were otherwise occupied. She'd started having concerns about how different she and Ron were and what she wanted her marriage to be. Even so, she pressed him for another baby and he went along, thinking that the busier she was with the kids, the less time she'd want from him.

When Gracie was born, he had the perfect excuse to take a chief of staff position and was just about never home. Pally didn't seem to mind at all, while all I wanted was for Bill to be home long enough to get me pregnant. But I was working a lot as well and it just hadn't happened yet.

I had been the last of my gang to still be single so now that everyone seemed to be married and moving on into adult life, whatever that was supposed to be, life seemed calmer. Andrew seemed to be gone more than he was around. We never talked about it but it felt like he was trying to let me try to have a new chance at life. Or at least one that didn't involve regular conversations with someone dead.

Even after things started to get hard, I didn't see a lot of Drew in the first years of that relationship. He'd show up now and then when I was lonely or troubled about something, and we'd talk, but not about Bill. He told me later that I was right, that he thought he owed it to me to stay out of things and give it a chance. And because I had no one to talk to, I started writing in earnest. Most of what I wrote took the place of the conversations I missed having with Andrew, and over the next two years I finished my first book of poetry, *Things We Keep*. I ended up finding a small publishing house through one of my connections at the bookstore, and it had a nice little run, that book.

I mostly published it for Francis, who always loved my poems and made me believe in myself. That was just one of the many gifts my father gave me that cannot be measured in dollars and cents. Francis had mellowed with age, and felt deeply the lack of time he had spent with his older kids while he was working nonstop trying to keep Maria happy and a roof over our heads. In the years since, he had really tried to reconnect. When he and Deborah had a son, it opened my dad up in a whole new way. He became the guy who said "I love you" every time we talked. He encouraged my writing and told me he was proud of me. And all of that pushed me to be brave. The most important thing about that book was that it helped me find what I knew I needed to do. What I had to do to keep that spark in me alive. After a little while, I moved from the bookstore to the publishing company, where I'd taken a job helping their writers manage the maze of promoting their wares. I traveled and spent lots of time in New York, where I fell in love with the city and the time I got to spend there. Nights away in hotel rooms and on airplanes also made for plenty of quiet time for me to work on my own writing. And to avoid the fact that even though I was married now, I was still pretty much on my own.

My position paid very well and thank god, because Bill wasn't much help in the paying the bills department. It also offered lots of perks, like a company car when I needed to chauffeur the clients around, an expense account for entertaining and travel, and lots and lots of parties. Most importantly, that time on the road, away from what wasn't working at home was exactly what my writing needed. I started a short novel about life in the sixties, based loosely on my brother's escapades in the world of rock-and-roll and my general observations as a child of that era myself. It took me three years to finish, but when I did and the book was published, Bill was happy about the money, if not my brief time in the spotlight.

But as the book became a small success, he started to resent the fact that I was bringing home the bacon, even though it had always been that way. He was verbal about it in private, and worse, in front of our friends. I started to crawl back into myself and downplay any praise or compliments I was given. When Bill told me if I wanted a child, I'd have to back off my own career, I stopped writing without a second thought.

For a guy who didn't have much sense, he did have a knack for knowing what made me listen. I'd always known I'd want children, and in those days, you didn't just go off and have a baby. You waited. You waited for the man, the marriage, the house, the whole thing. We still lived in the house I had rented, but we had first option to buy it when the owner decided to sell, and with my job and Bill's "jobs," even though they came and went, he went along with it when I wanted to take the leap and buy it. This seemed like the silver lining to the cloud I'd lived under for so long. He'd made it clear this all hinged on me focusing on our life, not my writing. I listened to my head, if not my heart, and gave myself up for the dream of a baby.

The funny thing was, once I committed, Bill detached. He started coming home really late or not at all, claiming he was working fishing charters with his new best friend, Al. He'd call sometimes, and other times, when he didn't bother, I'd sit by the window into the small hours of the night, wondering if he was coming home at all. At first, I was just mad at myself, because I didn't trust him. It was his idea to have a baby, after all, and he claimed to be working so hard to help us financially. But I never saw a paycheck, and was still paying all the bills, including his truck payment. The insurance I had at the time didn't have maternity, so we found an outside policy and I gave him the money to take to the agent. All the paperwork was done; all he had to do was pay them. I didn't find out till the morning I threw up for the first time (and somehow knew I was pregnant) that he'd pocketed the money and now we had no insurance at all.

Instead of fixing our marriage, my pregnancy pushed Bill over the edge. He'd never been responsible for anything in his life, not even a cat. The idea of having to support a child, and quite possibly a wife too, since I'd have to take off at least a month after the baby was born, scared him senseless. Which is saying something since the man was not exactly a rocket scientist. He started to drink more often, and he wasn't a nice drunk. Meanwhile, I had to save every penny to pay the doctor and the hospital in advance. The day Bill went with me to hear the baby's heart beat for the first time, he melted down in front of all the nurses when they asked him to sign the papers promising to pay any costs that might arise from complications. He looked at the papers, looked at me, and said in a loud voice, "there is no way I'm signing my life away for this," before walking out the door.

I was humiliated. Let me rephrase that. I was seven-and-a-half-months pregnant with my first child, deliriously happy about that, but clearly on my own with this and embarrassed that all the nurses now knew it. I made a joke about the inability of some men in these situations, while ignoring the couples who tried to hide their sympathy for me. I tried to smile and not cry, and signed the papers myself, right there on the line that said "sole responsibility."

Andrew came back that night and he's been around pretty much ever since. Bill hadn't just left the building, he'd left ME at the doctor's office and I had to call a cab to get home. When I got home he wasn't there either. I could tell he'd taken a bag, his golf clubs, his scuba gear, and some clothes, so I didn't know if he was gone for a few days, a week, or forever. And at that moment, I wasn't sure I cared.

I made myself a cup of tea and sat on my grandfather's old slide rocker on the big screened porch and stared at the trees. I felt the baby moving, soft and rhythmic like she always did. Like a fish, gliding around inside me. Yes, I said she. That's how sure of it I was. In those days, an ultrasound was a luxury and one I definitely couldn't afford without insurance. So since there seemed to be no other issues with my pregnancy, I relied on the doctor's opinion and he and all the nurses had guaranteed me I was having a boy. The way I carried the baby, high and in front, the rapid heartbeat, and my endless heartburn, all underlined their opinions.

But the reality was that the day I got the news from the doctor that I was indeed pregnant, I had gone directly to the beach that was a mile walk from our house, and stood at the edge of the water on a bright May afternoon and thanked the powers of the universe for my baby girl. I had not a doubt in the world that this child was a daughter, and for the nine months that followed I never wavered from that conviction. I asked my friends not to throw me a shower until after the baby came, because I didn't want to have to return oceans of tiny blue onesies. And I picked out two names that I held in my heart. Lo's middle name was Roseanne, so I chose Rosie, and Gemma, a name I'd heard and liked. In my mind, Rosie was fair, with roses in her cheeks, and Gemma was dark, like me.

And for a middle name, Ann, after my grandmother and my aunt. In any case, I knew, as all mothers do, that I'd know her name when I first saw her. And that's exactly how it worked out.

Drew spent a lot of time around me in those lonely days of pregnancy. I'd wake up to find orange juice and saltines by my bed in the beginning when I needed that to calm the queasiness of the early months. When I'd curl up on the couch alone in the evenings, and rest my hand on my ever-growing belly, Drew would put his hand there too and his eyes would widen and his smile would grow. All the things I'd wished Bill would feel and say, Andrew supplied.

Somewhere around the end of my 8th month, Bill showed up. He didn't explain his absence, he didn't apologize. He said he was going to keep working the charters with his friend Al and he'd be around. We didn't talk much. Something had happened that broke whatever hope I'd had for this marriage, and whatever that was, it had happened to him as well. So even though the space between Bill and I was growing, I was content and happy, knowing when this baby came, I'd never feel alone again.

When Miss Rosie Anne finally arrived, blonde and blue eyed and smiling, something wonderful happened to Bill. For the first year of Rosie's life, he turned into the father I'd once imagined he could be. He was there every day, holding her, playing with her, building things for her to play on, even when it taxed his patience beyond imagination. (Remember, it is a rule that all children's toys that must be assembled basically come with instructions printed in only two languages: Swedish or Japanese.) But he was present.

While he wasn't any closer to me, he was totally in love with this child, and that was more than enough. I still didn't love him in the way I knew I should, but at least I began to like him again. We had a good year and a half.

And then life happened. Rosie was nearly 2 years old and had a bad cold that she couldn't seem to shake. All new mothers are figuring it out from day one pretty much on their own. The one thing they don't tell you when you take that first child home from the hospital is the most important thing you could possibly hear: "Trust yourself." Trust your instincts, your gut. Because you are usually right.

Rosie had woken up with a strangling cough and she was obviously having trouble breathing. I'd read every page of the ten or more baby books I'd bought, been given, or borrowed, and at 15 months, had navigated colds, diaper rash, teething and first steps. But this was my first round with high fever and a panicked baby. I ran a hot shower and let the bathroom fill up with steam, and slowly rocked my screaming daughter until the hot vapor cleared her throat. I slept with her in my bed until morning and then took her to the pediatrician.

The strange thing is, at some point during the night, Bill left the house. While I was in the nursery, or in the bathroom soothing Rosie, I don't know. But he left. The good daddy ran. Bailed. Checked the hell out. And basically, to this day, never really checked back in.

The doctor ruled it croup and pneumonia, a rare and potentially dangerous combination. He agreed I could keep Rosie at home if I stayed home with her and followed a strict regime of medication and breathing treatments. I remember it was early fall, and I got a call the next day from Bill saying he was leaving for a month's charter trip in the islands with Al. I told him I couldn't work and needed some help with Rosie, and he said I'd have to figure it out. And that was that.

I called one of the girls who had pitched in at the bookstore for me whenever one of the regulars was out. Caroline was a painter who was on the way up, but she loved the chance to make a few bucks whenever she was in between shows or commissions. Annie would have gladly stepped in but she Ed were in the middle of a construction boom and working like crazy. But Caroline loved Rosie and the feeling was mutual, so we shared the work at the store and of caring for Rosie for the next few weeks. What began as a temporary fix turned into a long and lasting friendship. Without Caroline, who Rosie would later rename "my Ala," I'm not sure what I would have done. To this day, I have a portrait that Ala surprised me with of Rosie at that time, it hangs in the hallway and reminds me of those sunny days together.

Annie and Ed acted as our weekend relief. Along with my own grandmother they were thrilled to fuss and babysit and basically spoil Rosie rotten. Their own grandchild wouldn't come along for years, so Rosie reveled in that role (and still does). For me, I knew that I'd made the right decision when I had come to Florida all those years ago to rebuild my life, even though it was turning out to be very different than I'd imagined.

While she recovered, I slept in Rosie's room for weeks on an air mattress on the floor, with one hand up through the crib bars on her chest, so that I could feel her breathing. Eventually, she got wise to me, and would hold my hand while she slept. I don't think my left shoulder has ever been the same from the weeks of sleeping like that. But as any new mom will tell you, there really aren't any limits when it comes to a sick kid.

Rosie got better, finally. But Bill and I never recovered. When he finally returned home, it was to shower, shave, and head right out again. We kept up the charade for another year and a half, till I got tired of feeling like a dog he came home to feed, and only occasionally at that. I kept telling him I couldn't take it. That I wouldn't stay and settle for half of a life.

He ignored me till about a month before I finally left him. I paid all the household bills because that was the only way I could be sure they'd get paid, but I stopped paying his. First, I handed him his car payment and said, "I'm not paying this anymore, so you will have to."

He looked at me in a confused sort of way and said, "Uh, ok." A week later I told him I'd put the electric and phone in his name, and gave him the new bills. I said I wouldn't be living there much longer, so he should take care of them if he wanted lights, heat and a phone. He just stared at me like I'd lost my mind, and then shook his head and walked away. Finally, about two weeks later, I told him that I'd taken him off my health insurance and he would have to look into coverage for himself.

He stopped in his tracks and said with a goofy grin, "Are you trying to tell me something? "

"Bill," I said, with a sad smile. "I've been telling you for the last six months. I'm leaving, and I'm taking the baby. We aren't any more than an afterthought for you these days, and we are both worth way more than that." While he sat down at the table and put his head in his hands, I told him the movers were coming in a week and that I would leave him half of everything we had, plus the bed.

He looked up at me then. "I'll change. I'll do anything. Don't go."

I'll admit it, I felt bad for the guy. I always liked him, but that had never changed to love. After Andrew, my heart had decided on how much it could open up for anyone, and I honestly thought that I had made a good decision when I agreed to marry Bill. I thought I could be his friend and partner, and that someday, it would deepen into that forever kind of coupledom I'd always hoped for. Maybe it would have, if he ever spent any time around me. Or if I hadn't left my heart in a place in Georgia I'd never actually seen.

For Rosie's sake, I told Bill there was only one way I'd consider staying. He had to stop drinking, stay home at night with us, and go to a counselor with or without me. He stopped crying, looked at me, and said, "Ok." We spent the afternoon in that kind of tentative tiptoe dance you do when you're afraid that one false move will cause every delicate thing you've built to crumble. But we found a counselor and made an appointment for the next day, which was a Friday.

Bill wanted to go alone at first, he told me, because this was his problem, not mine. I tried not to hope, I really did, but when he sat outside on the lawn with Rosie for hours that morning, I'll admit the idea of keeping our little family intact made me smile.

Since Bill was scheduled for his first meeting with the counselor that afternoon, I took Rosie to the beach for a walk. It was late September, and the Florida air was unusually crisp, a condition that occurs twice a year in that land of humidity and heavy air. The late afternoon sun glinted golden off the water, and locals wandered in rolled up jeans and t shirts. I remember feeling that somehow, this was a beginning, a new life that I would unwrap like a gift from golden paper. But in the back of my mind, I wondered if I would begin it on my own, with just my daughter by my side.

I'm sure it's not a shock to find out that Bill didn't come home that night. He never made it to the counselor, or to the dinner I'd cooked and laid out with candles and wine on the dining room table, or to breakfast on Saturday. In fact, I didn't hear from him until later that next week, when he called from "a friend's" in the Florida Keys. He'd snuck into the house one day when I was at work and Ala had taken the baby out, and collected enough belongings to get by. He was drunk when he called, full of curses and enough epitaphs to clear a church. I didn't listen to the words he said, but could feel the meaning in the air that hung around them. I told him that when he came home, I'd be gone. I went to my lawyer's office and told him that I needed this marriage to be over, at any cost. And then I went home and had a good long cry.

The divorce took a year. For someone who rarely had the energy to go to work each day, Bill proved to be limitless in his ambition to get every cent he could from me. After months of trying to divide our possessions civilly, during an argument in the attorney's offices over butter knives and blenders, I calmly stood up without saying a word and walked towards the door. I put my hand on the knob and didn't turn it, but spoke loudly enough for everyone in the room to hear me. "Give it to him. Everything. Anything he wants, except Rosie's things." I was calm, and inside a smile was finding its way out. "I just want this to be over."

In the end, Bill got the van I had paid for, the household goods, and almost all the furniture. But he didn't get anything involved with my writing. He didn't want to push his luck I guess. When he agreed to sign over full custody of Rosie for the deed to the house, I signed a quit claim without a word and walked away.

When we went to court to settle child support, he told the judge he couldn't see why he should pay us four-hundred dollars a month, since he knew he could buy a BMW for that amount. The judge just stared at him and shook his head. But based on the earnings Bill reported, he managed to get away with $65 a week. All these years later, that is what he continues to pay, till Rosie finishes school. Or, more accurately, what he pays when he gets around to it, which is usually four or five months behind. Anyway, you get the idea. For Rosie, if not for me, I realized it was the right thing to leave. To keep writing and to make a life for her and myself. A however I could, to make it a happy life.

Ok, there is obviously more to that story.

Andrew chimes in, "OH so much more. That guy cracked me up." I glare at him. "Ok, mostly he cracked me up. Sometimes." I'm still glaring so he leaves it alone and pretends to stare out the window till I stop giving him the evil eye. I think I've told you enough that you understand why I left, and how good it felt right then to be on my own with my little girl. Bill would drift in and out of Rosie's life for years, never being the father I'd hoped for, and it broke my heart because it broke hers. I told her people do the best they can and well, his best wasn't very good in this area. And like all children in this kind of story, she learned on her own that his failings and distance had nothing to do with her. Like all fathers who abandon their child, it was his loss not to know this amazing child and the woman she would become. I was the lucky one who got to be there for every minute.

I had no idea what would come along next in my life. Whoever does, really? You hope for the best, plan for a rainy day, and mostly just muddle through. After so many years wasted with the wrong guy, the last thing I was looking for was another guy – even if he was prince charming. Or so I thought.

What did happen next was that I spent a nice long summer with Pally and Ron, living with Rosie in their new guest house. Ron's success had just grown more and more over the years as he became well known for his skill as a cardiac surgeon. The beautiful beachfront estate he'd bought for his family was his penance in a way for rarely being there for them. As always, Pally was generous and offered us a home for as long as we needed it. Since Rosie and Grace and Izzie were best buds, I agreed to her offer, and took on more work so I could save up for our own place. Andrew was around a lot that summer. He loved watching the girls play and took on the role of 'invisible lifeguard' when they played in the pool with Pally and I, and watched over Rosie like a hawk. When it came time to move into the small townhouse I'd found to rent, it was hard to leave the comfort we'd found there with our friends. But it was time for me and my girl to begin again.

The next two years would bring a lot of change. We moved in January and settled in quickly to a new part of town, finding a new preschool for Rosie and new everything for me. I'd been promoted at work, which meant I could be home more – which also meant more time in the actual office. But it was good. We settled in and even though my commute was longer, it was a real fresh start. Drew kept watch and showed up when I felt overwhelmed to provide entertainment, support and comfort. Rosie was about to turn four, a happy little girl full of smiles. And then, just when it felt like everything had found a new rhythm, the sky began to fall.

It started with my grandmother's unexpected death in late February. We'd been close since I moved to Florida years before, spending lots of time together, more in the years since my Gramps had passed. She'd always been frail of body but sharp of mind, and I'd counted on her advice and ability to help me see through even the most muddled emotions. And she adored Rosie. "Because she's yours," she'd say.

I had chosen our new place partly because it was literally minutes away from her and Rosie loved our visits where Nana would cook for me and share Rosie's Happy Meal French fries. We'd had our last dinner two nights before she passed, and I can still close my eyes and feel that last long hug. I was so lucky to know her, and for those years to be so close by. Like Annie, she had been a big part of how I healed my broken heart.

I mourned quietly for her and felt her around me a lot in those days. I was grateful for being busy with work and spending all my free time with Rosie and Annie who was finding the loss of her much loved mother very hard. We helped each other clean out her little apartment with the assistance of several bottles of wine and my Nana's favorite records on her ancient record player. We cried, and laughed and got through the worst of it together.

But there were more hurdles to come. Maria and Lana had also moved to Florida a few years after me; Lana had married the second of three husbands, and had just had her second child. Kelly had opened a couple of retail stores out west, and offered Lana and her husband the chance to run one of the businesses in Arizona, so they'd moved in March. And with the exception of my grandmother's funeral, I'd avoided my mother completely. She didn't like babies or small children so it wasn't difficult at all. She lived an hour or so north of the rest of us, and had found a job to supplement the alimony Francis paid and allowed her the lifestyle she'd never left behind. Maria was working her way through the doctors at the hospital near the restaurant she was managing and having a gay old time. Same routine for her, plenty of vodka and valium and a few new recreational escapes she'd discovered, courtesy of her new and often much younger friends. I guess it all caught up with her, because one day she just didn't show up for work. The owner of the restaurant got worried, because one thing Maria had never been was late for work. After a couple of hours when she didn't pick up the phone at her apartment, he went to her place and saw her lying unconscious on her living room floor. He called an ambulance and found the super to let him in.

I'm going to tell the rest of this part in the abbreviated form, for two reasons. One, because it won't be anything you didn't see coming, and two, because it just wears me out to replay in my mind. It turned out that Maria had suffered a major cerebral hemorrhage. No one at the hospital could figure out if it was the alcohol, the drugs, genetics, or a combination of all of the above, but in the meanwhile she laid in a semi-conscious state while they tried to come to an agreement.

Annie and Ed were away with their oldest who was off to college, and Lana was conveniently two-thousand miles away. Suddenly I went from disappointing daughter to next of kin. The hospital said they had tried to reach me, but I happened to be on an airplane coming back from the east coast when it all happened. When the doctor finally ran a test to see if Maria's arteries were blocked, she had a stroke during the procedure. By the time they reached me, she was unconscious in the ICU. I had landed in Miami, where my office was, and she was 45 miles north in West Palm Beach. I drove home, picked up Rosie from school, took her back to Caroline's where she'd been while I was away, and drove north to stand in the doorway of that room and try to figure out what I was supposed to feel.

For the next three months, I made the trek from home to Miami and back, then north to visit my mother, who invariably greeted me each time I walked in the door with a welcoming, "I wish your sister was here."

"Me too mom," I'd say. This went on as they moved her from the hospital to a rehabilitation center, and finally back home. Maria fought with everyone who tried to help her, and during the 16 weeks of rehab and slow recovery she lost her spark. The vivacious, glamorous party girl who tanned too much, drank more, and played tennis in short shorts became an 80-year-old version of her 62-year-old self. Only meaner, and bitter beyond description. She settled into that way of life and signed a permanent lease.

It was just after my mother was moved home that Francis decided to invite his children and grandchildren to Disney World for a long weekend. Exhausted from the four months of caring for an ungrateful Maria, I was desperate for the break. I packed an excited Rosie in the car and headed north for what would be a crazy few days with cousins and step-siblings and of course, Minnie and Mickey. I felt like I could finally breathe after so much loss in the space of a few months. I'd spent so much time caring for a woman who barely acknowledged me that I'd lost my smile. Here in the sunshine and warmth of my father's affection, it started to come back to me. But that trip became important in more than a few ways.

On the last day before we'd all leave for our respective destinations, Francis and I sat with our feet in the hotel pool, watching the kids splash happily. We chatted about a lot of things… my divorce, his sadness at my grandmother's death, whom he'd always adored, and in time the talk turned to Maria. Over all the years they'd been apart, after his marriage to Deb and even after his son was born, my father had always taken the blame for the failure of his first union. He blamed himself for the hours spent working to support a family of five, a home in the suburbs, and the lifestyle Maria demanded. He blamed himself for not being there in the lives of his kids more, not understanding the absence of affection when he wasn't around or the effect of Maria's abuse.

He stared down into the water and said quietly, "There are things I've never told anyone, you know." I didn't say anything. "Just once, I would like to tell someone the truth about that time," he added.

I leaned into him softly and said, "You can tell me, Dad."

For the next hour, he told me the story of Maria's affairs. How he had caught her more than once at her favorite haunts, cozied up to some man and drunk. How he'd known about one guy in particular and how much it had hurt him to have to leave her there at home with us while he worked harder and harder to make enough money to figure out some way to divorce her and still take care of us. It wasn't the life he'd hoped for, that was for sure. Finally, he told me the truth about the pregnancy that caused her to end up in the hospital. In all that time, I had never found out, though later I would hear that I was just about the only person in town who didn't know. As betrayed and angry as he felt, Francis knew his first obligation was to his children, so he'd made the decision to stay married until we were all grown and gone. And he worked hard to live up to that promise he made to himself, waiting until Lana turned 16 and turned on him, and he really had no reason to stay.

It's funny how you can "know" something in your heart, but hide from it until the truth finds its way to your brain. That's when it becomes something you can't deny. All those years I'd suspected what my mother was up to, but I'd never known for sure. I didn't have the pictures in my head, nor the details to bring the blurry images into painfully sharp focus.

All that was different now.

I went back home to my routine, but having all of this information tumbling about in my mind, I could barely look at Maria when I returned. I started working through the piles of paperwork and endless waits in crowded social services offices till I could get her on disability. And then I let the system and my siblings take care of her. Over the years ahead, I would take a step and try again with her, over and over and over till it became like a movie you try to watch, each time forgetting there was a huge defect in the DVD. It would never play the way it was meant to, and you'd always end up frustrated and disappointed.

Most of the year the eastern coastal shores of Florida are a dream place to live, sunny and warm and green and flowers everywhere. But summer in Florida is brutal. Humid, hot, and often rainy. By the end of August, we were all ready for a break. Pally and I decided to slip away to the cooler breezes of a small island town on the Gulf coast, a sleepy little place where the rent on a rambling beach house was crazy cheap.

We stole a whole ten days away and it was grand. Long walks on the beach, experimental barbeques (you cannot grill avocados by the way, but pineapple is awesome), and lots of Motown and dancing on the deck. I started each day with a three-mile jog down the beach followed by a swim. The girls were brown and full of smiles and the trip was deemed a huge success. We were meant to head back to reality on Friday morning, when during my last run I tripped over a rock and hurt my foot. Andrew hadn't been around much, but suddenly he was right there with a worried look on his face. It was bad enough that I had to hobble back the last mile, and I wonder to this day if my ghostly friend didn't somehow help me get home. By the time I made it back to the cottage, my entire foot was fairly swollen and starting to bruise.

Since Pally is a former nurse, it only took a quick survey for her to diagnose a bad sprain and possible torn tendon. She never travels without an armory of antidotes and remedies and she fixed me up good for the ride home. After a Percocet and an ace bandage and some ice I was down for the count. We arranged to stay one more night at the cottage, and the next morning we managed to pack up the girls and head back to civilization. We were home by noon. Rosie's dad picked her up a couple of hours after we pulled back into the mainland for his once-a-month visit (these seemed to coincide with his sister's days off, a fact that made me feel better about letting him take her anywhere, since I knew Sally would make sure Rosie was ok). The painkiller was wearing thin and I was afraid to unwrap my foot, so I started banging around the kitchen to see what the liquor stash was like.

About that time, Pally called. "How's it feeling?" she grinned into the phone. "Not numb enough," I growled. "Well, I've got the remedy," she half-sang, "unless you're sick of me." I smiled at the phone despite the twinge in my foot that was getting harder to ignore.

"Never," I said. "What have you got in mind?" "Well," she said, "Caroline just called and said that guy at the Barn she's dating says there is a great band playing tonight and he'll get us in." "The cute guy that you are lusting after gonna be there?"

"Shut up. Do you want to go or not?"

"You're married, Pal."

She laughed. "Yeah, I know, but I'm not dead. I just want to dance with him."

I knew this to be the truth, Pally had an eye for the cute boys, but not the heart for cheating, which it had become clear was not an issue for Ron. So how could I be mad at her for wanting to feel pretty and wanted once in a while? Didn't we all need a little of that, as long as we remembered what was important? Besides, she wasn't giving up.

"Come on. You know you want to."

"You got something that will help me forget about this foot?"

"Absolutely."

"And you'll drive?"

"I'm not letting YOU drive, silly!"

"Then I'm in."

A good three hours later, I skipped the pain pills and opted instead for a couple of ibuprofen, and pulled on my boots and jeans. When Pally had seen her target enter the bar, she made sure the bartender would keep me in supplied with those seemingly harmless fruity cocktails. The ones that slowly creep up and before you know it, well, you know. And suddenly a shadow crossed my heart, in the form of a tall stranger. Trouble in a leather jacket and with a charming grin. Trouble that would be so much more than I could have imagined. But I wouldn't have believed that then.

Pally had left me propped up at the back bar, and was canoodling with the object of her affections while I tried really hard to look cute and awake simultaneously. Not as easy as it sounds in my pleasantly pain-free but more-than-mellow state. At a certain point, I became aware of a face that belonged to that shadow. A pair of warm brown eyes, head full of black curls, and a serious five-o-clock shadow grinning wildly at me from across the bar.

But I was in no mood, not to mention that I couldn't actually form sentences at that point. I think what I managed was a sort of half grunt, half snarl. "What?"

The eyes just crinkled up and laughed at me. Disgusted, I refocused on finding the straw in my drink, which somehow was full again. When I looked up (because I am, after all, a girl, and those eyes were awfully cute), he was gone. Sheer willpower or the exact angle of the stool against the bar, one or the other, you pick, saved my head from slamming down on the bar in surrender. I wanted Pally, I wanted my bed, I wanted it to happen like it does on Star Trek. You know, I'll bet you've been there too. I remember saying it out loud, to the bartender's amusement. "Beam me up, Scotty."

And then, the shadow spoke. "O'Connor, James Rafferty," said the voice that was laughing in my ear. "Raff."
I couldn't turn my head because the room had begun to spin, and I wasn't about to risk a collision with my brain and the rest of the universe, so I sat still and pretended not to listen.
"You'd probably feel better if you ate something," he said.
Unruffled by my silence, he kept on. "My cousin works in the kitchen; I could get you whatever you want. Sandwich? Soup? Ice cream?"

Here and now as I sit staring out my window, open to a rare rainy summer day, Drew has arrived and he has a comment. To be clear, he has a few, and none of them are nice. I'll let you imagine what he has to say, since he had already guessed that this guy was going to be more than I could handle in a lot of ways. After a while of him stomping around the backyard mumbling just loud enough for me to hear through my open window, it dawns on him that I need to get this part of the story on paper, regardless of his or mine or even your opinion of what comes next. He mouths a silent "sorry" through the window glass and slowly fades before my gaze.

So, back to my new friend. Do you believe this guy? Me neither. Part of the reason I wasn't responding was obviously the combination of pain, alcohol, tiredness, pain, and really loud music. And pain. The other was that even though he was standing behind me all this time, I could still see his face like it had already burned into my memory. It was one of those times when you just know that life as you know it is changed forever and you aren't sure if that's a good thing or not. I hadn't responded but he didn't give up. I felt him lean in a little closer and whisper. "Or," he said, we could dance." And somehow, despite my distinct state of sleepy drunkenness, my broken foot, and everything else, we did.

I'm thinking about this now and wondering if I can actually do it, tell you this whole story. It's a big part of understanding my life, and there really isn't any way to leave it out, but it's already making me kind of sad. So enough for now. Sorry.

23~ Forgiveness

Later, after the rain clouds have cleared, Andrew is standing behind me as I watch Riley and his friend Matt in the pool. The sky slowly turns that grainy color between blue and violet that is so particular to twilight in this part of the country. He doesn't touch me but I feel him, and I'm struggling with the tears.

He says, for the nine-thousandth time, "E. It's not your fault. I mean, it wasn't your fault. E. Come on, you know this." I do, or I should, but I don't feel that way most of the time. Call it Catholic guilt, call it failed intuition, whatever you want, it's that thing in your brain that screams at you, "Why didn't you know better? Why didn't you see it coming?" And, on days that aren't so good, "Why were you so stupid?"

I've heard it from the shrink, from my friends, from clerics and fellow survivors, but it doesn't really matter when the echoing voice inside your head won't shut up and won't stop blaming you, even if the only person who got hurt was you.

I sit down on the wicker loveseat and stare for what feels like hours but is really only minutes. When I look at Riley, the unlikely product of the five-year bad movie of my life with Raff, it's the only time I think I am close to understanding the meaning of anything. There's a peace about the boy, in the middle of all his ten-year-old manic mayhem. He was born grounded, centered, with the soul of a Zen Buddhist. He drives his sister crazy because nine times out of ten, his logic is undeniable. Everyone has a gift, and this is his. I think it's because he got all the good genes that were buried inside his tortured father, and none of the drama that colored his life. That's when I think about it at all. Mostly, you know, I don't. I just love this boy so much. It might sound strange, but just having him on this earth makes it alright to forgive myself for all the other stuff. Because in the end, the other stuff fades away, and the love you have for your children never does.

I decide to give myself the next day a break from routine, thinking it might help me get through writing all the tough stuff I have to tell you. Because you might enjoy the visual, just imagine this. It's a Saturday in August, about 110 degrees in the shade, and I'm sitting in one of those arcades the size of a public school where the music is incessant and manic and designed to make you spend money. I've discovered for me it's a kind of white noise and I write better here than almost anywhere. For about ten bucks, it buys me a couple hours of freedom and my own particularly bizarre form of peace and quiet. There is so much noise you can't hear any of it, you know? I need that at the moment. It drowns out the voices in my head, at least the ones that don't come to visit me from the great beyond.   Ha, ha, ha. I crack myself up.

Anyway, I've been walking around for days with a feeling of anxious foreboding. I love the way that sounds, like something crazy is about to happen. "It's that PTSD thing you have. It's not real. NOT real." Drew pips up from the corner of the room, where he is watching a family sing Happy Birthday and eyeing the cake, which is shaped like a giant Scooby Doo. He's probably right, I decide, although the feeling is hard to shake and quite frankly, annoying as hell.

"Yeah, well, you are not helping, mister," I throw out mentally. I am, at least, careful not to talk to him in public. I mean, society has its limits and there is an advantage to being allowed to live outside of a mental facility. Drew is loving this place; every now and then I catch a glimpse of him watching Riley play the claw machine (I secretly think he is the big secret of Riley's unerring success at that game), and counting the small pile of stuffed prizes that are beginning to mound in front of my laptop. He is, after all, still 19 in a lot of ways. I asked him once what is was like, I mean, did he feel like he was changing over the years, growing older inside his head, even though he was, well, dead?

He looked at me with a puzzled expression and said, "I only know what you know, E. So, yeah, I guess." I have to wonder why he sticks around, because it hasn't exactly been all laughter and roses. And sometimes, when I try to wrap my brain around what my life would be like without him, that's when I understand everything and nothing at the same moment. You know what I mean -- that feeling that you can't explain or deny?

The boys rush the table yelling for the go-cart tickets, "Cuz the line is really short right now mom!" and then whoosh, they're gone again, and Andrew is right there with them. My heart does that ouch thing, and I wonder again what life would have been like if my boyfriend hadn't fallen asleep at the wheel.

I guess I need to fill in some of the blanks for you at this point. So here we go, back to the guy, the bar, and what happened next.

From the night we met, Raff made himself a constant in my life. He'd show up when I was at work with flowers or lunch, some small trinket he'd picked up because it made him think of me. He'd leave notes on my car windshield. He was that ultimate romantic, all give and no take. He was tentative with Rosie, didn't push, and she loved being adored, even from a distance. I resisted for months. And then I just fell. He was tender and sweet and strong and very, very sure of himself. That was what he showed me. That was what I believed.

Time passed, and things changed. It was three years after I'd met Raff, and one year and ten months since I'd started running away from him every chance I got. More accurately, since I'd started failing at running away. Because it never worked. Not even for a day. When you are in a relationship with someone like this, at some point you really have no control. And if the person who doesn't want to let you go, has all the power, and money to boot, well, there aren't many doors to run through.

When Raff came along with a sparkling laugh and eyes to match, the kind of crooked smile that would turn heads in a crowded room and an intellect that never failed to amaze me, I was quickly smitten. Even though he was almost 10 years younger, he seemed so together. So sure of what he wanted in life. So sure it was me. Everyone loved this guy. My family, my friends, everyone we met anywhere we went. My daughter. My damn cat.

Oh, there were signs, but I refused to heed them, even when they were pasted against my forehead by Andrew. He was the one who saw it first. After we had been dating for about eight months, Raff suggested that we move in together. Rather, that he move into MY townhouse, and share the rent until he finished law school. He'd work part time at the car dealership to pay his share. I wasn't that cautious and confused 28 year- old who'd gotten married to have a baby. I was 36 and had navigated parenthood, divorce and so much more. I was confident, and successful and my life felt complete except for one thing. I wanted someone real to love and to love me, and Rosie. I wanted a partner, someone to build a life with. The kind of life I'd dreamed of with Drew. When Raff asked, all I saw was the beginning of that life. I'd been so happy I never thought past the YES that flew out of my mouth before he had the question all the way out of his. I thought I'd found it. That dream I thought I'd lost forever when Drew died.

That night, while Raff went to pack his stuff out of his parent's condo, I made space in the closet. Drew spoke quietly from the bedroom. "Are you sure about this, E?" He sounded sad, not confused, so my instinct was that he thought I had finally left him behind. "Andrew Cosentino, you know this doesn't change the way I feel about you one bit," I said, smiling. "It's just that it's time for me to do this. It's time for me to move on with my life." "It's not that, E," he said, shaking his head with a worried smile. "I just get a bad feeling about this guy sometimes. Like just when you think you know him, he's going to turn into someone else." I must have had a confused look on my face because for a moment I thought he was going to hug me. Maybe he actually did because I felt the strangest feeling, like he moved through me or something. It felt warm but weird, so I shook myself out of the moment. "Seriously, Drew, do you know how weird that sounds?"

"I know, E. I wish I could explain it, but I wish you'd just think on it a while."

I was feeling like I had one foot on the road ahead of me and I was really scared that if I let myself listen to all the sense Drew was making, I'd never be able to drag myself away from his memory and the strange in-between life we'd sort of built. I pushed his words and all my logic aside. "Look, I've known Raff for eight months now and he's only been wonderful to me and Rosie. The family loves him and except for Annie and Ed, they don't even like me! Even my boss loves him. I need to give this a shot, because I want this kind of family. For Rosie. And for me. I want what we could have had but I want it real. I want a man who can hold me and protect me and stay by my side always."

At some point I'd turned away from him and tears were running down my face and the pain of losing everything I'd wanted with Drew cut through my gut. As I turned to him, the look on his face stopped me, and he said softly, "Oh, E. I messed it all up, didn't I?"

And with that, he was gone. I didn't see him again for almost six months. And when I did, I couldn't face him.

My dad was the only other person who had reservations and of course, felt the need to make sure I understood them. It started with his observations about Bill.

Rosie's father had been so indecisive, his friends called him "Maybe Bill." Case in point: I left him one time, standing in a hardware store as he swiveled his gaze, neck craned upward, hands on hips, as he puzzled over which of two ceiling fans he would allow me to purchase. The fans were nearly identical but for a three-dollar difference in price. I'm not sure whether he was paralyzed by the price difference or the fact that at some point if he decided, he would actually have to pull out his wallet and buy it.

That about sums up the whole relationship actually. We spent our time trying to convince each other of our life philosophies, which were polar opposites. I wanted to live life, he wanted to watch everyone else and save the tax.

Francis weighed in early and often where Bill was concerned, and was very supportive when I made the decision to divorce. "You did the right thing, babe," he'd say with a rough pat on my shoulder. "Guy was a wimp." "Guy was a loser." "Guy was clueless." Need I continue?

After years of trying to find Andrew alive and well and waiting for me in the person of some guy I was just waiting to meet, I woke up. I mean to say, I came to believe that it wasn't going to happen for me again in this life. I'd had my chance, missed the boat, pick your euphemism, and I'd settled for Bill. How we women despise that word. *Settle.* Why is it always the precedent to "for less"? You don't even have to say that part, it's just understood.

But here's what was going on in my head. I figured if I loved the guy but wasn't IN love, I couldn't ever get hurt again the way I had before. Of course, Bill had convinced me that I hung the moon, that he wanted me more than anything, and that he wanted all the things I wanted. This never once struck me as strange, since I don't think we ever discussed it -- what I wanted, that is. I don't know that I'd even have known at that point how to describe what I wanted, except for knowing for certain that I wanted kids. I have known since I was a child that I wanted my own chance at a family, if only to prove that raising children could be something other than a battlefield where everyone has to die a little every day.

When Raff came along, in the early part of our relationship my Dad came to town for a quick visit and we met for dinner so I could introduce them. Francis was charming and cordial. Raff was also charming and played the loving boyfriend, full of praise for me and adoration of Rosie.

Later in the evening, as Raff went for the car, my dad looked at me and spoke quietly. "Be careful, Elaine. This is not another Bill. Be careful." But just like Andrew's warnings, I filed this one away under "you don't know him like I know him." A mistake that would prove to cost me dearly.

25 ~ What's Behind the Curtain

"I love that you save everything for forever." Andrew pipes up from Rosie's room where I find him looking through our old yearbook.

"What are you doing? "I ask. He smiles at me and holds up a worn and folded handkerchief wrapped around a flower now brittle and brown with age. "Remember this?" he says, not looking up. I can't talk. I'm suddenly a hundred-years-old down to my bones and I'm so afraid that if I let the first tear fall, I will spend the rest of my life trying not to drown in the sea of my own sadness. The phone rings and I'm suddenly grateful we don't have to talk about this right now.

It's a few hours later, Drew is gone and I'm driving across town to take soup to Rosie. It was her when the phone rang, calling to say she's got one of her colds. Ever since she was a baby she's had the same issues as her mother, meaning every cold has the potential to become something far worse. She may be nearing twenty-one, but I still worry and fuss. I think she secretly likes it. Like any mother and daughter, we've had our share of moments I'd rather forget. But deep down, and you don't have to go that deep, we both know we'd kill for each other.

It's like that with your firstborn. This tiny round shiny baby with honey-colored hair and the most amazing blue eyes that so surprised me from the day she first looked up at me. I still wonder where she came from. She was the angel child, only crying when she was hungry, wet or tired. Slow to walk, slower to talk, peaceful and smiling. Easy. Happy. Wonderful.

When I finally realized that her father was never going to be the man she or I needed and we moved on, she never blinked. She made the best of it, and held on to me just a little tighter than before.

Rosie Anne, the child my heart wanted since that day on the playground. It makes you really wonder how all the universe unfolds sometimes. There are children you raise, and those who just let you watch them grow. Rosie is like that; she just figures it out as she goes and very rarely do I have to slowly push her back from the edge of things. I am in awe of her. Her values, her solid belief in certain things, her fierce loyalty to her friends, her fear of everything except anything that threatens her family or those same friends. Her ability to stay organized with work and school, all while living in an apartment that usually looks like it's been through an earthquake. Several earthquakes. Earthquakes where food is involved. She makes it all work and she thinks I don't notice. Well, I do. I see it all and no matter how many ways I try to tell her; she doesn't hear me. But I get it, and she gets me. I wish she'd had the chance to know Drew. If that'd worked out, well, she'd have had him for her dad. And if wishes were horses, well, you know.

Ok, back to the Raff thing. I think I was talking about my dad, right? Well, I don't know how the old Hoosier does it, but he has a sixth sense about things. A few weeks after that dinner, he called me. There was something about Raff, he said, something that made him worry for me.

"I messed up with you, I think," he said over the phone one night after all the pleasantries had been exchanged. I'll admit, that's quite an opener, and it caught me off guard. "What do you mean?" I said, not sure I wanted an answer.

"Well, with all that your mother put you through, and me being gone, you just had to be so strong. I never really helped out with that, and you are a pretty tough kid." I still wasn't sure where he was going with this, and for a moment, a smile lingered on my lips, thinking he was going to get emotional about the upcoming handoff to the new guy in my life. But I didn't expect what came next.

"This guy, he doesn't like his women strong. You're going to be you, Elaine, and one day that's not going to work for him." He sighed. "It's my fault I let you figure things out for yourself. Hell, I made you do it. And you did. You are strong. Some men have trouble with that after a while. So be careful, Elaine. Don't be too strong with this one."

Part of me wanted to laugh at him and tell him, no, no, you don't understand, he loves that about me, but my lips wouldn't make the words. Behind my ready defense, somewhere inside my head, I knew. I knew he was right. But after years of being sad, I wanted to be happy more than I wanted to listen.

So I just said, "Ok, Dad, I'll be careful. Thanks." And I hung up the phone. And my spurs. Or something like that. You know what I mean.

A couple months pass and Raff and I are living together, quite happily, and thinking about actually tying the knot. Dad and I talk every week or so. Raff has been hinting a lot and I am giddy with anticipation. I'm in L-O-V-E, the big kind. I'm blind, deaf, and dumb with it. We are in the pre-honeymoon honeymoon period: Little love notes on my pillow, small velvet boxes with diamond studs one day, silk nightgowns the next, surprise weekend stays at romantic hotels and long talks way past midnight examining everything from the meaning of life to which of the meals I've cooked this week he loved more.

You tell me, how could I have known? There was only one thing I knew about Raff that made me the least bit troubled. One night, after snuggling up on the couch to watch a movie, we opened a bottle of wine and put on some old Motown. He looked serious. The movie had been a story about a bunch of orphans and kept me laughing most of the way. I guess I hadn't noticed he had disconnected.

"What's wrong, babe?" I asked, as I settled in next to him. He looked up at me and I could swear there were tears welling up in the corners of his eyes. He couldn't hold my gaze and he seemed to struggle with what to say. "What is it Raff?" I whispered. "Tell me, I love you."

He reached for my hand, and held it between his own. He looked down and said, "There is something I need to tell you." I waited, sensing he needed to do this at his own pace. My heart was pounding and ten-million horrible and devastating scenarios played at warp speed inside my brain.

"When I was ten days old, my mother left me at an orphanage in Chicago. Carmela and Sal are not my parents." My heart dropped for him, as this was clearly still very painful for him to talk about. He continued, "They adopted me when I was nine months old. I've never met my birth parents and I don't think I ever will." He looked up at me. "How does a woman hand her child over to a stranger and turn around and walk away? HOW?"

I didn't recognize the look that took over his face at that moment. I know now that what I felt was fear, because I didn't reach out to hold him. I just sat there in silence, waiting for a sign to know what to do for him. In that moment, I saw how this abandonment had colored his life. Snippets of the family stories he'd shared came into focus. Years later, I would recall the warning thought that grazed my brain and flickered away (I PUSHED it away) before I could process it. But at the time, I kissed him to make that thought disappear, and it worked.

What I would have seen if I hadn't been so deeply in love was the truth about who he really was, and the thread that ran through his whole life. From the moment he'd understood that he'd been abandoned by his mother, he had developed some very strong ideas about women. He built them up, the ones who came across his path, put them on pedestals too fragile and unreal to hold for any length of time, and then, when they inevitably fell, he couldn't   take it. For him, it was the betrayal of that first woman all over again. And he lashed out with all the force of 29 years of that betrayal. He hurt so badly, the only comfort he could find was in giving out more pain than he'd been dealt.

The first time I stepped off the pedestal was six months after he moved in. We'd spent the evening at Carmela and Sal's, watching football. I'd had one glass of wine too many and entertained the family with my opinionated views about the game. I never noticed Raff's growing upset and was too wrapped up in what I thought was family affection and laughter to notice when he abruptly ended the evening by handing me my coat.

"I have to work early, let's go," he'd said. Looking back, I wish I'd seen the warning signs. But I couldn't for the life of me tell you how I would have known. I think it's like that for a lot of women who end up where I did; one moment your world is picture perfect and the next you have taken up what feels like permanent residence in hell.

"Seems like I could have warned you," Andrew chimes in from the corner of the patio where I'm taking advantage of a cool late morning in early October and trying to rid myself of writer's block that starts each September and takes its time letting go.

"How?" I reply "And even if you tried, I wouldn't have listened," I say. "I was too far gone." He's behind me now and even though I can't see his hands on my shoulders, I feel them. I feel comfort and warmth and a million other emotions. I can hear his unspoken assurances that everything will be ok. That I can do this. That the bad part is over and in the past.

"I know," I say, and I'm not sure if it's out loud, or just inside my head. "I know."

The phone rings in the other room, breaking the moment. I'm relieved in a way; I don't want to write the next part. I leave Andrew and the laptop and search for the cell, which is never where it sounds like it is. I get there a minute after it stops ringing. The caller ID says Pally. *Weird*, I think. Pally and I talk about once every six months. I tease her all the time by answering the phone with 'who died?' I hit the button to call her back but there's no answer. I try to leave a message but the signal breaks before I finish, so I'm not sure whether it took or not.

I make a mental note to call her later and go back to the patio, but the moment has passed and it's just the computer now. No Drew, and the sun is gone behind what looks for sure like a cold front moving in, even though it's Arizona and what passes for winter here is a long way off. I reach for the sweater I keep out in the little alcove I use as a writing room and stare into the trees, but nothing is coming. No memory, no words. And it feels just fine that way.

A few days later, when I do find the words, I decide I've waited long enough to tell you about my fall from grace. Or at least from that pedestal I mentioned. I guess what happened on Easter almost a year later started the night of that football game. At some point Raff hadn't liked something I said, and he'd decided I wasn't Perfect Elaine anymore. For my part, I was finally feeling like part of his strange family, and had found the kind of humor that worked with them: One-part sarcasm, two parts self-deprecation, like a conversational dirty martini.

It's always been my life jacket, the ability to find something that makes people warm up to me and laugh. It's really the only time I feel like a real person who can live in the world with other people and not just inside my head. That's what happens when you spend a childhood hiding in books, you lose the ability and the need to be real for most other people. Anyway, I guess he liked me better quiet and pretty in the corner, hanging on his every word or being the quiet helpful girl in the kitchen. "Quiet" is probably the key word here.

When we got back to the townhouse and Rosie was asleep, I started getting ready for bed. Raff was already laying down, still fully dressed, arms folded across his chest with a storm cloud dancing in his eyes. I sat down on the edge of the bed next to him and laid my hand against his cheek. "What's wrong babe?" I asked softly.

He hit me so fast and so hard with a closed fist that it took my breath away and I lost my balance and slid off the side of the bed to the floor, landing hard on my behind. I think my mouth must have been wide open in shock because all he said to me was, "Close your mouth, you stupid bitch," as he climbed over me and went to the kitchen and poured himself a scotch.

I don't know how long I sat there before I realized there was a trickle of blood running down my chin, from where he'd split my lip. I felt black inside, nauseous and empty all at once. So many feelings swirled around inside my head I couldn't identify any of them. I heard his voice from the other room. "You did this. You ruined everything. Goddamn you."

I know now that what I felt more than anything that night was fear, but I wouldn't have been able to tell you that then. I had been so deliriously happy till the moment he hit me; all I could think about after was how empty my world would be if the good part was over. But after a while, as I sat there on the floor, dabbing at my lip with my sleeve, I started to get angry. Just like I had since I was a child, I found a couple bricks inside my head and started to build a wall against the pain of what I was feeling. I'm really good at it, too. I can make a mean cement out of rationalization, self-loathing, and fear--and when I get started, no one is getting near me for a while. Not even Andrew.

I woke up on the floor next to the bed, with a pillow under my head and a soft blanket covering me. I opened my eyes and looked up, confused as to why I was on the floor, and met Andrew's eyes as he sat opposite me leaning against the bedroom wall. "Morning," he said, not smiling. I couldn't answer him. My face felt weird and I wasn't sure why, but as I started to sit up I saw stars for a minute and started to remember.

"Oh," I said, almost under my breath.

"Yeah," said Andrew, just as quietly.

Sitting up I pulled the blanket around me and glanced anxiously towards the bedroom door, which was open. I didn't hear Raff, but I could hear Rosie who was nearly five by now, playing in her room on the other side of the townhouse.

"She's fine," Andrew said to me, "and he's gone."

I don't know how long I sat there before standing up and moving to the dresser to look in the mirror. *It's not that bad,* I told myself. My lower lip was split and swollen, and there was a small bruise coloring my left cheek. More than that, it was the look in my eyes that scared me. I saw Andrew standing behind me now, and he was as angry as I'd ever seen anyone.

I suddenly understood the meanings of a thousand things about men, but mostly I knew he was angry at himself. For not being here, for leaving me. For dying. As if he had some choice in the matter.

I spoke to his reflection calmly, more for him than for myself. "It's ok. I know what I have to do." He didn't smile but I knew he felt reassured. I turned around to face him but saw only Rosie, smiling in the doorway instead.

Raff called all day, but I didn't answer. Instead, I dead bolted the door and Rosie and I spent the day watching movies and baking cookies and playing dolls and anything else that could distract us both. I was fine until after I tucked her in, when went to check the mail.

I opened the door to find a painter's five-gallon drum filled with what looked like a hundred roses, and Raff, who had apparently been sitting there for hours. He'd been crying. He was stone cold sober and very sorry. And I, like most women who didn't yet understand this kind of man, only felt grateful that he'd seen what a huge mistake he'd made. I believed him when he held me gently and swore that it had never happened before, and would never, ever happen again. I told him I believed he meant all of it, but that I needed a few days to think things through.

He shook his head and said he understood and that he'd be waiting and praying I'd take him back. He reminded me he'd never known love like this and didn't know if he could survive losing it. In other words, he said everything every woman in love wants to hear.

His reassurances drowned out all the voices inside me trying to warn me. He drowned out Andrew, who was louder than all the other voices combined. I felt the conviction of a woman in love. And the blind faith that whatever had hurt him so badly that he would lash out like this, I could fix it. I was strong enough, and above all, I loved him enough.

I smiled and asked him to call me in a few days. And as he walked away, I felt

again like I was in charge of my life, that time and love would fix this, and that

after all, I had made the rules.

Drew had drifted in and out during my first marriage, never saying what

he was thinking, like why on earth I would marry the mama's boy who couldn't

keep a job. I loved Bill as a friend, but what I loved even more was that he

really, *really* seemed to NEED me. I had shut off my "fall in love" valve after

Drew, having declared myself smart enough to know no one ever gets that

twice. I would settle for good guy, a good friend, and a potential good father.

Bill seemed to fit the description, and I convinced myself that he was sadly

misunderstood by everyone but me. He practically begged me to be with him.

How could I turn away from that? And you already know how that turned out.

Once Raff was back and we'd decided to give it a real try, Drew went on

what I will refer to as "vacation." To his credit, he tried to warn me, but I

wasn't listening. I didn't want to hear all the logic he had ready for me. And the

comfortable relationship ghost- boy and I had developed was starting to seem

like something I'd held on to for far too long, or so I rationalized when he

stopped appearing for long periods of time. Occasionally as things began to

disintegrate with Raff, I'd catch a glimpse of him in the bathroom mirror, with

a sad look on his face.

Later, when things got really bad, he returned, but at that point I couldn't look

at him. I was too ashamed. Ashamed of things that I had no way to control.

No way at all.

He's here now though. He's here standing in front of me, holding me with real arms, pulling me to him and whispering that it's ok, I don't have to talk about this right now. "There is time, E," he says. "Nothing but time, and you don't have to do it all at once." Because I know he's right, and because it feels so good just to let him hold me, I say "ok."

When Drew couldn't convince me to push Raff away, I thought it was his way of holding on to me. That he was in some way jealous that I could move on and have a life without him. When I told him that, his eyes filled with love and fear and sorrow. I knew I had hurt him. I knew he was right even as I stood there and fought with the awful truth of it all. It was a moment I would come to regret deeply as I lay in a dark room, naked, terrified, broken and bleeding on Easter morning a year later.

I needed a break, and not very coincidentally, today turned into a "not really writing" day. I kept busy with errands, driving Riley to a friends for an overnight, and made another soup run for Rosie. I skipped dinner in favor of popcorn and wine and an old movie that was just the right combination of make-you-laugh and make-you-cry. I drifted off to sleep on the sofa, with one dog on the floor and the outside cat who had recently decided to be an inside cat curled up at my feet.

I woke up in the middle of the night with the choking thing. Have I mentioned this? Usually I am having a nightmare, starring you-know-who, and I'm being pursued through a big empty house. What drives me crazy about this dream is that I love the house. I mean I really love it so much and the light is just beautiful, you know? It's that morning time just before twilight when the light is all perfect yellows and pinks, and all the edges blur so you can't see any of the flaws. Painter's light. I want to paint that house, except I can't because I'm running for my life, and at the same time I'm watching the whole drama play out.

The house is pale yellow too, with five floors, just a big box of a house, and it's on the beach on stilts and has lots of black rectangular windows. Inside, it's all wood, but not finished. There are walls here and there, but mostly it's just framing. And Raff is chasing me. I never see him; I just hear him. Smell him. Feel his anger. And the fear wells up like vomit and I wake up gasping and choking and crying so hard I can't breathe. Most of the time it takes me a while to realize where I am and to bring myself back to the now, where the dog and cat are staring at me, waiting for me to be the me they are used to.

In the daylight, I pretty much do a great job of forgetting all that happened before. But that's when I'm awake, alert, and in control. This, though, is what happens when I give in to sleep and dreams and memory.

Ok, do you think I'm crazy yet? But you see, you must see by now - there is just so much to tell. Yes, my life has had a lot of twists in 51 years. There has been a lot of time for all of this to unfold. Let's just say it's a life that has been lived. Not all of it good, not all bad. But full. And full of well, some pretty big stuff that I never ever thought would happen to me. But here we are.

I get up, make the coffee, and step outside into a sunny morning to let the dog and cat out. I look around at this place, the home I built out of sheer will. The warm yellow walls, the blue kitchen with pictures of the kids and Francis and friends. The stone and wood and green and blue of this outdoor oasis which is always filled with children splashing in the pool, laughter filling my head even now when there is no one here but me, alone with my coffee and the big stone Buddha in the garden.

I stop for a minute to let myself feel this moment. My life now is filled with so much that is good. So much I feared I'd never have. I let go of the memories that haunt me and take in the present with each breath. And when I hear the front door open with Riley's hello, I smile and return to the sweet land of mom. The rest of this can wait for a while.

Full disclosure: Months have passed and I haven't written a word. I tell myself I need more time. And as fate would have it, that's just what I've got right now. One of my authors is working through a major edit, and I've come to her hometown which also happens to be my hometown. October in Pittsburgh is a constant enigma. Some days feel like late summer, some feel like snow is just around the corner.

I love this place. I love driving up and down and around the green hills filled with pine and oak and maples resplendent in their autumn colors. I love knowing that any stranger I meet won't have to be a stranger for more than five minutes if you feel like striking up a conversation. I love that if you drop something and someone picks it up, they say "here honey," as if you're their best friend, then they pat you on the arm as they keep going. I love that easy and open way that these people seem to be born with, and how comfortable they are sharing themselves.

The people here make this place special. I'm so moved by what I think so many take for granted. Seriously, I wonder if other people feel the same way about the power of a kindness, when combined with a touch. It overwhelms me these days. No, wait, it always has. Even writing about it I feel the emotion at the back of my throat. Is it because there is no one around to make me feel warm these days? Could be a simple explanation, right? Who knows.

By a happy coincidence of my author blazing through her edit, the book is now safely in the hands of our publishing crew here, but instead of heading home, I'll be staying put. Deborah has planned a trip to Greece with her sisters, and when she came up with this idea, I'd offered to stay with Francis if I could manage it. The trip to Pittsburgh for work dovetailed beautifully into our plans, and so I get spend the next ten days with my father, who is now 80 and frail - of body, that is, definitely not of mind. Francis still has an elegance about him that was wasted on the life he has had. He knows how to use just the right amount of words to say something, and he always uses the pretty ones. Like "ecclesiastic" to describe food. Or "peripheral" to talk about how he treated his children when they were small, adding that his regret is "oceanic." I credit him with my love of language. And it certainly underlines his effect on the ladies over the years.

I've heard it said that timing is everything. In this case it certainly helped. Rosie had agreed to spend two weeks based in our house so she could make sure Riley was taken care of. I'm lucky enough to have a job I can pretty much do anywhere, from an office to a boat dock, or, in this case, the very same dining room table where I struggled over algebra thirty years ago.

And oh… this table. My father staged all the truly serious conversations at this table. Sometimes I felt honored, when he talked through a business strategy because it helped him to say things out loud. Other times, well, let's just say there where those *other* talks. It was quite apparent I was a disappointment in the math department. And he had serious problems with my wardrobe. As you know, the sixties produced some amazing fashion choices, so name the trend and I was trying it.

Last night we spent hours looking at old photo albums and I categorically denounced that blue and white checkered wool suit as well as every pair of glasses I wore prior to my senior year in high school. It was NOT my fault. Add the hair and the eyebrows to that list. My mother was cruel about things like wardrobe and makeup in ways that the best makeover show today would just not believe.

So. All these years later and it's me and Francis, long walks at the mall, dinner at Denny's or any number of local haunts, and lots of time to dissect the last three decades. In between our talks and outings, he sleeps. And dreams. John Wayne dreams mostly, he says. Sometimes he dreams of cars he had, or old girlfriends. He dreams in vivid and often quite graphic detail, but because I like you, I will spare you a full description.

That's been the oddest part of this visit. There must be something liberating about aging, at a certain point. When you rely on someone for almost everything, the only real independence you have is the control you exert over your communication. That is, whether you choose to converse or retreat into silence and sleep. As well as what you decide to confide to the daughter who has always thought you were normal, no matter what dream you were chasing. During this visit, dad has felt like telling me things he wants so badly for someone to know, like how he wished he'd been more present while the first four of us were growing up, and how he wished he'd understood daughters needed a lot of the same things he gave so easily to his sons. He has also been thinking that his marriage of thirty years appears to have become too much for his wife, Deborah. I point out that they were both old enough at the time they married to understand the implications of their age difference. I guess neither of them considered what happens when 50 and 27 turn into 70 and 47. How the touching would change. How legs that ran down steps two at a time would become tentative and slower. How eyes that offered a loving gaze would now flit away from the physical body, now that Francis spent more time in bed than not.

Things change, he tells me. And while he looks me straight in the eye and says she still is the light of his life, his angel, I know he is thinking that for her, he has become the worst thing he can imagine: A burden. She is kind to him, and takes care of him with a sweetness that comes when you share so many years with someone, good times and bad. But I can tell she gets frustrated too, when he doesn't want to come down for dinner or get out of bed. It's hard for her to not look ahead and understand what her life will be like when he fades away. She is still full of life, sparkling, cheerful. Madly in love with the five grandchildren she wants to spend more time with, and torn because visiting them means leaving Francis who cannot be alone now.

Deborah rarely complains, but I saw it in her eyes when we talked about nothing over coffee at the beginning of my visit, before she left. She is putting the rest of her life on hold. I want to tell her, at least it's not forever, but that would mean saying the words out loud. "When dad dies," Nope, can't do it. While she packed, I sat with her and we pretended, but there was an understanding growing between us. For the first time, I hoped that long after Francis is gone, Deb and I would remain friends. That, in a new and different way, came as a comfort. Then the moment passed and she was up and moving and building a small tornado of activity that whirled around me and Francis, and I saw that in all of it, all the attention and care, there was an ever-widening space between them. He wanted to talk about the old days and she wanted to talk about the grandbabies, both of them striving for a connection across a divide they could no longer cross.

Although we had made these arrangements months in advance, Deb waited until the day before she left to inform my father that she was going and that I would be staying. He pretended not to know me for the rest of the day. He was understandably angry. But more than that, he was frightened to be alone with someone new. Even if it was his daughter. Perhaps that was what worried him most, the inevitability that someone for whom he had been a pillar and a little bit of a god would now see him in all his human frailty.

I was angry at her, too, for what seemed like a very selfish move. She left before we were awake, leaving written instructions on the fridge door for meals, pills, routines. I sighed when I saw this, and realized then that no matter what kind of package it came in, this time with Francis was a gift. How often does a grown woman and her father of eight get to spend time together alone, and not at a holiday? So I smiled, thankful for this opportunity, whatever it would hold.

And sure enough, after the first few days of awkward and polite exchanges, Francis decided to admit that he did, indeed, know me, and began to open up. We talk about his youth on the farm, and what it felt like to go to school with only 20 other kids in the entire school. How he longed for education that he did not even know existed, much less know how to find his way there. He asks me to pull out a few old family albums filled with photos I've never seen, since his sister passed and his niece sent them to Francis. There are pictures of him at four, a cherub-cheeked little guy who reminds me of Riley. Another in a basketball uniform, the spitting image of my youngest brother Matt. One in a letterman's sweater with a shy smile.

We talk about the summer he and his brother Ralph went "up north" to work on a pipeline. Francis was only 14, but tall for his age and determined. The job paid five dollars a week, plus room and board. This was a fortune in those Depression days. The boys would stand by the ditch and throw large planks of plywood in for the pipe to rest on. One of the laborers somehow discovered that Francis was underage and tipped off the foreman. He gave him his week's wages and told him he was sincerely sorry to lose him, but he couldn't risk being fined. The laborer's brother slid right into Francis's spot. Ralph stayed on for a couple weeks, but was homesick without his brother so it wasn't long before he turned up in the soybean fields back home. They labored together on that land till they lost the farm a few years later.

Between drought and depression, and his father's failing heart, they just couldn't hold on. They sold the place and the land and bought a small frame house in Versailles, a pretty little town just over the river from Kentucky. The house had only two bedrooms, and the plan was to take in a boarder. Ralph joined the Navy, and Francis followed. After his stint, he and his best pal "Shorty" traveled throughout Indiana and Ohio working as salesmen, plying their trade door to door with gas heaters, vacuum cleaners, and even sewing machines.

Across the kitchen, I'm heating up his soup for lunch when I hear him say in a voice I remember from childhood, clear and strong, "Good Afternoon, Ma'am. My name is Francis Evans, and I represent the Hurley Heating Company. Now, ma'am, you know the coal heater you got going down in the basement is old-fashioned, and I bet you get tired of hauling that dirty coal down there every night, right?" I could just imagine his younger, dimpled smile, as he removed his hat, and continued. "Now what if I told you I had a new gas-style heater that would never require a piece of coal, and that would heat your whole house for just pennies a day?" He went on for about ten minutes, delivering his entire sales pitch from 60 years earlier as if it was yesterday. I had turned around and stood leaning against the counter, stirring the soup during this impromptu performance.

I mean, seriously, how often do you get to witness your own father's life in this way? I was moved, but didn't want him to see, so I just filled the bowl and set it in front of him, putting my hand on his arm. He looked up before I could turn away, and with his eyes moist with emotion, said clearly, "I'm not so proud of some of the things I did back then, just to make a dime."

I sat down with him at the table then, and he went on to tell stories of the days when he and Shorty lived on stolen crackers and ketchup soup, sharing a small room in a boarding house on the north side and sleeping in Shorty's car when they didn't have the weekly $5 for rent. Sometimes the coal heater in the customer's house was just fine he admitted… till he or Shorty gave it a kick. To try to get a stake in something, he took a second job, selling vacuum cleaners door-to-door in the afternoons. Shorty had a girl he was sweet on, so he went to work in a movie house, sneaking her in with him at night. But Francis was all about the work. Soon he'd proven himself to be the potential workaholic he would become in time and Goldman, the owner of the small appliance store, made him manager. Now he had one job, a decent paycheck, and even with the money he sent home dutifully each week, he had enough before long to buy a car.

And not just any car. A shiny yellow Mercury convertible. He and Shorty moved up to Point Breeze, just off the streetcar line, into a first-floor apartment in the back of an old prewar with a big wraparound porch. That car was his church, and every Sunday morning, he worshipped over a big bucket of suds as he cleaned and polished within an inch of its life. And that was how he met Maria. You've got to hand it to that woman; she knew potential when she saw it. He didn't have much, but she quickly learned that what he did have, he would willingly spend on her. And in the meantime, she could love the Mercury if not the man.

But that was a million years ago, and now he's had 30 years with Deb, and his fair share of good times and bad. Business success and investment folly. He's seen the world, from South America to Japan and even Russia, something a small-town farm boy never imagined. And now, as the time gets small, alone in this house where so much of our lives happened, he just wants to talk.

I love these stories. I steel myself as he doesn't spare me the details, remembering romances over long ago, and laughing along at tales of mischief with his Navy pals. But sometimes when he finishes recounting a memory that's left us both teary-eyed with laughter, he drifts away to a different place. More accurately, he comes back to now. It's as if he suddenly realizes that 80 years have passed in what feels like a heartbeat, and he's not quite sure how he landed up here in this kitchen, a row of pill bottles in front of his dinner plate and an ever-present cane at his side.

It's incredibly sad for me to listen to him talk about loneliness. I tell him finally, interrupting his slow attempt to make me feel that it's nothing, and he's ok, that he has only to say the word, and I'll gladly take him back to the desert with me. I have the room -- in my heart, in my life, in my house. I work hard to make this sound light while inside I am melting into myself.

I can tell he's taken aback. He looks at me straight on, and says a simple, "Thank you." We don't need any more words for now. Life with Francis has had its share of ups and downs, and like any father and daughter we didn't always see things in the same way. I think back to all the times it didn't work, and settle into the gratitude for how things are now, how time and life melt away all the hard edges of our hearts, and how all we both want is the comfort of love and memory. Here in this house, the memories come, of times I'd lost when I let all the love slip away. The memories come back. And I begin to remember myself before my life changed.

My last night there, I dream in technicolor. I have just turned sixteen. Francis and Jeff, a pal 20 years his junior, decided it's time for a trip in the Cherokee 180 4-seater plane they purchased a few years ago. It happened to be spring break, so his excuse to Maria was that he was taking me and Pally to Florida to visit my brother Evan, now known as Jesse, who was living in Fort Lauderdale and playing in his first real band. Even though Jesse is barely sixteen, the band was starting to get an audience and even my dad was curious. It would be the first of many attempts at reconciliation my father would navigate over the next decade or three. Jesse and Francis had, till the very end, a relationship that could best be described as confusing.

You see, Francis had the gift of music that Jesse clearly inherited. Riley has it too, by the way, and with each generation, the gift gets bigger. Francis was so proud, but resented that Jesse took his talent to a completely different world. Francis had to be content with singing folk songs and old country tunes to his kids until they were old enough to avoid him anytime that old guitar was out of its case… while Jesse held hordes of young girls in the neighborhood in a teen-dream thrall every time he and his band of long-haired buddies struck the first chords to "Louie Louie" in our suburban garage.

Francis came from the school of Elvis, while Jesse worshipped at the altar of Jimi, Janis, and Jim (Morrison, that is). While each had some appreciation for certain aspects of the other's affections, it fell just short of respect. And that was the mortar they were missing in the foundation of their relationship.

The rest of us watched over the years: Two bricks up, then something would trigger a break and everything would fall again. It broke Francis's heart more than once, and I never heard him blame anyone but himself. This happened long before the days of Dr. Phil, self-help and open dialogue about anything between fathers and sons… so I truly don't know how it could have worked out any other way between the farm boy and the rock star.

Back to the now-infamous spring break trip. Pally's folks wanted no part of her girl flying to Florida with a "hobby pilot," so that left my other partner-in-crime, and one of my dad's favorites, my friend Dee Kelly. Dee (short for Doreen Eileen Mary Pat) was the fifth child of ten of a volatile and vivacious couple known to all as Frank and Franny. The two had been moderately successful actors in New York in the '50s living in a fifth-floor walk-up in the Village.

They'd both left the Southie section of Boston looking for a life far, far away from the one they'd watched unfold around them time after time, one where parents had too many kids, worked too many hours, and downed too much whiskey. Funny how it worked out for them, because after the third child in four years, they'd migrated to Pittsburgh, where they could buy a small house in my neighborhood for the price of their annual rent in Manhattan. Frank got a "real job" during the week working for the newspaper, and Franny stayed home to raise the ever-growing brood.

It was so much fun to hang out at the Kelly's. The kids were all ages and everywhere. The house was a riot of clothes, sports equipment, and ballet slippers, and where was always something strange and wonderful cooking on the stove. Franny and Frank swung wildly between passion and a Taylor-Burton kind of madness. Seriously, it was more fun than the movies. They were nice to me and called me "Silent Beauty," in homage to my long dark hair and quiet reserve. Franny would drape an arm around me, twirl my hair up into a French twist, and tell me I was pretty. For the child of Maria Capella, this was like fantasy makeover camp.

Dee would grin her wide wonderful smile across the kitchen counter, loving every minute of my shy delight. She was a sprite of a girl with a mischievous twinkle that terrified and tantalized at the same time. And she had the same effect on boys, adding to the allure of being in her circle, since there were always those guys who spun out of control and into the web of whatever girl happened to be nearby.

I swear, if it hadn't been for Dee during those times when Drew and I were on the outs, I'd have never have had a date. I saw her recently and I swear, except for a few stray grays, the girl still sparkles. Some things really do never change.

Dee's folks barely noticed when one of their ten kids was gone, and since Dee did her daughterly duties mostly without fuss, they agreed to let her go with us. Drew was off visiting colleges with his dad, as he'd been offered a boatload of scholarships for wrestling, and he was struggling with the decision.

Even in the dream, Drew shows up to contribute. "I didn't want to leave you… but I didn't want to disappoint my dad." This he offers from the big chair in my father's living room. I glance over my shoulder and smile at him, sprawled out, legs splayed, head back with arms folded behind his neck. "I was a wreck, so I stayed away so you wouldn't see, you see?" He mumbles. We grin at each other.

"Yeah, well, I was pretty mad at you right then," I say. He nods, "Yep, I remember that part." Actually, we'd had more than a few arguments since the first of the college offers had surfaced, and he'd been gone nearly every weekend, with tournaments out of town or these college trips. I missed my "not boyfriend." I was out of sorts and ill at ease, and neither one of us had figured out exactly what we were or wanted. Isn't that how it works? I mean with the big loves? "BIG HUGE LOVE," pipes up Mr. Regional Wrestling boy of 1971.But I am not allowing my friend's attempts at distraction. Back to this crazy dream…

Spring break, 1970. Think very small halter tops and short shorts. Mini baby dolls and wild bikinis. Coppertone. Aviator sunglasses. Surfers. At least that's what Dee and I were dreaming of. Dad, Jeff, Dee, and I set out at first light, around 5:00am, for the five-hour trip in fair weather. Halfway there, around Charlotte, North Carolina, we stopped for fuel and barbeque. Francis could never land at that airfield without a quick walk down the road for ribs and some collard greens (or since it was still morning, grits and sausage biscuits). After that we headed south, aiming to land before dark and then find Jesse's place. We were finally in range to land and Dee and I were slumped in the backseat, half-dozing as Francis and the air traffic tower shared coordinates in preparation for him to drop his wheels.

"Go ahead 'Zero Three Lima' - we can't see you, but you are cleared for landing on runway 624." Francis banked hard to the left and slowly began to bring the plane down, when suddenly Jeff sat straight up and said, "Jesus Fritz, why are there cars on the runway????!!!!"

Francis let out with an "OH SHIT!!!!!!!!!!!!!!" as he pulled the throttle back hard and took the plane back up. Dee and I were open-mouthed and big-eyed and holding on for dear life! After a glance to the backseat and a forced smile, Francis was as calm as a cucumber, once he got his bearings again. Jeff pulled out the map, and after much conversation with the tower, everyone figured out that we were about 15 miles north of the actual airstrip over Florida Atlantic University which is built… wait for it… on an old runway.

Let's just say no one wet their pants, but it was close. In those days of minimal technology, folks mostly flew private planes that size with what is called a VFR, or visual flight rating. So while Francis could read and interpret the critical instruments on his airplane, he was pretty much reliant on a compass, a map, and an air traffic controller for the rest. And air traffic had only sonar; if they saw a blip, and someone was chatting them up, many times they just assumed they would see the plane before they had to guide it in. The craziest part is that almost nobody ever crashed. Well, at least we didn't.

We finally landed, parked the plane, picked up the rental car, and set about finding my brother's "pad." This turned out to be a commune-like residential motel sprawled across a block of prime real estate two blocks from the beach. The band had several large apartments in a row on the second floor, overlooking a large and sparkling pool. The whole place smelled like beer, girls, and marijuana. And that's what we found there, along with several long-haired scraggly musicians with eyes happily glazed over from the effects of all three.

Jesse greeted my dad with a half-smile, mumbling "hey dad" under his breath and allowing himself to be shoulder clapped a few times, the male equivalent of jumping up and down and squealing that teenage girls are so good at. The oldest guy in the band -- a guy also from Pittsburgh named William who went by Joshua -- and his wife

Harmony were the de-facto "house parents" for this unruly bunch. As I mentioned earlier, Jesse was only 16, but he'd been on the road for a year with these people and he seemed years ahead of me. I wish I'd known that a year later the weed would lead to pills, the pills to heroin, and the heroin to the next ten years of hell for my sweet brother. And even knowing that knowing may not have mattered one iota, I can still wish.

It was only 2:00pm, so Dad headed with Jesse and Will-Joshua to the rehearsal studio to check out the sounds. Jeff went to the grocery store to buy us all some basics, after checking out the meager contents of the pantry. He said cigarettes, Mateus Rose, and beer weren't exactly a breakfast of champions. And Dee and I? Well, we donned our psychedelic neon bikinis and our Coppertone and our white Jackie-O sunglasses (each of us had packed several suits and shades, so it was a daily decision which bikini and accessories to choose), then set out for the deck chairs by the pool.

Now, if you are not from the three rivers tristate area, you may not understand what clear blue skies and sunshine mean to a person who spends nine months a year under gray humid skies, often accompanied by snow. And all this in March! We couldn't wait to be sunburnt and then golden. Even though Dee was as Irish as they come, she was blonde Irish, so she tanned without a problem. And of course the best thing in the world for my olive skin was a little extra pink.

I think we must have stayed out there till dinnertime, because the one thing I remember was a shadow over me and a deep smiling voice saying, "Hey gorgeous." I opened one eye and squinted. He was standing right in front of the sun, so all I saw was a skinny guy in jeans and no shirt. Vincent, I think was the name. About 20, definitely too old for me, and twice as tempting. Bad news, trouble, you name it, and most definitely NOT what Francis had in mind for his baby girl. But charm just oozed out of this guy as he sat down on the lounge chair next to mine and tried to get me talking.

After a few minutes and when I was fully awake from my sun snooze, I glanced around for Dee and realized I was alone. Her towel was on the bottom of my chair but she and her Coppertone were nowhere to be found. I started to get nervous and shy all at once, so I mumbled, "Nice to meet you, better go now" and skedaddled up to Jesse's place. The entire crew was now gathered around what served as a communal dining table, a large door on several sawhorses and a mess of mismatched chairs donated for the occasion from each of the rooms on the floor.

Jeff was cooking up a huge feast of pasta, salad and garlic bread, and the smell of real food alone was enough to sober up the entire household. Dad and Will-Joshua were on the communal patio/ balcony talking, and I could tell from the glance Francis threw my way as I tried to sneak past him to change that he was less than pleased about my new friend. Obviously, he'd observed our meeting by the pool from his perch there at the railing.

I put on my most conservative and "not cute" t-shirt and jeans, despite my already tingling sunburn, and kept quiet the rest of the evening. We were all beat from the journey; Dee and I grabbed the futon as far away from the noise as possible and were asleep by 11:00pm. Don't remember much after that, till I woke up around 9:00 the next morning. I got dressed in the bathroom, wondering why Dee hadn't woken me when she got up. I noticed that the house was super quiet and figured I might be the first one up, then tiptoed around and headed to the kitchen for coffee or soda, anything to help me wake up. I also needed to find something to take the sting out of my shoulders.

When I got to the end of the hallway, it became immediately clear that I was alone in the place. I mean not a soul. Everyone was gone, airlifted by aliens or, well, something. My emotions ran from confusion, to more confusion, to fear, to more confusion. Then, after a quick scan of the pool and parking lot from the balcony, I was PISSED OFF. They'd left me! I mean, did they KNOW they'd left me? Or did they just forget me? And if they DID know they left me, WHY did they? Has this ever happened to you? It's no fun and I'm pretty sure I cried into my cereal while I sat and wondered what to do. An hour or so passed. No note, nothing. Nothing to do but sit and wait.

And I waited. Boy, did I wait. For about two more hours, dozing on the couch, leafing through the stack of magazines Dee and I had lugged along on the plane. Then anger and boredom combined to create a dangerous cocktail in the hands of a sixteen-year-old. I put on my tiniest bikini and my aviator shades, grabbed a towel., and headed for the pool. I left a note, taking satisfaction that I was far more considerate than those who had so callously abandoned me. Smug and somewhat excited about the independence of my situation, I stretched out and spent the next few hours in and out of the pool, turning like a chicken on a spit to make sure my newly burgeoning tan was even. Around 1:00pm, still no sign of anyone. I ventured upstairs to check the answering machine, but still nothing. I grabbed a Coke and went back to the pool. I had barely settled in on my tummy when I felt that shadow again. "Morning sunshine," said the velvety voice. I turned my head and squinted up, but this time his face was in clear view. What I'd missed the night before was the full impact of this face. In today's terms, let's just say no one would notice Brad Pitt if this guy was in the room.

Vincent, as it turned out, was an artist for a local ad agency, sort of the underground headshop variety for the bands, bars, and other small businesses that thrived on the idiosyncratic needs of locals and tourists alike. He had a small studio (or more accurately, a large drafting board next to his window and a bookshelf full of pens, markers and other supplies) in his apartment, where he worked when he felt like it. The rest of the time he spent surfing, fishing, and hanging out.

We talked art most of the afternoon, and I did make my way upstairs to check the machine at least two more times. But at some point, I crossed a line and let my new friend get me a "cool drink," which turned out to be a wine cooler. Let me paint you the picture. Despite the Italian curves, I weighed about 95 pounds soaking wet, including my hair. And I had a lot of hair. I hadn't eaten anything since the cereal, so the wine went straight to my head. We got in the pool and swam and played around for a while, and I was sitting on the steps in the shallow end while Vincent showed off his diving skills and I laughed and squealed at his antics. And that's when I saw the car pull into the parking lot and man did I sober up fast. Vincent saw it, too. He grabbed his towel and said, "Hey, come over for dinner tonight? I want to cook for you. Do you think you can?" I was close to freaking out, but still considerably pissed, so I said I would try as I gathered my stuff and headed up to the apartment, throwing a shy smile over my shoulder. I threw on a baby doll mini, pulled my hair into a ponytail, and washed my face, positioning myself at the table with a magazine. And that is where I sat as my father, Dee, Jesse, and the rest of the crew entered, laughing and sunburnt.

They looked somewhat shamefaced when they saw me. I think Francis was trying to figure out how to apologize but Dee had enjoyed being the star of the day a little too much. "OH, E… you missed it," she began, and rattled away with her account of their adventure. "We went to the beach for breakfast, you were still sleeping, and we like seriously meant to come back for you but then we decided to rent one of those boats and take a ride, and then we went to that little island and had lunch, and then it started to get really windy so we had to wait, and OH then…" she looked at the guys who all began to laugh too.

I'm not sure what she was going to say next but I'd had enough. My tears were on the edge of my eyes and I stood up and said, "Well I'm glad you all had a great time WITHOUT me. So I hope you all don't mind, but since I had no idea when you would all be back, I've made plans for dinner and I need to take a shower."

My dad's head snapped around at this and he started to say, "What's that young lady?" but Will- Joshua put his hand on Francis's shoulder and said, "Aw, don't worry Fritz, she'll be fine." Then, looking over at me in his half-glazed sort of way, he said "Vincent?" and I nodded with a superior "I am SO MUCH more mature than you think" toss of my ponytail.

It was the first time I'd sort of gone off and declared my independence from my dad. He looked a little sad, a little amused, and a little like he knew it was his fault. But strangely enough, he didn't even try to stop me. I threw on my hip huggers, a halter top, and added a pair of hoop earrings, mascara and lip gloss. I surveyed my suddenly more sophisticated, burnished brown image in the foggy bathroom mirror, then headed out the door before fear got the best of me.

Vincent was, as it turned out, a master at many things. Watercolor, basic illustration, and the art of seduction, at least when there was enough innocence and a fair amount of naïveté involved. There was something wonderful simmering on the stove, a bottle of wine opened, and candles lit. The air smelled like patchouli, incense, and weed, and the raggedy trappings of his small rooms were transformed into velvet and silk, shimmering in the glow. He held my hand while we leaned against the counter and tasted the wine. He called me beautiful. He listened to me talk about my dreams, and we even talked about our "real lives" – mine in Pittsburgh and my "not boyfriend."

As for Vincent, let's just say I came about as close as I would get in the next few years to letting go and giving in. In the end, I have to give the guy credit, because at some point during the make-out session that ensued after several glasses of wine, he pulled away and looked me dead in the eye.

"You, my dear, are definitely wife material."

I laughed nervously, not at all sure what he meant. I didn't know what to say, so I just shook my head.

"No, believe me, you are the kind of woman I need to meet again in four or five years…" and reaching out to touch the tip of my chin, he finished, "But for now, I need to stop before I forget that."

My mind was a jumble of the right and wrong of it all, the emotion and the physical sensations and how good I felt at the moment, and of course… Andrew. I knew there were some things that we could overlook, forgive, and move on from. And I knew that I had only been saving myself for one man, and that wasn't Vincent. I smiled and unfolded myself from his embrace, said goodbye, and crept back to the balcony of Jesse's apartment. I spent the night on the hammock with a contented smile on my face. I'd just figured out what all the fuss was about, you see, and now I couldn't wait to see Drew again. The next day we all went to hear Jesse's band and they were so much better than anyone expected. I could see the pride on Francis' face and the unspoken exchange between them later as we prepared to head back home. Somehow in those few short days, my dad had accepted what he'd fought for so long. Jesse had his own life now and there would be no coming home again for him, at least not as my father's son. He'd become a version of the man he is today, and the long road of twists and turns that lay ahead of him was not a road that he would take with us. Over the years, I'd come to be grateful for that, despite the aching wish I could have helped him make a different choice.

Francis sleeps late, so I'm up early for a walk up and down the hills of my youth. The neighborhood has held up nicely, and each house on the path down the hill to that long-ago monkey bar playground holds a memory or two. Interestingly enough, the four or five houses surrounding mine still hold the original residents; they recognize me, thirty years older and almost blonde, without a moment's hesitation. Without even trying I am steeped in long ago, and a few minutes into my walk, I'm jogging toward my memories.

What greets me is a dried-out hillside, sans playground, and bearing instead a large marquee announcing the coming "Lebanese Food Festival" this weekend. "Don't miss it," The elementary school is gone and there's some kind of Orthodox church in its place. I walk to the place on the ground where I think those monkey bars once stood and sit down. And the tears come. But Andrew doesn't, and that gets my attention.

Rosie is on the phone with her grandfather when I come in and they are deep in discussion about the unfairness of college professors. Francis Evans would have given more than his right arm to go to college so he sets her straight pretty quick. He smiles into the phone as his hand starts its Parkinson's dance, and says "So long, kiddo" as he hands me the phone. "It's the gorgeous one," he says.

"Hi hon," I say, still out of breath from my run up the hill once I realized I'd been sitting on the hill crying for way too long in broad daylight.

"Where are you? I ask, as I start finding the breakfast ingredients in Deb's overstocked (as in, if there is a nuclear bombing, go to THIS house and there will be enough for everyone) kitchen. "Driving home from work before school" she says, yawning.

"You ok?" I ask, half listening as I survey the fridge and try to remember if it's peaches or raspberries he doesn't like these days.

"MOM," she says, at just a decibel too high. I stop and focus. "I know, I know, I'll just listen and not do anything else."

"Good," she says, and launches into a long and detailed accounting of school, boys, friends, work, my devil son who she may allow to live until I get back but no guarantees, the whiny dog who may also live, and a host of other things that no matter how hard I try, I cannot explain to you.

At the end, I repeat my well-rehearsed lines. "I'm sorry honey. Just try not to stress, everything will be all right." (In person, it's important to add to this mantra a very sincere hug. Oh, and hold it. She can tell when you are faking.) Then she hangs up.

I put the phone down, sigh, and serve dad his oatmeal and peaches. I walk back to the kitchen and that's when I see him through the window, sitting on the back steps staring out into space. I never thought about it this way before. Andrew has been with and around me for so long, but for the last ten years, we've been in Arizona. And before that, Florida. Not here, where his whole life took place. Where he is probably buried. Where every street and every tree are part of him, just like they are part of me. I suddenly feel terribly selfish, and I have no idea what to do for him. I love this boy. This man. This ghost. I love him with my soul, and there is not a lot I wouldn't risk for him.

I know that sounds insane. I mean, I know, he's not even alive. Somehow, that doesn't change a thing at this moment.

I tell Dad I need to run the trash out, and he is happy looking through the pictures we left out on the table last night, so I slip out the back door and down the steps. I sit on the step behind Andrew and lean into him. "I'm sorry Drew," I whisper, or maybe I don't even say it out loud, but he hears me. He leans back and we blend into each other, or at least that's how it feels for a moment that could never last long enough. He turns his head, and looks into my eyes. "It's ok. I come here sometimes, you know."

But I didn't know. I never considered he might go other places. See other people. Have *them* see him??? Suddenly I am afraid and jealous all at once. "You do? I mean, who, um, where, oh, I don't even know what I'm saying."

He grins. "Not the way I'm with you, E. It's not like that with anyone but you. But I used to watch my folks before my dad left. And Lucy, I like to watch her with the twins, but they tend to know I'm there so I don't do that much anymore." I'm taking this in, processing, staring across to the hillside where he grew up, the one I could see from the kitchen window growing up. But now the trees are so full I can hardly pick out the houses anymore.

I'm surprised when he starts to talk. In all these years, everything we talk about has really focused on me. On my feelings, my struggles, my needs. Being dead, I mean, he doesn't have a lot going on in his own, um… well… afterlife. It's odd to hear him as he begins to tell me what he's feeling.

"This is really different for me," he says. "Maybe because it's that except for the time you came back from Chicago, you and I haven't really been here together. I mean, not since. You know?"

I nod. "And being here, it just makes me realize how different things could have been if I hadn't been so – I don't know. I wanted to keep driving till I got to you and everything that we had planned, and I should have stopped. I should have stayed awake." He's crying now and I'm feeling really strange. "I don't know why any of this happened. I wanted a whole life with you, Elaine. And I see people all around me who waste that every day. It makes me angry. Why do I still feel all these things? What did I do so wrong that I had to go away, that I lost you, and everything we wanted? And now all I am is this! He slams his hands against his chest as he finishes. I look at him with all the love I have always and will always feel, but I have no answer. I tell him it feels the same for me. That I love him as much today as I ever have, maybe even more. He puts his head back against my chest and we sit in the bittersweet memories and lost dreams.

He fades away while I'm blinking back tears. I remember Dad and run back into the house, where we sit and chat. He sees I'm distracted but mistakes my distance for a need to work, so he heads upstairs for a nap, promising to meet me later for our afternoon rendezvous at the mall. And today, I will be glad for the mile walk alone with one of the few men on earth who gets me. That is, until, Andrew decides we could all use some cheering up, so he decides to come along. Have I mentioned he has only gotten more creative in his role as the invisible prankster?

I'm not certain the "Pick-me-Up" Coffee Cafe girls believe it was a huge draft that blew all the cups, straws and displays across the food court. But it was funny to watch them wonder.

I have to bite my lip to keep from yelling at him to stop it, but Dad seems oblivious so I just enjoy the show, which continues with moving mannequins, display disturbances, and a more than a few hilarious sightings of the mallrats losing their ball caps without warning. It's clear that Andrew has not lost this gift. This talent for making me smile.

The days with Dad are long and full of small jokes that only the two of us understand, stories told over his walker at the mall, over pizza in the food court and ice cream in the evenings. We sit on the front porch and talk about everything from my job to his regrets over what "I didn't do when I had time." I remind him that he's more than made up for it since then, buying and restoring low-income housing and then renting it for barely enough to cover the mortgages. He's done this for thirty years and I remember so many times he let tenants slide on the rent when they'd hit hard times. I remember the Christmas I went with him when he filled our old station wagon with groceries and gifts which we left on two dozen porches in the dawn of Christmas Eve. He shrugs off any compliment and says, "It was never enough. I always wanted to do more."

And I realize he's not just talking about giving. He's talking about his life. A few days later I'm packing after Francis has gone to sleep for the night, trying to remember everything I've spread around the house over the last two weeks, when I hear a sound in what used to be my bedroom. It's the nursery now, for the smallest grandchildren, Deb's daughter's and Matt's babies. They are the only ones with babies anymore. Riley is the youngest of the first group and at twelve, he's hardly fit for this room. As I walk down the short hall to the room I hear the noise again, like small stones against glass. As I walk to the window I smile, knowing who I will see when I look out.

Drew is there, grinning wildly, as he reenacts a scene from our teenage romance. He used to come over and park at the bottom of the hill, then climb through the neighbor's yard and sneak into ours. He'd wake me up in this same way, I'd creep out the back door, and we'd walk down the hill to our playground to swing and talk for hours. As I look at him all these years later, it isn't hard to remember why no night was too cold, and sleep was the last thing on my mind. We cut through the yards and walk to our spot. Or I do, and I feel him with me. I'm careful not to talk while we walk, as I don't want the old neighbors' last memory of me to be the one where I'm talking animatedly to myself in the middle of the night. We sit behind the big marquee and lean back to look at the moon half hidden in the clouds. You can feel the chill that foretells an early winter. Even this morning I noticed the beginnings of autumn in the red and gold hints among the trees. Andrew asks me if I ever think about moving back here. It's funny, because these last two weeks are the longest time I've spent in this town in thirty-odd years. And I've thought of little else. I miss the seasons, but not the humidity. I miss the kindness of the people, but wonder if the endless speculation of the overheard conversations would get to me after a while. Pittsburghers love to wonder. About anything. And everything.

It's comical for a while, but after a long wait in line at the grocery the other day, it was all I could do to keep my well-traveled opinion to myself. And I miss, most of all, my father. But how would I feel once he was gone? I think about saying this out loud, but before I can Drew says, "Yeah. I know what you mean." And I smile.

Jet lag. My arms and legs ache, my brain is on s-l-o-w- and I can't think of any reason to do anything but lay around. Riley has his personal chauffeur back and is full of reasons why we NEED to go to Blockbuster right now for a new video game, and can't we please go get food because his sister has not fed him ANY-thing decent in two weeks, and it's a miracle he's still alive. I just look at him and I'm too tired to answer. To make the 5:00am, five-hour flight home even more entertaining, it was filled with Steeler fans on their way to a game here in Phoenix. I will spare you the in-depth description, but let's just say the plane probably needed to restock the liquor supply by the time we landed at 9:00am Arizona time. Yeah. Go Steelers. Yawn.

Last night after reclaiming my house (two weeks in the possession of siblings takes a toll), I fell into a hard sleep, the cat happily curled around my ankles. It was one of those sleeps that leaves you slogging through the morning, gasping for coffee and looking scattered. I found the coffee and wandered out to pet the big dogs and sit and stare at my pool, which had somehow managed to stay blue for two whole weeks without me. A small miracle, believe me.

I sit in the big wicker chair, blanket around my shoulders, knees up against my chest, coffee mug warming my hands, and try to shake off the feeling of sadness that somehow claimed me during the night. I need something to get me back to writing this book and finishing the story but I can't seem to move quite yet. At some point, I'm going to have to explain the whole Easter thing and all the rest, I guess. But for the moment, I lean back and savor the quiet Arizona morning.

Settling back into work provides more reasons to avoid writing. The fall moves fast. The holidays come and go in a blur. Rosie is home for a week, then gone again, this time leaving her cat Mister with me since her landlord has begun questioning her about the "noises" she claims are coming from the pipes. I've just brought home a new pup. A chubby little Yorkie we've named Henry I agreed to take from a friend because I've missed my Lola so much. This dog is a whole different species though. Mister and Henry have become attached and once again I'm running a small zoo. But it's good when the house is full. And when it's full, there are lots of excuses to avoid finishing this book. Oh, and business has been busy too. I've been to Boston, Chicago, New Jersey, and London. I've had four new books to promote and four authors to keep happy. In other words, a universe of rationalization at my fingertips.

Even spring brought new excuses not to write. Rosie was in the throes of writing a major paper for school and took up residence on my sofa. It was far easier to be *her* sounding board for a while than to deal with the voices in *my* head. Then it was summer again and Riley was off to camp with his buddies for a while, and I spent June and July navigating a challenging book tour for a self-help author who might just need to read her own work a bit more closely. So now it's late August and almost time for school to begin. And I've run out of excuses. And all I want is some down time, maybe a quiet place with no distractions so I can find the words to write again. So I pack up the car, Riley, and his pal AJ, and head for one of our favorite spots in the universe.

Quiet. I was hoping for, dreaming of, quiet. I remember that, the kind of silence so soft and deep you can curl up in it. I remember it fondly. At the moment, Riley and AJ are tapping, clicking, humming, and burping their way through what should be fifteen minutes of homework, but is turning out to be more like a long painful hour. I'm trying to pick up where I left off in this story months ago amidst all of this. Despite how much I really do love them, they are seriously getting me to the point where I am hovering between screaming and looking for a real weapon.

This is all happening here at the beach in California for what has slowly become a tradition, now in its tenth year. We rent the same condo that sits right on the sand in between the pier and the YMCA surf camp. It's a sleepy little town with stacked waves where anyone can learn the art and mystery that is surfing. Sometimes it's Riley and Co. with me, and sometimes Rosie and a pal. But since college began, it's hard for her to get away. And even though technically Riley's school has started, I have a deal with the teachers since my schedule keeps me on the road so much of the year. They understand that vacations mean a lot to us, and as long as Riley does his assignments and writes an essay about the trip, and AJ does the work his homeschool teacher (his mom) gives him, it's all good. Especially now that the boys are older, I have real time to write.

(After the homework is done, that is.)

But for now, the sun has finally made an entrance, after a soggy morning that cancelled our original plans for the zoo. Instead, I endured a two-hour horror movie, made tolerable only by the fact that John Cusack never really gets hard to look at. Even when he's scared and kind of creepily insane.

But I digress. Anyway, Riley needed this trip. He's twelve now and the questions never end. He wants to know all about his dad, but the questions are random and spread way apart. I get the feeling he is thinking about my answers all the time in between. I try really hard to make sure the answers are just right, whatever that is.

See, I don't really want him to know the truth about his dad, at least not the really bad stuff. What's the point, after all? I've been through this with shrinks, friends, preachers, basically anyone who knows the story, and they all agree. Nothing good comes of telling your son that his father tried to kill you. More than once. On the other hand, I do share all of the good things, the qualities that Raff's genes passed so abundantly to his son. The quick-witted sense of the absurd, the goofy laugh, the ability to charm even the most skeptical adult. His athleticism and grace, his love of music and the drums and spicy food. The tenderness that is such a surprise in this boy. I'm not sure where that came from, but I sure do like it. He's the first one to defend the littler kid in the group and to help a stranger with a bag at the grocery store. But he'd rather chew off his arm than help his sister. Unless of course no one is looking.

In any case, Rosie and I are the only people Riley has to ask these questions, and while it wears me out, it just about kills Rosie. See, she really loved Raff at first, and he absolutely adored her. At four, and even five, that was all she needed. But at eight, well, she could see things weren't right, even though he did his best to only hit me when she wasn't around. And he did always buy me the expensive cover-up makeup when the bruises on my face just didn't fade fast enough. But as time passed, she could see me starting to disappear. I think that's when she started to realize something was wrong and that it started and ended with Raff. This time together makes everything else slip away. His questions, my fears, the stress of wondering if anything you are doing as a parent is the right thing. We just settle into sunrise and sunset and the golden sand. And that works just fine for me. I've got this. Or I thought I did.

The boys have decided I need to teach them to surf. Let this be a lesson to all of you- sixties rocker-surfer hippie types: Be careful of how you enrich the truth when you regale your children with the tales of your younger self. I did not lie when I said I had spent more than a few summers surfing on the beaches of northern Florida.

Ok, maybe I did embellish… but the truth is more like I spent more like a few months spread out over many years. If I recall, there was a guy, and there was a surfboard, and I was on it. And that lasted for at least two months one endless summer. And then another, maybe one more. The reality is I managed to get up a couple of times each summer during this trip. But now, even if I could, I really don't have the stamina to fail in front of these boys. And since I broke my ankle last year, it's become a handy excuse for escaping anything physical I'm not in the mood for. (Except grocery shopping. Rosie wouldn't buy it.)

Back to the beach. The small town we have come to love is inhabited by a few students, some old hippies, and a ton of surfers. I figure the guys at the surf shop will be able to hook us up with someone who can give the boys lessons. I promise that we will head down there to find out about all that, as soon as Algebra and Social Studies are out of the way.

This kind of place is an anomaly these days. I mean, it's literally about a three stoplight stretch of beach with one main drag, two supermarkets, one at either end, and outside of the usual chain feed stops, a couple of worn-out but comfy restaurants.

Folks don't come here for the food, they come for the lack of tourists and the waves. And the long expanse of sand that changes color as the sun moves through its daily dance of pink, to bright hot yellow and then again to lavender shot with sunset. It's a rare enigma that seems to have escaped the greedy race for tourist dollars, and there isn't a high-rise to be found. Scattered beach houses dot the shore, and the locals live on the side streets in apartments, small wooden houses, and a combination of dwellings that remind me of a surfer's Venice... all secondary to the location.

On the street level below the condo we rent here is *the* local surf shop. For such a small town, this size and variety of the offerings in this rather intimate space tell the true story of who comes to play in Imperial Beach. There are boards, long, short and in between, wetsuits, flippers and snorkel gear, and a clothing selection of surfer-appropriate attire that rivals a small department store -- all inspired to make the observer say "dude." Riley is frustrated at this point; he's grown almost five inches since last summer and as much as he's happy he will not be as small as his mom and sister; he hates having to try on the "men's" wetsuits.

I notice a guy who's obviously doing some kind of repair or construction inside the back area of the shop. He is quietly encouraging my boy and I wonder at what he must have said to coax a smile from him. I see Riley nod, and the man hand him two suits from the top rack and gives him a quick pat on the shoulder when he heads off to try them on.

While the boys are at it, I venture a query with the surfer dude behind the counter about the possibility of surf lessons this late in the season. The clerk scratches his head and says, "Probably dude, but I like need to check with the manager dude, he won't be back till later. Dude."

I don't bother to mention to him that dude is probably not relevant in my case, as it seems a waste of words. Besides, it feels good just to smile, and this works. I thank him, and just as I'm about to hand him my card and ask him to just let me know what he finds out, the carpenter dude who has been standing nearby comes over.

He says, "I know a guy, he's 20, but he's great with kids and cheap. And safe. I don't have his number with me, but I could give you mine?" As I consider, he looks back at Riley, now happy and carrying the suit that fit, and asks, "Yours?"

I smile and nod. "Both of them?" he asks again, eyebrows up.

"Oh lord no," I say, "Just my son and his pal. You know, two are easier than one sometimes."

The stranger grins, looking me in the eye this time. "Actually, I do. I seem to remember my son at that age, and we always had more than one at the table." We laugh over that one and he introduces himself. "Eli Duncan," he says. He goes on to explain that he's a local, a contractor whose guys are working on the rebuild of the beach house a few hundred yards down the beach. "But the owner of the shop here, he's my pal and I just stopped in to see what he needs for his new board rack. I still like to pick up the hammer now and then, you know?"

I smile, introduce myself, and say I do. The kids are ready to go, so I thank him again and promise to call for the referral. He tells me he'll be home after five, and won't have the number till then. We exchange a handshake, and the boys and I head back to the beach, short boards in tow.

The boys can't wait for tomorrow. Tomorrow always seems like a month away when you are just about thirteen. They suit up, and even though it's nearly five, they head out dragging their boards, full of determination. I gauge the waves and decide it's probably just about right, nothing too high, and even though it's low tide and the reef stretches out for what seems like a quarter mile, they hike out with a pair of anticipatory grins to match.

Sometimes when you've been through your own life tsunami, it doesn't take much to make you remember how lucky you are to be alive. And there is something about the combination of ocean, sand and sky, warm sun on your face and your children caught up and happy that heightens that emotion. I settle in to the beach chair and focus on the boys, who are slowly getting the hang of hanging ten. Or at least five, for now.

After about an hour, they are done and relapse into the boys they haven't quite outgrown, settling down on the edge of the water to build yet another sand sculpture. One never knows what these will be, and I'm just grateful they haven't moved into the mermaid area just yet. I'm sure it's not far away, so I'll just be happy I have some time before I'm dealing with semi-nude sand goddesses. Or the real kind.

I decide I need some stretching so I head down the beach for a long walk. I'm not one to look for shells anymore. I have exhausted the number of places I can store them after all the years of coming to this beach. But I do appreciate the beauty of the mosaic they create as they wash ashore. I'm more likely to get completely lost in the colors and shades, ever changing as the sun moves slowly towards its watery end. It absolutely empties my brain and for this, I would pay a lot more than this trip is costing.

All this is to say, when I nearly chest-slam the carpenter because I'm so lost in that emptiness, he has to grab both my shoulders to keep me from falling right over from the shock of it.

"Hey, fancy running into you here," he says, laughing. The moment is surprisingly comfortable, and I laugh as I gain my balance, inside and out.

"Don't mind me," I smile, "I get kind of in the zone out here sometimes." "No worries," he says. "I get that." I realize he's looking straight at me, which is strange because most men don't do that. They sort of look, and then look away, or if they do hold your gaze for more than a minute, they have an agenda. But this is somehow different.

For a few minutes that seem more like an hour, we don't say anything. Finally, he breaks the silence cheerfully. "Oh, yeah, right, I was hoping to find you guys because I have that number for you. The surfer guy?"

"AH right," I say, noticing he's changed into jeans and a T shirt since I last saw him and the look works for him. As I take in the full picture I see thick brown hair with a bit of curl, a muscular but lean build and an arresting pair of deep brown eyes. I suddenly realize I might have let my gaze linger a bit too long. As I feel a blush start to color my cheeks, I turn away to look over my shoulder and realize the boys are up and heading for the water again.

"It's not going to be light much longer, I better head back to play lifeguard." He smiles, and asks if I mind if he walks with me. I return the smile and shake my head. "Are you heading that way?"

"I am now," he says. And we head up the beach. We talk about our kids -- he has one son, Sam, 22 and living in Italy while he studies architecture. I tell him about Rosie and we commiserate about all the things we seem to have in common, at least about kids at college. Before we know it, we've found a seat on the sea wall and are watching the boys. The sun is a tiny dot of hot pink shimmering over a cerulean sky, something right out of a movie. And a minute later the boys are right in front of us shivering and begging for the hot tub.

"Well," I say, laughing as I start to collect towels and all the other paraphernalia of the day, "I guess we'll be heading up." I point over my shoulder to the row of condos and say, "We only have two weeks here, but for now it's home." Eli hands me his card, and turns it over to show me the number for Shawn, the surfer dude. But just as I reach out to take it, he pulls it back.

"Maybe I should actually call him for you?" he grins. "I mean, he knows me and I could find out what he charges and then, um…" (wait, is HE blushing???) "I could call you and set it up?"

I answer carefully. "Sure, that'd be nice, Eli." He reaches into his back pocket and pulls out a pen but there's no more room on the card. He looks around kind of helplessly for a minute, and then, just like high school, I take his hand and the pen and write my cell number across his palm. Then I smile and walk away before he realizes I'm having trouble controlling my smile.

Andrew is sitting out on the rocks when we get back up to the condo an hour later, after the ritual soak in the hot tub and the boys' daily review of their progress on the boards. I can see him from the deck where sip a glass of wine and watch the colors change while the boys take turns in the shower. We're opting for burgers on the boardwalk tonight so I'm off cook duty. I watch Andrew and wonder if he has just watched the whole scene with Eli, and what he must be thinking. He doesn't show up later when the boys fall asleep on the couches in front of the SpongeBob reruns they never get tired of, or when I sit wrapped in a shawl on the deck staring into the blackness of the midnight ocean. And it's ok. There is so much in my brain that I'm happy just to sit and let it swirl around until sleep finds me, too.

I guess the wine and the long day in the sun must have really done me in, since I slept the whole night on the chaise on the deck. Luckily, I'd been fully dressed and wrapped in a blanket to begin with, so aside from feeling my age clear down to my knees when the sunrise hit me, I guess I slept pretty well. No dreams at least, and that's always a plus.

I make my way to the kitchen to put the coffee on, and remember that I'd used the last of it the day before. I jot a quick note for the boys, slip on a fresh t-shirt, and head down the beach to the little coffee hut for something with espresso for me, and donuts for the kids. I'm leaning on the sea wall sipping my cappuccino when I hear a now-familiar voice.

"Up early, I see," says Eli, leaning his elbows on the rail next to mine. I smile to myself and turn to him with a quiet, "Morning." We stood like that for a while, as I remember. You know that feeling when you meet someone and you just know that you have a thousand things to say to them, but it can all wait? That's how it felt. "Boys still crashed out?" "Uh huh," I reply. "My favorite time of the morning." We both chuckle softly.

"So, I talked to Shawn, and he's free around noon. He kind of owes me a favor, so he said he do the first lesson for free, how's that sound?" He grins.

"Oh, I can't let you do that," I tell him, straightening up.

"No, really, it's cool, he is crap with a hammer and it's really the only way he

can pay me back, so come on, it's a favor to me, actually." He has this

amazing grin and a twinkle in his eye, so of course I smile and agree. We

decide to meet on the beach in front of the condo at noon, stare at each other

for a minute, and then he says, "Ok, well, bye for now then," and turns to go.

"One condition," I add as I turn back to the ocean. He stops and waits,

turning his head with a smile. "I'm making dinner tonight. Both of you have

to come."

Eli nods solemnly. "I think I can do that. Can't speak for the surfer dude

but I've yet to see a 20-year-old male turn down free food. See you later,

Elaine."

With that, we head off in different directions to start our day.

The boys dive on me as I enter, the smell of fresh pastries calling them more

loudly than the sound of my key in the door. I pour them both big glasses of

milk and they settle in on the deck, foregoing the TV in favor of a morning

watch for dolphins on the horizon. I find a bathing suit and pull my hair back

in a ponytail, put on the sunscreen, and ok, I'll admit it, spend a few more

minutes than usual on lip gloss. I check the temp outside and it's still pretty

chilly, so I grab some yoga pants and a hoodie. Late September at the beach is

always a toss-up, but usually by late morning the fog burns up, the clouds

blow away and the sun warms everything to just the right temp. I straighten

up the house and take out the ground beef from the freezer that I will use make meatballs later. The boys are already working on the day's assignments at the table (without a word from me!), as they know there is no surfing in their future until they are done. I finish my coffee and the newspaper about the same time they offer up their work for approval. We're on the beach and settled in by 10:00am.

I'm lost in thought as I keep one eye on the boys who are mostly

content with playing in the waves as they adjust to the cooler temperature. I'm

waiting for the fog to break so I can shed my jacket, but it's so beautiful even

with the mist on the water that I really don't mind the slight chill. We are just

about the only ones on the beach this weekday morning, and it's quiet except

for the sound of gulls fighting over their breakfast.

Andrew sits down on the sand next to my chair and leans against my

stretched-out legs for a minute.

"Hey," he says.

"Hey yourself" is my reply.

"I could hang out here forever," he offers.

I laugh. "You could, you know. Lucky."

He smiles up at me. "Ha. But only if you stay," he says. "I'm not done with

you yet." We sit watching the boys for a while. I know what's coming. "So, this

guy…" he pipes up.

"Eli," I say.

"Yeah, Eli."

"He's ok," he adds. I don't say anything. I'm not sure why he feels the need

but it sounds like he is offering his approval. I'm too settled in to this rare state

of comfortable quiet to start a big conversation on the subject (never mind that

I am on the beach and someone might notice me having a major discussion with, um, no one), so I just smile at him and run my hand quickly through his hair.

He smiles back.

I make my daily picnic run back to the condo and the kids have waited the requisite hour after eating and are back in the water when Eli and Shawn arrive. Introductions are made and the boys and their new teacher wander off to a discussion of boards, wax and waves. Eli points to the beach chair next to mine and asks, "Mind if I hang out and watch?"

"Of course not," I laugh, trying not to show how much I hoped he'd ask. We chat for a while, the usual getting acquainted kind of chat. He asks where I'm from and I laugh, say it's a long story but originally from Pittsburgh. Now it's his turn to laugh. He looks down and shakes his head, then starts singing softly. "Steel-town girl on a Saturday night."

I punch his arm playfully and say, "Wait. Really?"

He says, looking up, "South side. You?"

"You're kidding," I answer. "That's kind of crazy. South Hills." We take a walk down that hometown memory lane -- why we left, where we are now, and how we both think about going back someday. "I lucked out with my place here, though," he says. "I hope I never have to let it go, but I could sure use some fall colors now and then."

"I hear you," I reply, and then both together we say, "and the people." We laugh at the timing and the sentiment and go on to talk about the unique familiarity of the Pittsburgher, those folks who never seem to meet a stranger. There is a definite chemistry that makes laughter and conversation flow like we've been friends a long time, and it feels good to both of us. I wonder if it's as rare for him as me, and am about to ask, but he beats me to it. I can't answer with words, so I settle

for another smile and we go back to watching the boys.

Ok, don't start with me, I know this is all sounding a little bit syrupy and

smiley but hey, what the heck? You've seen the other crap I've had to deal with

and you must at least be saying to yourself, hey, the old girl deserves a little grin

now and then, right? Besides, I've got the boys with me night and day so

there's no way this will turn out to be anything anyway. Right?

Eli heads off to check on a few projects and I remind him that dinner is

at 7:00pm. I point out the condo steps and promise to meet him at the gate if he

gives me a call when he is heading over. The boys have finished their lesson and

are off practicing. Shawn manages a few words to say they did well and he will

be back for dinner too.

Eli brings a big bottle of Chianti like any good Pittsburgh boy would do

to an Italian dinner, and after we eat Shawn and the boys watch a horror

movie while Eli and I sit out on the deck. Shawn pokes his head out to thank

me for dinner and to say "Night dude" to Eli, and the boys are soon asleep in

front of the TV.

We talk late into the night until the temperature drops and he notices.

"Come on, let's go inside, you're cold," he says softly. We head in and he grabs

his jacket from the back of the kitchen chair and asks, "Uh, Elaine, what are

you doing next Friday? "

I think for a minute; it's more than a week away and I haven't thought

that far ahead. "No plans so far," I say quietly.

"Ok if I call you tomorrow?" "Sure," I smile, "thanks for Shawn, and the wine, and well, everything,"

He takes my hand but leans in to kiss me on the cheek. "No problem," he says, smiling. And I close the door before I let myself smile back.

Andrew is missing. Have I mentioned that? Ever since our chat on the beach and his quiet endorsement of Eli, he's been noticeably absent. He's done this before, and since I really don't have any great understanding of how this whole afterlife thing works, I always figure he's checking in with the big guy or something. But he'd been around so much lately I just have a bit of a weird feeling. It's starting to get to me. The next morning, I'm wishing he'd show up as I sip my coffee and squint into the distance hoping for the arc of a dolphin or two. The customary fog has burned off early, or maybe I slept later than I thought, since the sun is already warming my face. I push any thought of the previous night from my head, since I have other words to find and the distraction is just too easy to let in.

But before I can start to plan my next move, I'm interrupted by the boys, already in wetsuits and brandishing finished homework. Newly armed with their "mad skills", they lug the big surfboards down to the beach with a promise to wait till I follow before they hit the early morning waves. Anxious to begin the surf ritual, they deposit boards and towels and run back up to help me with the rest of the supplies. Before I can say "more coffee please?" I've been deposited, notebook, iPod and sunscreen in hand, on the stretch of sand they have claimed for me, like early explorers with a beach umbrella for a flag.

The writing. It isn't going so well. Or to be more accurate, it's not going... period. The lazy roll of the waves and the incredible theater of the sky over ocean as it glows and fades through the morning are far too hypnotizing. My brain is tired; the way your body feels after an eight-mile hike. I know what it is, but I don't want to acknowledge it.

I want Andrew. But there is something inside that tells me, this time, it's just not fair to do this to him. This time, I need to figure it out on my own.

The rest of the week passes in a blink. Eli stops by now and then in between work, and on Friday night he brings a bottle of wine to the condo after dinner to see if I'd like to sit out and watch the sunset. We've become something like friends, and whatever that is, it feels good. As he leaves that night he gives me a hug and another kiss on the cheek. He's still holding my hand when he mentions he has to go down the coast for the weekend to check on a job, and promises to stop by Monday, if that's ok. This time I don't even try to hide my smile as I tell him that would be nice.

Sunday night brings dreams and not the good kind. I know somehow that until I write the rest of this story none of that will go away. I'm still missing Drew. I stumble through the morning till the fog breaks, and head down to the sand with the boys. I feel like I have an emotional hangover, and I'm not sure what to do about that.

A few hours later, I'm working up the energy to go inside and put together some lunch, when Eli arrives. He's carrying a big cooler filled with sandwiches and fruit, juice for the boys, and iced coffees for us. He grins as he hands it over… "I'm beginning to share your caffeine fascination, lady." I shake my head laughing. He's so easy to be around, and even this impromptu lunch doesn't feel pushy. He apologizes for the intrusion on our day as he hands out the food.

"I had to come back to the surf shop today to get my crew going, and I wanted to see how you are doing. And to thank you again for that dinner." I laugh and say that a thank you for a thank you is, well… nice just the same.

The boys sit a few yards away on one of the boards eating like no one's fed them in weeks. Then they stretch out on the sand and fall asleep, saving me the "Wait till your food digests before you even think about getting back in the water" speech.

Eli and I sit in comfortable silence for a while. He doesn't look at me when he asks, "How much longer are you guys here?"

"Just till Sunday." I hear the note of regret in my voice. "I should have booked the condo for at least another week. The boys are missing school but keeping up with their work, and while I've been here, I've decided to take some time off from work. I need the time to finish something I've been working on, and it would be the perfect time for me to take a break from work to do that. But the condo's booked so we are just going back to Arizona."

He stares at me for a long minute, and then looks away. "I have to go up to Santa Barbara next Friday for the day to check in on a project. It's a pretty drive, and we could stop on the way for lunch in Malibu?" A day away before you head back?" He cocks his head with the question in his grin. I smile but shake my head. "The boys," I begin, but he stops me with an even bigger smile.

"Shawn and his girlfriend are taking his brother Kyle, who is Riley's age, to the zoo on Friday, and they offered to take the boys for the whole day. They are totally responsible, you can trust them, and we could have a day." He's got my hand somehow without me noticing and he gives it a squeeze. "I know it will just kill you to miss the gorillas, but what if I promise to make it up to you?"

I'm not at all sure, so I tell him I need a couple days to think about it and is that all right? It's only Monday, so he laughs and says "of course, I just wanted to get my bid in early." We both laugh and chat a bit more about random things, and then he heads back to work and I try to find my words, without much success.

33~ The Absence of Fear

The next two days float by. I find myself walking on the beach and writing in my head, and I can't wait to get back to the house and my computer. Something about just letting go is starting to feel right. When you live in fear and panic for a long time, it can make you want to hold on to anything that feels like control. All these years later, I'm starting to understand this. And more than that, I'm starting to truly understand and believe I don't have to be afraid for myself anymore.

I wish I could really find the words to explain how that feels – the absence of fear. But for now, the best I can do is say that it feels like you've been a cold dark place for a long, long time, and someone moves the curtain aside and lets in the light. Suddenly you can step into that sunbeam and feel the warmth. At first, the light hurts your eyes and that's ok. It's ok to let yourself heal at your own pace. To grow new skin over your wounds. To let your eyes, and your heart adjust to the light.

Eli stops by on Wednesday on his way home from work to see if I've decided about the day trip.

"If I'm still invited, I'd love to go," I say. And I look right into his eyes when I say it. Friday comes before I realize and I wave to the boys as they head off with Shawn, his brother and his girlfriend for the zoo. Eli comes up behind me and puts a hand on my shoulder. I can feel him smiling without looking back.

"Ready?" He asks as he squeezes my arm.

"Yes," I say, and I wonder if he understands all that I feel in that simple question and answer. I guess we will see.

The drive up the coast is sunny and bright for the first hour, then the sky changes and the fog rolls in out of nowhere. Without me asking, Eli calls Shawn and checks on the boys. He smiles as he hangs up.

"Still sunshine down there," he grins. "I don't mind a bit of grey, living where I do," I say. We drive for another hour, talking about the coastline and our memories of California from twenty years before, when we'd both been there for work, for holidays. Why we love the beach down south so much. We talk in a comfortable ebb and flow, settling into silence then back into conversation.

"You know," Eli says, "it seems silly for you to go back to Arizona now." "I know," I say, "but I can't really afford another week here. All the cheap places have been rented." Eli is silent for a few minutes, starts to speak, then stops.

"What?" I say, as it's obvious he's trying to tell me something.

"I have to go to Pittsburgh to check on my house there, see my mom and take care of some business. I'll be gone about ten days or so. You guys could totally stay at my place if you wanted." He doesn't look at me, and I can tell he's nervous. "Look," he adds. "I know it feels like we just met."

I laugh and say, "Because um, we DID just meet?"

He keeps going; he's found his voice and he's rehearsed this, it seems. "But I think we trust each other, and it would actually be nice for me to have someone there to watch the place, and to keep an eye on the dogs and plants and stuff. Instead of owing Shawn a favor for that. Yeah. You'd be doing ME a favor." Now he's grinning because he got through the speech and he is quite satisfied with himself.

"Ok, I'll think about it," I tell him as I smile. That seems to satisfy Eli for now.

I almost don't notice that we've turned off the coastline to the other side of the road and onto a road that climbs and twists up the hillside. The further up we go, the more the vegetation changes, the landscaping intentional but indigenous. There are fruit trees, sago palms and flowers everywhere. A low rock wall edges the gravel road on both sides. We drive for about two miles and finally reach what looks like a private drive. Two ancient-looking iron gates open when Eli presses a remote clipped to the visor above his head. As we enter, I don't know where to look first. There is no one here but us, although this place is obviously under construction.

As we get out of the truck, I start to walk to the flagstone terrace that is being laid facing the ocean. I can see where the trees have been carefully moved so that the view is not obscured, but the house remains private.

Eli stops me by taking my hand. "Not yet," he says. "Come with me first. I want to show you from here." We walk back towards the front area that faces the sea to a three-story modified A-line structure. It lays against the hillside as if it was carved into it. The wood beams fit together almost like Lincoln logs, the top beams laid into a cutout at the top of the slightly wider supporting beams. "Mortar and tenant," Eli says to my unspoken question. "The wood is wet when it's placed together and as it dries, it swells and locks in place. No nails. And it won't fall down."

"Very cool," I say. The front of the house is almost all two- and three-story windows, and where the walls have been laid, I can see that the exterior will be mostly smooth rock and cedar. The house will almost blend into the scenery when it's finished   "This is what you do," I say, more a statement than question.

"Uh huh," he murmurs.

"Wow," is all I can muster. "Do you always work with this architect?" I ask, walking and exploring the twists and curves of the house with my hands as I talk.

"Well, I do these days," he says. Something in his voice makes me turn and look at him.

"YOU?" I gasp, "you designed THIS?" He has been waiting for this, I can tell. "Oh my god Eli, it's, well… it's spectacular!"

"Well shucks," he says with feigned modesty. "I'm pretty proud of it, but it's about a year from finished. I just don't get much time to work on it." I take another step back. This time I stare straight at the house, not looking at him at all.

"Of course," I nod, then shake my head, "you're building it too. By yourself?" Now I'm thinking out loud. "Are you some sort of amazing renaissance man?" I'm picturing him laying tile, putting in windows, managing the electric and the plumbing, all on his own. I laugh and shake my head. "Wow. Just, wow."

"No, I'm not that crazy," he laughs. "I have a crew, and whenever I have some money, they come out and do a little more. I bought the land twenty years ago, right after I moved here, so that's paid for. And one day, it'll be done, and maybe I'll live here."

"Maybe?" I still can't look at him. Too many thoughts are spinning in my head. It's like meeting someone in a museum who is staring at a painting and speaking aloud the thoughts you thought were only in your head, then telling you they are the artist. Every single thing I see in front of me is just how I would design it if it were me making the choices. That's a bit scary and wonderful at the same time, let me tell you.

About this time, Eli takes my hand and says, "follow me." He takes me inside and across what must be the main living area, up a wide flagstone stairway and to the left, and back towards the ocean. "This will be the master suite," he tells me. The windows here are two-stories high and they fold back into themselves to provide access to a flagstone deck outside. The wrought iron railing is reminiscent of those I'd seen in Florence, oiled bronze with swirling details and bold design.

Eli takes my hand and turns me around, telling me to close my eyes. He turns me again, and leads me forward till we stop, with him standing behind me with both hands on my waist.

"Open," he says softly. I open my eyes and lose my breath. We are above the massive pines below, and yet close enough to the sea to see the turquoise water and hear the crash of the waves. "The sunsets here are pretty cool," Eli whispers. I can't speak, really. It's misty and the air is lush and cool, and I'm feeling like I'm exactly where I should be. This is not a feeling I am used to. I start to shiver a bit, which turns quickly to shaking. I'm holding onto the railing with a grip that turns my knuckles white. Eli can't help but notice.

"What's wrong Elaine?' he says, concerned. I still can't speak. I'm afraid
I will break down if I try. I just shake my head, unable to look at him. I don't
understand what I'm feeling. It's overwhelming though, and when Eli turns
me around and holds me, my head against his chest, I don't try to move. I stay
in that spot, eyes closed tight, and slowly let myself breath into the moment.
I feel his chin on the top of my head after a while as he rubs his hands up and
down my arms. "Let's go inside, it's getting cold out here," he says. I don't
want to move,

but I follow him back through, and down the stairs. We head back to the truck
and he hands me a dark blue V-neck sweater from the back seat.
"It's big but I bet you'll look great in it," he smiles, "and it's warm."
"Hungry?" he asks, and I smile and nod, still not meeting his gaze. I look out
the window for a last gaze at this place he is creating, and my eyes water at the
simple beauty of the image before me.
"It's so lovely, Eli," I finally manage. "You should be so proud." I can feel his
happiness without turning to see him. The sun dips closer to the water as we
head back down to the coast highway. About the time we hit the main road it
becomes obvious the weather has

turned. A dense fog has rolled in, obscuring every inch of the shore. And the
road ahead is barely visible. Eli is leaning forward in the truck squinting to see
when the rain begins to hail down on us. He backs up the truck and turns back
up the drive we'd just come down, then stops and looks at me. "I think we are
going to have to wait this out, it's just too dangerous to drive down the

mountain in this." I nod, and before I can say a word, he says it for me. "The boys. I know."

Let me call Shawn now. He can take them to my house. They'll be safe. We might not get out of here for a while." I really don't have a choice, so I say sure. I just want to talk to Riley.

After a quick conversation with the surfer dude, Eli has Shawn put Riley on the line. They have clear weather where they are, still at the zoo but about to grab a soda before they head back to the condo. Eli hands me the phone and says," Shawn's got this."

I hear Riley before I even say hello. There's excitement in his voice as he shouts to AJ "…overnight at Eli's beach house… YES!" We chat for a few minutes but I'm not sure he's heard anything but my last "ok, love you bud."

I hand the phone back to Eli and he tells Shawn where the extra keys are, and to go ahead and get the kids fed at the zoo, he'll cover it when we get back. Then he hangs up.

By now the rain is falling so hard we have to creep up the hillside to get back to the house. "There's really only the one room with a roof at this point." Eli says as he stares at the rain. "And no electricity. I think we might be better off waiting this out in the truck."

I laugh and say," Don't worry, I've slept in worse places." He hops out, pulling his hood up as he climbs in the back seat and lowers them down. He pulls a couple of blankets out of the back and roots around in the cooler he always keeps to find a couple of beers. Then he turns and looks at me with a strange grin. "Hang tight, be right back."

Before I could say anything, he was out of the truck and running into the house. A few minutes later he comes back with a package, the kind you get in the mail from Amazon or one of those online places. He jumps back into the back seat and smiles. "My mom sent this to me – she still sends me care packages. Like I'm still in college or something. But she's gotten better at what's inside, since she discovered online shopping." We both laugh. "Can you climb in between the seats and come back here? We can't have a proper supper if you are up there and I'm back here."

The maneuvering it takes to squeeze over the console to get in the back from the front proves too much, so I give him a look, ask him to unlock the side door, and manage to jump out and back in without getting drenched. There's one of those big construction flashlights in the side bin on the car door, so we light that up, as darkness is setting in fast.

"Mood lighting," I say. Eli, in the meanwhile, has begun exploring the package. "I brought this up here last time I came up because I thought it might be nice to have some emergency supplies…" he chuckled. "Because, you know, you never know when you are going to have a guest. In your truck. For the night."

Eli's mom has, as it turns out, excellent taste. There are vacuum sealed cheeses, the good kind. Two bottles of wine, crackers, Italian hard salami, some dark chocolate, and a wine opener. "She's always hoping I'll meet someone," he says quietly. "And she's not subtle."

We start talking about that part of our lives as we sample the delights of the care package. You know, the big old past loves and stuff. I tell him about Bill, and how it all ended. After a minute, he says, "That was a long time ago. No one since?" I kind of look away and take a breath. And then I tell him that there'd been another man. Riley's father. His eyebrow raises and he asks gently, "What happened there?"

"Long story," I say. "Maybe another time?" There must have been something in my voice that makes him respond, "Sure, no worries." Then it is his turn to talk. I ask him about his wife.

He looks me in the eyes for a few minutes. Then he says, looking down, "Ok, but I need to tell this kind of fast. It's become like ripping off a Band-Aid. If I go fast it won't hurt too much." I reach over and put my hand on his.

"I met my wife Callie when we were both in college. Freshman year. She was from Ohio, from a dairy farm. She came to Pittsburgh to study Special Ed and become a teacher. Her whole life she wanted to come to the city to work with kids who struggled in school. She had a brother who had struggled a bit and it had been so hard on him till he had the right teachers. So we met there. We became really good friends until about a year later when she started dating a guy in my architecture class. I didn't like the guy, but I didn't really have a reason. I tried to just let it happen and then I realized I was just incredibly jealous. I finally told her I wanted more with her, and she grinned and said, 'I wondered when you would figure that out.' We were engaged by the end of sophomore year, married a month after graduation. We wanted kids, but it took a while, almost five years. Then we had Sam."

He stops and turns his head to look out the window and at the rain, which has become more like a fine mist. He wipes the window with his hand and looks back at me. His eyes are so full of pain.

"Sam was perfect. A little boy full of energy, full of jokes all the time. A real handful. We were happy together. We used to say we felt like we got everything we ever wanted. We didn't want to take that for granted. When Sam was six we went to the farm for a weekend to visit her folks because her mom had slipped and fallen, and Callie was worried. It was about a five-hour drive, and because Callie thought she might want to stay longer, we took two cars. We spent a few days but I had to get back to work, and Sam had just started first grade. I drove the truck and took Sam home, while Callie stayed to help her Dad with meals and the house while her mom took her time recovering. About a week later, she called to say she felt like she could leave, and was heading out that morning."

He stops again, and when he finally speaks, his voice has changed. He sounds like someone reading a message, like he has disconnected from the story, and is just reading the words.

"I got the call around 2:00. A semi crossed the median in southern Ohio and hit Callie head-on. She was killed instantly."

He looks at me. I don't know what my face must have registered, because his own pain seems to vanish and is taken over by concern for me. "What? Elaine, what is it?" I just shake my head. I can't speak. I pull my hand back and cover my mouth with both hands. I start rocking back and forth and crying silently. I know I am saying, "I'm so sorry, so sorry," over and over and over. Eli scoops me into his arms and holds me and tries to calm me.

I feel like somehow all the tears I'd never cried I let go that night. At some point, we fall asleep on the blankets, until sunrise and the cold of the mountain morning shake us awake.

I lie there, looking into his eyes. I'd registered that they were a beautiful deep brown, but never noticed the flecks of gold and hazel. I'd spent most of our time together stealing quick glances, not letting myself land there for too long. We are chest to chest now, wrapped in those blankets, and we don't say a word or even move for the longest time. Then he reaches over and touches my cheek. "I don't know what happened last night. But I'm so sorry too."

I just smile and promise I will explain. After we get somewhere warm and dry that sells coffee. He nods and smiles. Then I do what I know I have to do. I kiss him for the first time.

It's one of those moments you don't want to end. At least I don't. And he doesn't seem to either. But after a few minutes I start to shiver, and then shake from the cold and damp as my body comes awake.

Eli laughs and says, "Let's get out of here, this party is too noisy." I smile and we get ourselves together, then head down the mountain one more time.

When we check in with the kids, Shawn sounds sleepy, but coherent and reassuring. He says the boys are crashed out in the den with some videos and that all is well. The rain has made it down the coast, so Shawn says to take our time. They will be fine till we get back.

We drive in the quiet of our thoughts about all that we'd spoken in the hours that had passed since the storm began. You know how you can be so comfortable in complete silence with some people? It's like that. At one point, Eli reaches over and holds my hand. He doesn't let go till we find a small beach café that's open.

Over breakfast I tell him about Drew. The simple version. No ghosts. Nothing about how I still hang out with my dead boyfriend after all these years. I tell him the important parts… how he'd been there through all of the Maria drama, how we'd started out as best friends and ended up, well, where we ended up. And how that dream died with my best friend on a highway in Georgia. I tell it quick, like he had told me his story the night before. I hold his hands across the table and look at him when I can. The tears come for him before me.

And all he says is, "Oh." But he squeezes my hands and for the first time in a long time, everything feels something like ok.

The rest of the drive is a blur of emotion; the kind you get at the beginning of what you know will be a big adventure. You don't really know how it will work out, but it feels like what you have to do, or at least try. And you kind of want it to start right away.

In the end I let my heart lead the way. I decide to drive the boys back to Arizona and school because the weather has become kind of unpredictable and surfing isn't safe for them for a while. AJ's mom agrees to host Riley for the next ten days while I go back to California, to Eli's beach house.

No, it's not what you might be thinking. I get there just in time to drive him to the airport for his trip back east. The plan is to stay at his place, take care of Gus and George, his giant golden labs and the plants and, well, myself. And to write, or at least to try. I have exactly ten more days till another author tour will take me on the road again.

I pull the car up to drop him off and while he gets his bag out of the trunk, I walk back to hug him goodbye. And I get a kiss that will keep me warm for the next ten days. When he turns to leave, he laughs and tosses a pretty good Schwarzenegger "I'll be back" over his shoulder.

When I get back to the beach house, I take the dogs out for a run on the sand. They're well-trained and seem to like me, so after a bit I start to jog a little with them. They treat it like a game but then suddenly stop and look at me. I pull my hands out of my hoodie and say, laughing, "What? No treats here guys. What's up?" They're both sitting staring just to my right. That's when I realize that they could see him. Drew. He's come back.

My best friend comes up from behind me and gently bumps against my shoulder. "Hi," he said quietly. "Hi," I bump back.

Even though the sun is on its way down and there aren't many people
on the beach, I think it might be better if we talk back at the beach house, so I
call to the dogs, who are still frozen to the spot.

"Come on guys, let's go home." And I said to him, "Meet you there."

The dogs quickly settle in their beds down in the den, worn out from
our run. I go upstairs to the room I've been sleeping in, with its beautiful view
of the ocean from the French doors. There is a small loveseat positioned just
inside the doors, and out of view of anyone passing by. In other words, a
perfect spot for a conversation with my favorite ghost.

"Sorry I haven't been around much." For Drew, he is unusually
quiet, but when I look over, he's smiling. "It felt like I should give you some
space." I just nod. "It's ok. I mean, I missed you, but it's been ok." He smiles
again. "I know. I'm glad."

I look out at the water, silver and gold in the light from a sun slowly
sinking into the horizon. I feel like I am at new place – in my head, in my
heart. "It feels weird," I say quietly. "I know," he says, "for me too."

"Are you ok? I ask. He looks at me and this time I see his eyes are wet. "As
long as you are ok, I will always be ok, E. That's how it works for me. So you
just be ok. Ok?" Then we both kind of laugh.

"Are you going again?" I say, not looking at him.

"I'll be around if you need me. But I think you need to finish this book already.
Especially now."

I look at him and ask what he means. "Why now?"

He shakes his head. "Because if you get it all out on paper, it will make telling Eli so much easier. And you know, at some point, you need to do that. Right?"

I'm shaking my head no, but it slowly turns into a nodding yes. I put my hand out and I feel Drew take it in his. And we just sit and watch the rest of the magic show that is tonight's sunset.

The next morning, when I wake up, this beach house with its old desk up against an ocean view turns out to be just the thing to get me writing again.

I've told you all of the important stuff about my family, how I grew up, and what Andrew means to me. You know the whole Bill saga. I bet you can even picture my kids. And while I've told you how the whole Raff thing started, let's just say I haven't begun to scratch the ugly surface of what would unfold over the next few years, and how it would change everything.

For the next nine days I write for hours and hours at the beautiful old desk in front of the beach view. I walk on the beach when it gets too hard, and fill up my lungs with the sea air. The dogs and Drew have become fast friends and provide a lighter touch when I get too lost in memory. Then I find the strength to go back to this work that means so much. I write some of the hardest parts that I think will help you understand all of the stops and starts in this story. And I hope, I really hope, that as you understand, you will forgive me for that.

So, where were we? Oh, right. That night.

A few weeks after I'd asked him to leave, Raff and I gave it another try. Or I did. But in his eyes, I'd fallen off the pedestal once and for all, and a few things that happened next didn't help at all.

We went slow. In fact, we went back to dating. Raff stayed at his parents and we saw each other once or twice a week, away from Rosie for about 4 months. And then it began to feel like that night never happened. He was gentle, open and mostly very sorry. And I believed all of the promises he made. Because I wanted what he promised more than anything. A home, a family life and someone who would love and care for me for the rest of time.

For the first few months after he moved back in, things were almost as good as they had been at the beginning. Raff passed the entrance exams for law school and started classes. He had a trust that Sal had set up years before so he used some of that money, but he was always afraid to tap into it too much, so he started to work nights at a car dealership. A year went by and everything was good. We were both happy for a while.

Law school proved to be a bigger challenge than he'd anticipated, so along with classes, there were lots of days spent in the library, working with study groups and then barely having time to eat before he headed to his night job. Even his weekends were spent at the dealership, so we became like ships that passed in the night.

All work and no play made Raff a mean boy. He started stopping off more and more frequently for "a drink" with the guys from work on his way home, which meant by the time he'd made it home he was good and drunk. And that meant one of two things. Either he was loving and lusty or mean as a snake. The worst part was there was no way of knowing until he'd been in the house for ten minutes or so. If the mood was good, he'd pull me away from whatever I was doing and want to stay up all night drinking more and making love. But the more he drank, the less loving he got, so eventually even that turned ugly. If, on the other hand, he started out mean, it usually meant he'd end up saying things that hurt me and slowly began to whittle away at my self-esteem. He hadn't hit me again at that point, but I was starting to believe it was just a matter of time. And it turned out that time came sooner than I thought.

I bet you are wondering at this point why I was still there. Letting him be in my life. In Rosie's life. I would be, if I were you. But it had all started out so good. I had no idea what a normal relationship felt like. Looked like. I thought this was what "working it out" looked like. And for a while, the bad times were brief, and far apart. In between he'd be charming, loving, happy, funny Raff. Till everything changed. Andrew had tried to talk to me about it time after time but I wasn't listening. And eventually he stopped trying. But he was always there, whenever I was alone, even if I wasn't ready to hear what I knew was good advice.

About four months after the first incident, there was another. And it was bad, I mean scary bad. But what happened after might help you understand how I ended up staying in that relationship for the next four years. Raff was anything but predictable. Anything could set him off. It was usually nothing that got him going. One night he came home well after ten, and I'd fallen asleep on the couch waiting up for him. I woke up when he kicked me in the stomach. I barely had time to react when he grabbed me by the hair into the kitchen.

"Cook me some goddamned food," he snarled. When I went to stand up, still trying to get my wits about me, I didn't get up fast enough. He slammed my head into the wall oven, and I felt my cheekbone shatter. Blood was pouring from my nose and my ear and he looked at me with disgusted eyes. "Bitch," he grunted, then walked away into the other room.

I remember being terrified, thinking he was going for a weapon or some other way to hurt me. This was different than anything that had happened between us before. I sat on the kitchen floor and tried to figure out what to do, how to get Rosie and I out of there alive. After what felt like forever I stood up and walked to the hallway where I could see the living room. Raff was on the sofa, completely passed out. While I shook from what had just happened, I tried very quietly to clean up the broken glass from the oven door, and then myself.

That night, I listened to the voice inside me, and this time the message was clear. I quietly packed a backpack full of our clothes from what was sitting in the laundry basket I'd left on the stairs, carefully woke a confused Rosie, whispered to her to be very quiet and bundled her up. I grabbed my purse, and left before he could wake up. I didn't have a clue where to go but I knew I should get my face checked out for sure. I was shaking so hard I wondered if I could get the key in the ignition, and even as I drove away I kept thinking he'd pop up in front of me to stop me. Women who have been slowly and deliberately made more and more afraid, whether by verbal or physical cruelty are easy to spot, if you pay attention. There is a quiet anxious energy about them, like an animal who's been abused. They wear that fear like a coat that is too big and heavy to move around in. It slows them down and wears them out. It fogs their mind and breaks their heart in ways you cannot imagine.

At least that is how I felt as I parked outside the 24-hour diner about ten miles from my house at 3:00 in the morning. Rosie fell asleep as soon as I had her in the warm booth, snuggled under the blanket she'd never let go of, even now at five-years old. As I nursed a cup of coffee and counted out the few bills in my wallet, I made a plan. I'd wait there till morning, then drop Rosie off at daycare and go to Pally's. I could stay there and call in to work.

Pally must have known what was going on but she wasn't the type of girl to talk about it. Until you were ready. She just went along with whatever story I gave her. I don't blame her, back then people didn't talk about this kind of domestic abuse, and too many figured the woman who got beat must have done something to deserve it. I don't think Pally thought that at all, but just the same, she didn't know what to say or do, but she was always there when I ran. And though this was the first time, it certainly wouldn't be the last.

After Rosie was safely checked in at her day care, I explained to the staff there that I'd had a bad fall that morning and was on my way to the doctor. I'd put a large bandage on my face and hidden most of the bruising by carefully arranging my hair. I stopped at the pay phone outside and called the bookstore and told them I'd been in a car accident and asked my assistant manager to cover for me till I was able to get back. I left a message for my boss, too. Then I drove to Pally's. When she opened the door that morning, with the sun barely up, it was still bright enough for her to get a good look at my face.

I didn't realize how bad it was till I saw it in her eyes. "Oh shit, Elaine," was all she could say. "Oh shit." She took me by the hand and pulled me inside and sat me down at her kitchen table. Her girls were already at school, but she took care of me like I was one of them. She cleaned my cheek and took a good look. "You need to be seen, E. We're going to see Ron right now." I didn't argue, as it felt so good to have someone else in charge of me.

She called Ron from the other room and drove me to his office. He ordered an x-ray and wrote me a script for some pain pills, and then gave me a talk about how I needed to leave Raff. I told him I knew, but I had no money and nowhere to go. Raff's name was on the lease, so if anyone had to go it was us. Ron was never much of a husband to Pally, but he was a decent guy and a good father. He told me, "Just get out and you guys can stay with us till you get on your feet."

Suddenly I felt hopeful that I could do it. At this point, you see, even though things with Raff had been bad, I didn't think I could leave. There is this place you get to when someone finds the tender places in your heart that are still bruised from a lifetime of injury, and they know just where to press to bring back all of your insecurity and fear. You become lost in the pain, and over time you begin to believe all the things that person says. And you lose that strength that took so long to build up. You settle into something like a daze and just get through it.

But this wasn't like anything that had happened before. It was the first time I realized that he could really hurt me. Or worse, he might turn his anger against Rosie. I'd begun to see that when Raff got to the point of that much anger, he simply had no control over how bad it got. He didn't even know it was me he was hitting. You could see it in the way his eyes glazed and lost focus. He turned into a trapped, snarling, raging beast. And I knew that I couldn't win a fight with something like that.

And I woke up from that daze, and I knew I had to do. Hearing Ron's offer brought back some of the old Elaine. I sat in the car as Pally drove me to my apartment to pick up my things, but when we got there, I saw Raff's car still in the lot. That meant he hadn't gone to class. He was waiting for me. I started to shake and without a word, Pally turned the car around and took me back to her house. Raff had only met her once and didn't know where she lived, so I figured I would be safe there. When we got back, she told me to go in the guest room and rest. She said she would wake me up in an hour or two and we'd go get Rosie.

Raff called Pally's house about two hours later around 4. I let the phone ring, but she didn't answer it, and when I saw the time I knew she was probably outside waiting for her kids to get off the school bus. Still half asleep I went to the kitchen and picked it up. When I heard his voice, I was surprisingly calm. And unafraid. "Why aren't you at work?" he said, sounding concerned.

"Well," I said, "I didn't want to have to explain the black eye and all the bruises."

"Oh Jesus," he said, choking up. "I'm sorry, Elaine." I didn't respond. "Are you ok? I'll come get you right now. Where are you? I mean, I know you're at Pally's, but where is that?"

I said, "No, Raff, I don't think that's a good idea." "Why not?" he said. "What do you mean?"

"I mean," I said, "that I don't think we are good for each other and I am afraid to keep going on this way. I don't think you meant to hurt me, but you did and it's really bad. Rosie and I are just going to stay here for a while. You can stay in the apartment and I'll send Ron over for our things in a couple days."

Suddenly I felt exhausted. It was Bill and the divorce and my giving up everything but my daughter all over again. But what else could I do? I was so focused on what I needed to tell him, I didn't hear Rosie at first. But then, when he didn't say anything, I heard her voice in the silence and I realized she was there. With him. But how? I started to shake and the terror I felt at that moment I really can't describe.

"What did you do, Raff?"

"What do you mean, honey?" He spoke in a voice that was completely changed. It was the voice from the night before. The voice of the man that hit me, the same voice that pulled me by the hair down the stairs, the voice that had more than once called me names and put me down.

"I picked up our girl from school, to save you a trip."

I hadn't ever put his name on the pickup list so I hadn't thought to say anything to the staff. I was infuriated and confused but I couldn't take the time to figure that out now. I knew I had to get to her.

"You better come home right now, Elaine," he said in that voice. "Ok?"

"Yes, I said. "Of course. I'll be there in twenty minutes." I grabbed my purse and looked at Pally's as I passed and said, "I'm sorry. I have to go back. He has Rosie".

I could drag out the rest of this for chapters, but I won't. For the next three years, I tried to live through what my life had become. Because he had managed it once, and because my fear overtook the part of my brain that might have figured out another way, I decided that it wasn't worth risking Rosie to try to leave. He would find me. He would hurt me, or so much worse, he would harm her.

I held a job, lied through my teeth about black eyes and bruises, lost my friends and couldn't face my family, or at least the ones that mattered, Annie and Ed. They adored Rosie but Raff knew they were my only real chance at getting out and away, so he forbade me to see them without him. And he threatened to hurt anyone I tried to pull into my life for help. And I'd realized he wasn't at all afraid to follow through on that promise.

By this point Annie had figured out something was terribly wrong, but I wouldn't admit it so there wasn't much she could do. There is so much shame associated with abuse and it feels like the final failure to admit it. I know now that this what the abuser counts on. And when the ones who could have helped have been threatened by someone you know will follow through on those threats – you just cannot bring yourself to ask them for the help you are so desperate for. Even though I tried everything I could think of to get out and away, with Rosie in the picture he had me up against the wall. He was crafty and resourceful, and worse, he had plenty of 'family' connections who would easily do bad things for the right amount of money.

Just a few weeks after I'd tried to make my getaway, and after a particularly ugly fight, which left me with a scar at the base of my throat from a knife he held there for three hours, he looked into my eyes and told me if I ever left him again, he'd hurt Rosie in front of me. Or he would make her "disappear." After everything I'd witnessed, I didn't question his sincerity for a minute.

When things had started to spiral out of control, I did the worst thing I could have done. I told Andrew to stay away. It felt like the only thing I had a say in, and as weird as this may sound, I wanted to protect him. I pushed him out of my mind and decided that this was my pain to bear alone. And the pain of losing him again somehow made all of the other hurt I suffered fade into something else I can't really describe. But somewhere deep inside I kept a tiny spark of hope because I felt like I'd finally done something that was my choice, and mine alone.

Raff was old school in his love/ hatred of me. He didn't want me, but didn't want me to go. He wanted me to be perfect, but hated me for any attempt I made at making a life for us. And he bitterly resented that I had fought through so much for custody of my daughter and that I loved her more than him. Deep at the root of all of this, I was the mother who abandoned him and kept her other children. He was bubbling and boiling with that bitterness all the time. And in the back of my mind, far beyond the numbness that had overtaken my body and soul, I knew it was only a matter of time and circumstance before he would lose control and that would be the end of me. And worse, I knew the only way out was if *he* decided to leave me. It had to be his decision.

"Stop for a while, E," I hear Andrew say softly. I can't look at him; I don't want to even breathe right now. I peel my clothes off as I walk through the room, and turn on the shower as hot as I can stand it and get in. And I cry from all the shameful memory. From sadness for all the friends and family I pushed away so they wouldn't get hurt. I cry for all the years I lost while I tried to find a way out of that nightmare.

And I cry for the others who knew what was happening but turned a blind eye. For the friends I had to leave behind because they refused to see. The ones who'd see me bruised, broken, and slipping away and stop calling. For my brother Kelly who knew, who asked me if what he thought was true, and when I confirmed it, he did nothing. No one who could have defended me even tried. No one protected me. No one helped me fight back.

And while I don't blame them for what was happening to me, I don't understand why no one -- not one person except for Pally and Ron -- ever asked what was wrong. If I was ok. If I needed help. After the first year, I'd tried one more time to run, but when I got to the car in the middle of the night, after sneaking out when Rosie was spending the night with friends, I found that he'd let all the air out of my front two tires. And when I started walking towards the bus, suddenly he was there in front of me before I was even out of the parking lot. He was laughing. And then he broke my jaw.

That was the end of the running. I was alone in a hell with no exit, imprisoned by a fear that would cripple me for years after all the reasons to be afraid were gone. And for the most part I never cried a tear during all that time. There was this feeling that I was standing that whole time on the edge of an endless abyss… and that the first tear that I let fall would be the one that would push me over.

Somehow, writing it down now felt like I was saying it out loud for the first time. And finally, letting myself feel the pain again. So now I cry for all of it. And then I dry myself off, pull on one of Eli's flannel shirts I see hanging on the chair and fall into a deep and dreamless sleep.

I know Andrew is sitting here by me all night, making sure I'm ok. And when I wake up, he says he is sorry he's been gone so long. He promises to stay with me through the rest of this. Even though I know I need to count on my own strength and not on my dead boyfriend to keep going, I have to admit that I need to hear this, and I'm hoping he means it.

The day before I'm due to leave the beach, Eli comes home. I am

so happy to see him that the fog I've been in all day lifts for a bit. We spend

the evening laughing and catching up on his Pittsburgh trip. He asks about the

writing but all I can really tell him is that I'm making progress, and I'm so

grateful for the time here. I think he knows that I'm in a fragile state and that

I'm not ready for anything more than what we are at this point. We curl up on

the couch, wrapped in blankets and fall asleep in front of the fire.

In the morning, I pack my laptop and the rest of my things. I hug the dogs

goodbye and let Eli hold me for a long time. Then I whisper, "Talk soon. I

promise," and head back to the desert and real life. Because everything with

Eli still feels like a dream.

Now it's been a month and a half since I left the beach. We've had one

of those long summers that seemed to last forever. It was still in the 80s when

Halloween hit, which even after all the years I've spent here in this desert

never seems right. Drew decided to follow Riley and his friends through their

trick or treat ritual and some of my neighbors will never be quite the same.

Use your imagination. Pumpkins that appear to be levitating. Fake gravestones

in the yard that appear to be moving. You get it. The kid in that ghost has

never really let go of his mischievous instincts. I laugh and shake my head but

I really wouldn't want it any other way, except, well – you know.

It's nearly December when we finally begin to feel the chill in early

morning and after sunset and the seasons are falling into place. I've finished two back to back tours with a couple of ex-groupies who thought the world needed just a little juicier info about the Beatles. Rosie helped out while I was gone as she's finishing her final semester at college and is only taking two classes. She's working and trying to figure out what comes next. It's nice to have her around more, I have to admit. I love the woman she has grown into and can't wait to see where her life takes her. And I'm grateful she is here while she finds her way.

I'm working from home for the rest of the year as we have no road trips planned. All the books have been released and are in the shops in time for the holiday rush. I've got two new books and two new authors lined up for January, but between now and then, aside from some conference calls, and a little end-of-the-year paperwork, the business has all but shut down. Happens every year. This year somehow it feels different. And I realize it is because this free time has suddenly taken away all of my excuses to finish my own book. And to make it worse, or better, or hell, I don't really know, something else has kind of happened.

I'd left part of my printed pages with some notes on my desk one day when I was in the office. I was late for a meeting with Nora, a new author's agent. and when I got to my desk, she was there ahead of me. Reading my pages.
She looked up with a grin. "Whose is this? And why haven't I seen it yet?" I just stopped and stared. Then I think I stuttered something like "um, it's my uh, well, it's nothing, it's ok, it's mine. It's my book. Um, I just printed some pages to work on over the holiday. It will probably never be anything really. Sorry."

She looked at me over her reading glasses. "No, I'm sorry. It has to be something. Because I'd kind of like to know what happens next."

I sort of sunk into the chair across from her and we talked for the next hour.

The conversation ended with my promise to give the finished manuscript to her and only her by the end of spring. And that still seems like I made it up in my head, but she sends me emails every week asking how it's going, so yeah. That happened.

I talk to Eli a few times a week. In a way, he's in the same place as me. All of his jobs have finished up with new work lined up for the new year. With the free time and the weather holding up, he's been working on the house in Santa Barbara and calls me to report on his progress. Sam is coming out for Thanksgiving and they will do some fishing and catching up. He misses me. I miss him, too. I told him about Nora and he's joined my unofficial book support group. He says if I'm not in California and I'm not working then I need to be writing. It feels somehow that all that is standing between what happens next – with us, with me and my life – is just this story that needs to be told once and for all.

At this moment, somewhere in the house I can hear my cell ringing but I have no idea where it is. I've been writing for a while so I stop, hit the save button and take notice that the light outside has changed to that color of violet and smoke that makes me forget to hate the desert for a minute.
I wander till I find the phone, on the sofa under a pillow. It's Deborah and she's worried about Francis.

Let me back up. Over the last year, since Deb's trip to Italy, it became obvious that Dad had made a decision. He wanted out. He'd stopped walking at the mall, stopped getting up at all. He no longer came downstairs for lunch, and then dinner. We talked, and She'd talked to my stepsisters who love him like their own father, and my siblings and our half-brother Matt, and then finally, she called to talk to me.

"Elaine, I have to do something for your father and I don't know what." I told her I trusted her and if it was time for him to be somewhere easier, then of course, it was time. So it began.

First, he went to live in a small studio type apartment with 24-hour care. He seemed happy there for a while. But he refused to engage with the other residents, even though we had all thought he would finally have someone to talk to about all the times he loved to linger in. Instead, he slept more and more. That fall, my work took me east a lot, so I managed a few visits on my way home, and even got Riley back there for a wonderful few days. He flew alone for the first time, now nearly fourteen and becoming more and more of the music freak that his grandfather, uncle, and even his own father had been. I will forever hold those images of him and Francis communing over the strings for hours, my father coming to life in those small moments. I will hold those pictures in my heart always, even if they still make me cry.

And now Deb is on the phone to say it feels like he is slowly slipping away. And she doesn't know what to do except stay close, and let him know we all love him. I ask if I should come, and she says no, he wouldn't want all of us rushing to his side. I want to talk to him. More than that, I want him to hug me, and kiss the top of my head and tell me how proud of me he is, just once more. But I don't know how to say this to Deb, so we just agree she will let me know how it's going. And I'll stay here and hope things take a different turn.

The three of us in our little family had decided on a quiet holiday. Riley had negotiated his way into going snowboarding the day after Christmas with the neighbor's kids in New Mexico and staying till New Year's. Eli was stuck in a typical Pittsburgh snowstorm for three days after we'd planned to try to catch up in Cali. We were growing closer with every phone call, but the distance was a good thing for me. It kept me from doing what writers love to do – find a reason to do anything but write. And when the reason is someone like Eli, well it can be pretty hard to resist, so I was, in a strange way, grateful for that snowstorm. Rosie decided to hang out at her best friend's new apartment which left me alone. I didn't mind, since I had a lot to work out. I felt ready to do what I'd been putting off. I sat down and wrote for the rest of that week, and now there were only a few hard chapters left.

Isn't it funny when things start sorting themselves out and you suddenly feel strong and in control, that's when everything around you starts falling into a thousand pieces? I'd spent the weeks before and after Christmas writing and remembering, and was getting closer to the last few chapters. The kids were back home, but I had a week and a half left of my leave, so I got up at dawn to drive up to the canyon lake and see if the fresh air could help me work through what needed to come next. Halfway there, my cell rang but I didn't have a signal so it cut off when I answered. I turned off the phone and just let my mind go all the places it needed to go.

Once I got there, I stood for about fifteen minutes staring into the water and suddenly felt like I should get back home. I'd left the house before the kids were up, and realized all at once that I hadn't thought to leave a note or anything. It was still really early, so I headed back to the house, thinking I'd get there before they were even awake. The phone had three missed calls, and I was about to listen to the voice mail but it rang again and it was Kelly. He wasn't in a good mood and when he gets like that, you just need to let him huff and puff and get it all out.

"It's our sister," he said, in what I secretly refer to as his "Francis" voice. "She's not doing well at all, and I think you should go over there." I sigh and let him finish the story.

It's nothing new. Lana is out of money, Lana is sick again, Lana needs our help. The problem is that every time we bail her out, get her to a new doctor, get her what she says she needs this time, she takes off. And usually with the last guy on earth she should be with. Within a few months, we're at it again. Somewhere along the way as her kids grew up, her marriage fell apart. And then she got sick. And like many people who have to deal with too many things all at once, the pain pills became too easy to turn to. And then they became a problem.

Now don't get me wrong. I know that she is sick. She's had the same issues for years, but she hasn't ever been willing to do what she needs to do to get better. To quit a toxic job, to take better care of herself. I just wish I had known how to help her. But she wouldn't ever let me in. So she learned how to kill her physical and emotional pain with prescription meds and anything else she can get her hands on. And it's changed her from the funny, loving sister I finally thought I'd found to someone I don't know at all anymore. At this point, it's hard to tell if it's the illness or the drugs, or the loneliness that are slowly taking her away.

Maria lives here too now. When I ran here after that fateful Easter, Lana was already here, running one of Kelly's stores, so it wasn't long before Maria decided she needed to be here, too. The funny thing is I came here to be near Lana and her kids, so Rosie and I could have some of the comfort you would think would come from the proximity of family. But in the fifteen years I've lived in Arizona, not two blocks from her, Lana has been in my house about ten times. And half of those she came to the door, and not inside.

Maria moved here to "be near her grandkids," but it turned out she didn't like them any more than she liked me. After her first stroke, she just got more and more bitter and mean. And over the years she's let that bitterness take her over and no matter how many times she's forced Kelly and Lana to help her move house, she can't seem to leave that anger behind. It follows her like a lost dog. Lana and my mother are cut from the same cloth: They live for the drama, and their best day is when they tell someone off. They hate the grocer, the doctors, the insurance agents and the people who take care of them.

I wish I could hate them. But I just feel empty in that place where "mother" and "sister" are supposed to sit inside your heart.

And Francis?

Francis is gone now.

There. I wrote it down. I'm sitting here alone in the almost dark and I need to tell you this part. It's been six weeks and still doesn't feel like six days sometimes. Or it feels like six years. I can't explain it. It's ok and horrible at the same moment. I miss him.

That visit with Riley turned out to be the last time I saw him. We'd talked a lot. He'd told me I'd done a hell of a job with my son, and that he was proud of me. We smiled and I kissed the top of his head. And when I said goodbye, I think I knew it might be the last time we smiled into each other's eyes.

After that call from Deb, it seemed like Francis began to let go a bit at a time. Matt, his son with Deb was in the Air Force by then, married with a little girl. He'd been deployed to Iraq and Francis worried over him daily. Deb kept him informed and brought him news as often as she could. In the end, as we all predicted, Francis held on until Matt came home safely to his wife and little daughter. And then, as fast as snow in spring, he slipped away.

I remember feeling like it wasn't real, but it was right. For him, it was right. His last living brother, my uncle Ray, had died on Labor Day, and the week before dad, Ray's wife Glory had gone. He told Deb, "They are all there, and they are waiting on me. I need to go." Then he stopped talking and it was just a few days before it was over. It happened too fast for any of us five "first" kids to get there. Deb was there with her girls and Matt, helping him let go. And I was what felt like a million miles away, holding onto the phone.

I've had two men in my life that I'd loved beyond words, and now they were both gone. That kind of empty hurts in a way I have no words for. It's a hunger you cannot chase with comfort or any kind of food or pills, or liquor. It's been weeks now and it's still there. I know it will get easier with time, but it will never be the same.

So back to now. After I hung up the phone, after I told Kelly that I just couldn't come to Lana's rescue one more time, knowing that it just made it easier for her to stay in her awful pattern. I agreed to pay the premium on her insurance so she'd at least have that, but beyond that he'd need to figure it out. I suggested another try at rehab, but that suggestion would have to come from him, because not much had changed in 30 years. She still had no use for advice from her big sister.

39~ I Have a Theory

After my January tour, I spent February working with my new author to try to get her ready for road wars. She was a reserved and extremely shy introvert, so I was nervous that the book tour would be miserable for her. She surprised all of us by being able to turn on her personality for the cameras and the bookstore crowds like a hidden switch. When that tour finished, I had a break. And now, since I'd promised Nora, I was facing a deadline of sorts. I made a decision and since the timing was perfect at work, I asked for a six-week break. I promised myself this was it. It *had* to be.

I wake up after having spent the first two weeks of that break alternating between writing and crying. It's like that when you walk into the pain of the past and let it surround you for a bit, so that the words you find are the right ones. And it takes a toll. I feel worn out, done in, and in need of serious sleep even though I'd just woken up. But that would have to wait a bit.

The winter, such as it is in Arizona, has made its escape. And the weather is what we waited for all year. Cool mornings, warm afternoons with sunshine and blue skies, and just enough chill in the evening to warrant a sweater. Easter is a week away, Rosie is here for part of her spring break and I hear her laughing in the other room and she's not alone.

"Mom!" she's yelling. I don't want to face her. I know I must look like hell. "MOM!" she calls again, "look who's here."

I force a cheerful "just a minute honey" and think, 'oh good lord', who is it now? I'm so not up for company. I take my time in the bathroom, throw on some blush and mascara and a pair of jeans, and pull my hair into a ponytail.

"Hey babe," I say, as she meets me in the hall. Behind her Riley is dragging our visitor to the back to show off the dogs and his latest "fort," and I'm still confused.

"Mom," she says, "it's Eli! He drove all the way here, he said. He called you and called you and no one picked up so he called me. He had the number from when you guys were at his place. "Remember?"

"Mom. He came all this way to see you." She grins and shoved me towards the patio doors.

When Eli turns around, I want to run for a minute. I'm so afraid he'll look at me and see only the broken girl. The ruined woman. All the mistakes. But he grins at me with that lopsided smile of his and I kind of forget all of that.

"What?" I say, "what are you doing here?" He just bear-hugs me and lifts me in the air, right in front of the kids, and kisses me. And then the strangest thing happens. As he puts me down and I open my eyes, over his shoulder I see Andrew. And he is smiling.

I'm in a daze, but it's the good kind. I sit at the table outside with Eli while Rosie makes coffee and Riley plays with the dogs. Eli explains that he'd decided that I was just too damn far away and he wanted to see me, so he hopped in the car and started driving. It wasn't till he crossed the state line into Arizona that he realized all he had was a phone number. He hadn't even thought to grab my letter for my address, or anything. So he started calling and when I didn't pick up after a couple hours he got worried. He still had Rosie's number in his phone from when I'd borrowed it one day to call her, and so he called her, hoping she'd be home. I guess I'd said enough about him to make her know it was ok, so she'd met him at the interstate and he'd followed her to the house.

I'm still a little bewildered by the whole turn of events, but they're both having a pretty good time telling the story. It doesn't matter to me how he got here. I'm just so glad to see him it scares me more than a little.

It's been a while since we've seen each other. We've talked on the phone a couple of times every week, and played with plans to meet up. But the more time that passed, the easier it has been for me to talk myself out of it. Eli says he figured that would happen, and he wasn't taking any chances. After a minute or two I realize I've hardly spoken and I'm just staring at him like I've found my lost dog. I'm pretty sure I have a big sloppy grin on my face the whole time, too. When I realize both the kids are staring at us and no one is talking, I decide to do the only thing I can think of. I stand up and announce I'm going to make breakfast.

Over scrambled eggs, bacon and cinnamon toast, the kids and Eli talk about life. I seem to be stuck in the role of observer, and quite content to just sit and watch them get acquainted. In my house. At my table.

Rosie has to go to work at her part-time job at the hospital and Riley wants to go to AJ's to skateboard, so before long we have the house to ourselves. Together we wash up the dishes and make another pot of coffee. The morning air is still holding onto a slight chill, but it's about 85 degrees in the sun. We sit by the pool with our feet in the water.

"I really missed you," Eli says softly, "but I guess you figured that out by now." I smile up at him. "Ditto."

"What are we going to do about this?" he asks. I just look at him and shake my head. "I don't know, Eli." He doesn't respond, just puts his arm around me and squeezes me to him. "I guess we'll figure it out. We'll figure it out in time."

That night after what has become kind of a favorite dinner ritual of pasta and wine, I tell Eli about my plan to write the rest of the book in the next few weeks. He smiles and says he's beginning to understand that this isn't just any book. He doesn't look at me when he adds, "I get that this is really important, E. Do you want to tell me what the book is about?"

I'm picking up my wineglass as he speaks, and when he calls me "E," I drop the glass, spilling wine all over the floor. "Oh," I say, but I can't move. No one has called me that since Andrew, and it sounds so right in Eli's voice. I start to tear up and I don't want him to see, so I get up and go for some paper towels to mop up my mess. But he's right behind me.

"What, Elaine?" He's standing behind me. "What is it?"

I turn into him and just hold on. "God, I say. "I'm always crying. I can't think what you must think. But this, it's good. It's, well, you just feel so. I don't know. It feels so…" I'm all choked up again. And we don't have to talk anymore. We lie down on the big sofa together, my head on his chest, not saying anything but feeling everything.

We spend the whole night like that, as though it was the most natural thing in the world.

Andrew is sitting on the kitchen counter when I walk back in the house from seeing Eli off the next morning. He has a big job in Malibu, repairing a friend's house after the sudden fires last month, so he has to get back. We've made a deal that I'll finish what I need to do, and then fly out for a long weekend to talk about what happens next. Riley's at school and the house is quiet and full of sunlight. Andrew is standing in the kitchen looking at me like I just dyed my hair purple or something equally out of character. "I like the guy," he says. I nod, "Ok."

He's staring at me, very serious now. "Don't mess it up." I look at him laughing. "Well, OK, mister boss man," I say as I turn to do the dishes.

He grabs my hand. "E," he continues. He's not joking around. "Listen. I know you, I know what kind of man you need. What kind of man you deserve, and? Eli is the real thing. And its time. Hell, its way past time."

He's standing an inch away from me and looking straight into my eyes. He is real. I smell him and feel the heat of his body. I tilt my head back to look up at him and he kisses me, not like the boy I remember, but like the man I want to know. The man he might have been if he'd lived, with all the passion and longing and ache, all the promise and dreams and everything I've imagined for all these years. When he's done, he pulls back and has tears in his eyes.

"It's done, Elaine. Nothing can change what's happened. But everything we had - it's never going to leave you. Us, I mean. The us that we were. This love, it's the kind you keep. These are the memories that you need to keep, not like the other ones. Finish the book, write him out of your head once and for all. And then go be with Eli. It's what you want. It's what I want for you. I'm going to need to leave soon, and this time it will be for good. I've never known how much time I had here, but I have a feeling once you are through with this book, and I know you are ok, I won't be able to stay. I might be wrong. I hope I'm wrong, but if I'm not, then I need you to know what I think." He walks away from me and sits down on the couch, staring outside. "I know you think I died too soon, Elaine. But I had a great life. And I had a great love. You, E. You loved me with everything you had. I never felt alone, I never felt scared from the first time I kissed you. Most people don't get that in a whole long lifetime.

I had enough. I lived enough. You were enough for me. You need to know that."

I have this theory. I think if you look at a man's face when he doesn't realize you are looking; you can see just about everything he's ever lived through. How he's loved, what he's lost, and what can still break him. I look at Drew looking away from me, and I see all the years he didn't have. But for the first time, I also see what he did have: A good life. Too short, yes, but really, really good. And I suddenly understand things in a whole new way.

I close my eyes for a minute, so grateful to hear that he feels that way and to realize he was happy all those years ago, and still is now. When I open them and start to speak, I am alone. But at that moment, I know I'll never wonder again about all the "what ifs."

Every worry, every question I've had, is somehow gone from my heart, and I   knew I

can just keep on living and that he will be, that he is, ok.

My dead boyfriend is just fine.

I used to be the kind of mother who lived for holidays and all the little things you do to make children smile. Easter was fun for Rosie and me. We'd dye the eggs, paint our own little baskets, and tell made-up stories about the bunny. One time, when Rosie was about four, we went to the mall and there was this guy dressed up in a giant oversized bunny suit scaring the Holy Jesus out of every kid in the place. Rosie calmly walked up to him and tugged on his very long arm. He looked down with ears flopping wildly and she said, "You are really much too big and its kind of awful." The bunny guy nodded and said, "you are a VERY wise little girl," then promptly went to change. That's my girl. Always has known how to handle a problem straight on.

The last Easter we spent in Florida was the one that changed how I felt about that holiday forever.

After we gave up the townhouse because Raff wanted to save money on rent, we moved into an old Spanish style house behind a bunch of clubs and bars in old Hollywood. The Florida Hollywood which was nothing like the California version. t Raff had chosen I with care, so I would be a block from his new job as a paralegal in one of those 'ambulance chasing' law firms. He'd lost the will to gut it out at law school and dropped out, leaving a boatload of student debt behind. So now he could show up to 'check on me' without any notice at all, any time of the day. After running out of excuses for the work I missed due to Raff's more brutal moods, and the bruises that resulted, I'd quit

working for the bookstore and took a job as a reader for a smaller publishing

firm in New York that needed an editor. They didn't care where I lived, so long as I

turned in my work on time, and the money was decent. No matter how it looked to the

outside world, I was just living day to day, and looking back I know the only reason I

survived this time was Rosie. I loved her more than I loved myself and so I did

whatever I had to, to keep us both safe.

To make myself and Rosie happy, this little prison of mine was decorated to the nines

for spring and the arrival of Mr. Floppy Ears. Rosie and I had spent all of Thursday

dyeing eggs and making little egg towns all over the house. The plan was for her to

leave on Friday to spend a rare weekend with her dad and his newest wife, and for us to

celebrate with Easter baskets and an indoor egg hunt when she arrived home for dinner

Sunday evening. Raff was supposed to work all weekend, so I made plans to take Annie

to lunch on Saturday.

I'd really missed her and I was ready to tell her the truth about my life. I

needed her to know that, and that I'd found the courage, and a way, to   leave Raff.

I'd managed to save every dollar I could by having work divert a big   chunk of my

pay to a bank account in NY. I'd been doing that for more   than a year, and between

the pay I'd saved and a few rather large bonuses for   some work I'd done for

my old boss on the side, I was nearly ready to put my   plan into action. I covered by

telling Raff I'd had a pay cut. He was just happy   I still had a job and it gave him that

much more ammunition when he felt like   putting me down. I was biding my time and

playing his game.

I'd also come up with a way of managing him – sort of. About six months earlier I'd gotten really sick. I had a few fainting spells as it turned out, a bad case of the stomach flu. And I discovered that the one thing Raff could not stand was a sick woman. It was so weird, but it brought out some kind of caregiver in him. He simply took over, took care of Rosie, took care of me and was the soul of kindness.

So what else could I do? I developed a chronic illness that would come on unexpectedly – or so it seemed to him. The doctor had told him it could last for a while, and had me checking in regularly for a few months.

When I finally did get better, I just didn't tell him, giving myself a reprieve that I thought would last for at least a while. On Saturday, with Rosie at her dad's, and Raff at work, I picked up Annie and we went to DeLillo's, where we'd spent so many happy times. I told her everything. It was harder than I could have imagined, but at the same time, so liberating. We cried together, she hugged me, and we made a plan. I had added her to my account in NY and she would keep the money safe for me and Rosie.

The plan was that the following Sunday night, when Raff was away with some buddies from work on a Vegas trip they'd been planning for months, I'd take Rosie and go to my neighbor's house. Minna had seen enough of my bruises to agree to help me. She'd take me to Annie's and I'd catch a flight that night to NY. From there I'd stay with a friend till I could secure passports for both of us and then go to England, to the home of one of my oldest friends and authors. Raff wouldn't know where to begin looking for us and I could start over and get stronger. It was a plan we both believed would work. And it would have, if I had only had $20 when I got home that night.

I'd finished the laundry at the neighbor's house about a half-hour before Raff came home. It was stacked all over the dining room table and I was in the middle of putting it all away when he blew through the front door. This house was one of four that had a common backyard, old Spanish stucco-style with a tiny galley kitchen, a door to the outside, and the front door. Only two ways out. I knew the minute I saw him that it would be a long tense evening. He'd been drinking, and had a mean look going before he even noticed me. In fact, he noticed my purse first. I'd left it sitting on the table, along with my car keys. I hung back in the hallway in the late afternoon shadows and watched him, holding my breath and wishing I could disappear.
He pulled out my wallet and cursed when he didn't find more than a few singles. With a snarl of disgust, he threw the wallet back at the bag, then noticed the receipt that had fallen to the floor in his search. It was the tab from lunch, fresh with a date and generous tip clearly marked.

He almost looked bewildered, like a child who picks up something written in a foreign language. For a minute I could see him as a young boy, wondering at all the things he could never understand. And for that minute, it broke my heart, everything he'd been through. But before I could move past the thought, he'd snapped his hand around my throat and held me off the floor against the dining room wall.

It's so strange, I can still feel what that felt like. I can remember the strange pale yellow walls and what the shadows across the room looked like, the stillness of the late spring afternoon, the desperation in his voice. He held

me by the throat and asked me if I wanted to die He asked me if I had the right

to live while it was clear I was stealing from him and spending my days out with someone else.

I was frozen, I didn't even try to respond. I could feel myself slipping into blackness and was almost grateful that this might finally be the end. And then I saw Rosie's tiny pink nightgown slip to the floor from the table, and the anger at what he had made of me rose through me like a wind storm.

The battle that ensued can still play through my memory's rewind at a moment's notice. Like a well-choreographed movie scene, step by step. When he let go of me and turned his back, still growling out the terms of my punishment, I made another critical error. I turned to run for the back bedroom and the window. But halfway into the doorway, he grabbed my hair and forced me the other way into the bathroom. He swung for my face and I put up my right arm instinctively to protect myself, but instead I caught the blow full force. I heard my wrist snap but I don't remember the pain. I must have looked so surprised as he drew back and this time hit his mark.

When he was finished, in less than five blows, he'd shattered my brow bone, my left cheek, my wrist, and broken my nose. I was bleeding and my eyes were beginning to swell. He pushed me in front of the mirror and said, "you're lucky you won't have to live with this face." He dragged me by my hair to the bedroom and tore off my clothes. The blows were coming so fast and hard that I fell to my knees curling up into a ball to somehow protect myself. I felt blackness closing in and the last thing I saw was a pool of my own blood forming on the floor in front of me. There was so much blood. That's all I remember.

And I can't say I'm sorry about that. When I woke up, sometime in the middle of the night two days later, he   was laying across from me staring at me and crying. In minutes, the pain was overwhelming, and I realized I couldn't open my eyes all the way. My mouth and cheek were alive with searing pain and I suddenly realized I was naked under the thin sheet.

I started to shake uncontrollably, afraid that I was about to face my final moments. But Raff just said, "I'm sorry. I hope you understand why I'm leaving you here. If I stay it will be bad. You are really bad for me and I think we both know this. I'm going away for a few days. But when I come back, you need to be gone. Do you understand?"

I think I must have nodded. I really can't tell you how long I slept after that. When I woke up I knelt on the floor by the window and saw his car was gone. I crawled to the closet found a pair of jeans and a sweatshirt and somehow got dressed. It felt like hours as I tried to confirm he was gone, and locked every door and window, and searched for a phone. My cell was missing, but the house phone was on the floor in the bathroom. I picked it up but couldn't force myself to look in the mirror.

I called Pally. "Please. Please come now. And bring Ron. I need to be gone when he gets back."

Next, I called Bill and his new wife Corinne, and told them I'd come and Pick up Rosie, but that I'd been in a car accident and was on my way to the hospital first. Corinne, who doesn't have a thoughtful bone in her body, said not to worry, as long as I got there by six before their dinner plans, it was fine.

Hours later, I lay sedated in the hospital security ward. Pally and Ron pulled every string to get me somewhere Raff couldn't find me. They'd taken me north to a private hospital, the same place Annie worked, but Raff didn't even know that place existed.

They called her, and I begged her not to come, but she wouldn't have it. The anger and sadness on her face was more painful than any of my injuries. She sat and held my hand while Pally picked up Rosie. The next day, she and Ron hired a mover and together they all went to my house and packed up everything I owned but the furniture and loaded it into a truck. And just like that, I left Raff.

It took three weeks for the surgeries to repair my badly broken wrist and my shattered face. I was still swollen, but we all stuck to the accident story. It sold well enough to anyone that mattered.

The problem was that my left ear had caught one of the blows, and my eardrum was shattered as well. I'd never get all of my hearing back in that ear but they'd manage to stitch me up so that at least it looked normal from the outside. My equilibrium would stay messed up for a while, so flying anywhere was out. My blood pressure and the time it would take to heal meant I had to find a place to stay until we could follow through with our European escape plan.

That's when I thought of Arizona. It seemed like a good idea at the time. Pally, god bless her, rented an RV and she, Rosie, and I drove across the country over the next three weeks. I'd called Lana to say I was coming out for a visit, and she'd actually seemed happy! I was hoping my bruises would be well faded by the time I arrived, but I took a lot longer for the swelling to subside than I could have imagined.

Funny thing was, Lana was happy not only to see me, but to have someone to take care of. She'd had three kids by now, all in a row, and was pregnant with twins. She had a thriving business and a husband who doted on her even if he was more biker boy than businessman. And she had just bought a big rambling house that she was more proud of than her offspring.

She promptly dictated that I should stay till I was completely healed, and that she would put me and Rosie up for the duration. She'd been in the process of building out a small mother-in-law apartment in the back of the house for whenever Maria visited, so we could stay there. I must have taken one pain pill too many, or maybe it was just the fear of going anywhere near Florida again that made me accept this offer with a grateful "yes."

For the next few weeks, I thought. And I mean that's about all I did. I thought and I floated in the pool and I thought some more. I'd told my job the same accident story that worked with everyone else, sent photos and a doctor's note that said I needed at least a month to heal and that I'd be living in Arizona for the foreseeable future. They didn't care where I lived as long as my work was good, and were kind and understanding about my circumstances. I took the kids to the park and let my mind drift around all the new possibilities of my life. Although I'd later find out that he was there when I woke up on Easter morning, I hadn't seen Andrew since that day. I was so ashamed of what I felt deep down was somehow my fault, and still in so much pain and fear when I thought about any of it, that I was happy to stay in that happy fog for a while. And so I blocked him out of my mind, and kept myself from seeing him. Ghosts only appear to those who let them in. I was afraid to look into his eyes and see how badly I'd failed. Again.

When Lana and her live-in nanny took the kids to the zoo for the day, I drove to the mountains about twenty minutes away and walked up the trails as far as I could. I sat on a bluff and stared out into a new landscape, so different than anything I'd ever seen. I'd lived through a hurricane of hurt, fear, and regret, and suddenly it seemed like there were only possibilities stretching out as far as the desert before me. I convinced myself that this is where Rosie and I could start our new life. Out here, where the air was clear, and all my mistakes seemed far beyond this valley of the sun.

My phone rings and my rhythm breaks. I hit the save button and stand up slowly, looking around for my mobile. I'm finally breathing normally but realize I've been sweating so hard that my tank top is soaked and my jaw hurts from typing so long with clenched teeth. I know from the ring it's not either of the kids, and I just don't know if I have the strength to answer the call, so I wander to the other side of the house. I lay down on top of the covers of my bed and let myself let drift into darkness.

40~All the Feels

The sound of Riley's less than subtle entrance as he makes his way through the house is my wake-up call. He plants a kiss on my cheek from above the back of the loveseat, saying he missed me while he was away with AJ and his family for the last spring snow of the New Mexico season. But I should know that snowboarding is awesome and super cool and even an Olympic sport so maybe he will do that. Then he leans in and nuzzles my shoulder while doing the "momma, momma, momma" song he is so good at. I ruffle his hair, grown long over the winter months, and linger with his warm cheek soft against mine.

This boy, this baby, now so big. My heart, my saving grace. My reward for all the weary roads I've traveled. More than I deserve and everything I love. This miracle of mine.

Turns out it was Eli on the phone last night, so I dial him back as I moved around the kitchen foraging for something that could turn in to dinner for the hungry boy. "E," he says, and I hear the smile in his voice. It's been a few days since we talked, and he promised to give me room to write what he knew would be the hardest part of my story.

"Hi," I say softly. I'm smiling despite the fact I'm finding it hard to speak. I can't find the words, but he gets the message in my silence. "How much longer, Elaine?" he asks.

"Soon," I say. "Very soon."

The days pass. And I find the words to tell the rest of it. How Drew showed up in Arizona and tried to warn me. How Raff showed up two days later, on Lana's doorstep. How this time, I was a lot stronger. I was also ready as I'd filed a restraining order as soon as I'd arrived, just in case this happened. It took six months of his calls, and threats and showing up without warning, but I didn't waver. He finally left and went back to Florida. Without me.

I had four months of peace, and I'd actually begun to believe it was all over. I'd called my old boss at the publishing company and told them I was ready to come back. They were busy and were happy to take me back. I had a month before I would pick up my new author and her tour. Rosie and I found a small apartment in a quiet neighborhood on the edge of the city where Lana lived, and we began to settle in. It was good. Lana had her babies, two little girls to complete her family, Avalon and Alexa. They were good little babies and their brothers quickly broke them in. Rosie loved having cousins and when the school year started I put her in the same elementary school as Lana's kids. Life began to feel real.

But in the back of my mind, or my heart, or deep in my soul, somewhere where I should have known better, I was anxious. And for once, I paid attention to that feeling. It would turn out to be the smartest thing I'd done in years. Maybe ever.

Back in real life, Rosie has just arrived, new boyfriend in tow, and she's laughing hysterically at some joke he's just made when she sees me across the room, trying to hide the fact that I've been crying over my laptop.

"Oh, mom," she says quietly. I don't even realize till she comes closer and sinks to her knees in front of me that my face is wet with tears. "It's ok, babe," I say.

She buries her face in my lap and I stroke her hair, remembering how close might have come to losing her. She remembers too, I know this without her saying a word. She's been my silent companion throughout this journey, knowing without my having to say it that it's as necessary an act as breath. The boyfriend has found Riley and the video game blasting from his room so we have this moment alone.

I put my hand under her chin so I can see her face. "Rosie" I say. "It's almost over you know. A few more pages, a few more words. Then it will finally be over." And she smiles this blazing smile, this quiet girl. A smile that   needs no words at all. Then she adds one that says it all. "Good."

Drew is teasing the dogs. It's one of his favorite games these days, when he's around but we're not talking much. My spring deadline is nearly here, and I have two more weeks to get the rest of this out and on paper once and for all. Once and for all. I like the sound of this.

I watch the big goofy dance of dogs and ghost boy around and in and   out of the water and let myself just soak up the sight of this man I have loved   for so long. It's bittersweet, what I am feeling, though I'm not quite sure why. I   don't want to know so I stop thinking and turn back to the computer.
But I can't write. Something is stuck, it feels like it's between my heart and my mouth, you know? Like I swallowed something too big to digest. Suddenly the   house is too

full and too happy and I start to think if I do this here, I will ruin it for everyone. I began this journey far away from here and now I know where I need to go. I grab my cell and stare out the French doors in the back. Andrew's sitting on the edge of the pool and stirring the water with his hand, the water falling slow motion from his fingertips catching the last of the summer's day sun.

"April?" I say, as my old friend answers the phone. "How are you?" She is the same, as certain as the day is long, and we make small talk for a few minutes before I confirm that the creek house on her land is empty for the next week. We agree I will come up the next day and the kids and Eli will join me on the weekend. It's still 20 degrees cooler in the mountains and I think the chill and the distance will keep me centered as I put the rest of this to paper.

Thank God for Rosie. She gets it, and doesn't make me feel a bit of guilt as I pack up my computer and some warm clothes fit for the evening chill that comes along even on the warmest spring days. I call Eli and explain my plan, inviting him to meet the kids in a week and come up to the cabin with them on the weekend. He's heard me and the kids talk about this place since we met almost a year ago, and he's happy he won't have to wait much longer to see me so he says yes before I can finish asking.

I drive up that afternoon and reach the cabin just as twilight breaks and the hillside begins to sparkle with the house lights of the cabins that dot the mountain. I park the car and hug April when she comes out to greet me, make my way to the warm familiar wooden house, and light the fire that April has laid and ready. I decide to write and not stop till it's finally all on paper. And yes, this time I mean it.

Raff came back three more times over the next two years. Each time was more or less the same. He'd show up, threaten Rosie and I'd fold. No matter what I tried, nothing worked to keep him away. When he found me alone one day at Lana's I flaunted the restraining order at him and he hit me so hard I was still unconscious when her oldest kids came home from school. I called the police and when they found him later that evening outside Lana's house, they arrested him. But 24 hours later, courtesy of Sal and Marie, he was out and hell bent on making me pay for his night in jail.

He found me again in the parking lot at the grocery store and this time he had a gun.

After that, all my courage sort of melted, and I just fell into doing what Raff wanted. He moved in with us and I didn't know how to stop him. He threatened Lana and her family and that was it for me. I kept up a front and did my best to keep Rosie as far away from the madness as possible. He'd stay for a few weeks or months, find a job, get fired, beat me up and then leave again. I lied to everyone, because no one understood how hard it was to get away. I was slowly, but decidedly disappearing.

And then one day, I got sick, this time for real. I think I must have had the flu, but I couldn't stop throwing up. He took care of me, and I was too weak not to let him. But as soon as I could sit up, he packed and left. About three weeks later he called and asked if I was better. Something told me to lie, so I said, "No. The doctors don't know what it is. I can't seem to kick this."

That kept him away for another month. While before I had faked illness and it had worked for a while, now it seemed like I couldn't really get well. The sickness acted like a shield for me, because of Raff's aversion to it. Many, many years later I would find out that this was just one of many symptoms of post-traumatic stress disorder. It's a coping mechanism many women find for dealing with what can be unimaginable pain and fear.

I remember one doctor visit, when Raff had decided to be really noble and take me to urgent care. The doctor had taken one look at the large bruise just under my ribcage and the fingerprint bruises on my upper arm, and asked gently, "What's really going on here?"
I remember looking up at him through the tears I could barely hold back, so moved by the simple act of being seen. I remember leaning in close and asking,

in a whisper, "Can fear make you sick?" How he had smiled sadly as he answered. "Pretty much."

He'd given me some valium, a whole bottle I could hide in my purse, and a script for some other medicine he said would help with the vomiting. But we'd both known I wouldn't even fill it. When I spent the next weekend in bed, Raff packed and left again. And in a few days, when I was sure he was back east, I started to feel better.

When another month passed and Raff stayed away, only calling occasionally, I thought I might finally be rid of my enemy.

In early September, Raff called in the middle of the night. Rosie was staying the night at a neighbor's house with a bunch of school friends, so I answered without thinking. He was obviously drunk, or drugged, but he was in Florida, so I let him talk. Within a few minutes, he started crying.

Through tears, he said, "I wanted you to hear while I did it."
Still groggy, I asked, "Did what?"

He laughed, but he was still crying. He started to curse, calling me names. "Whore." "Bitch." "Cunt." "Piece of shit." All through clenched teeth. Sounds and words I knew so well, but that usually accompanied by blows, kicks, punches, and body slams.

I felt the nausea start unbidden, rising through my gut. I started to   shake. "I'm in the bathroom at my parents' house. Those bastards are in the other room asleep. I'm going to yell and wake them up as soon as I do it. I want them to find me bleeding on their precious carpet. I want all of you to pay for this.

All of you. Listen bitch. Can you hear me? I'm slicing the vein now. Can you hear me?"

I suddenly snapped awake. As horrible as it felt, I wanted to just sit there and let it happen. But instead, I did the only thing I could think of. I hung up the phone and dialed the area code for Hollywood, Florida, and the operator. I told her what I believed was happening and begged her to call 911, giving her Marie and Sal's address. I stayed on the phone with her till she connected me to 911 and I knew the ambulance was on its way. And then I hung up and sat in the chair by the window across the room, staring at the phone till morning.

At about 9:30 the next morning, the phone rang and it was Marie. She told me that I'd finally gotten what I wanted, and that Raff was in the hospital. He was far from dead, she said, so I'd better watch out. I asked her if she knew it had been me who called the ambulance, and she uttered a few expletives and hung up. That sick and twisted relationship she had with her son had finally taken its toll, leaving them both without any kind of love, only twisted and bitter anger. Listening to her spew such hateful words, it was clear where Raff had gotten his talent for cruelty.

I checked in with Pally and she said he'd been released but had to do some mandatory psych care before they let him leave. She told me to be careful, and stay safe. I promised I'd do my best.

It was weeks before I heard from him, but the dread had started to build up. Fear is an animal all its own. It stalks you like shadows and footsteps in the darkness, lingers around the corner in bright daylight. It sleeps beside you and lives in the   corners of every room, in every quiet moment. It was wearing me down all over again and I didn't know how much longer I could take it. The money I'd put away for years had grown, it was more than enough to run. But a stubborn part of me that loved the life I was building in between the interruptions of Raff's unexpected visits, wanted to stay and fight. So I kept feeding the bank,   but I stayed where I was. And since I did, when the time came, I was right where he could find me.

It was September. Andrew had been around for weeks. Maybe that should have been a sign. I had stopped for a coffee with one of the local writers I'd met at the bookstore. Hank was quite a bit older, married, a great fellow. He'd lived a bit, and I'd almost come clean with him about the whole Raff thing. But trust was something I'd left behind years before. Still, he was a great sounding board for my own efforts, so when he called and suggested we meet for chat and a cappuccino at the patio café down the road from our house, I said "Sure."

I felt Raff before I saw him. I saw Hank's look of concern and I heard footsteps, and then the hand on my shoulder. "Babe!" he almost shouted as he pulled me up and into his arms. "Who's the old guy?" he growled into my neck as he forced an embrace.

I worked to extract myself from his grasp, already feeling the sweat begin to build on my forehead. "Hank, this is Raff," I said, trying to smile. Hank saw my eyes, though, and he extended his hand as he rose.

"Sir," he said, as formal as the bowtie he always wore. "A pleasure."

"Same," said Raff gruffly, not at all pleased at such a public meeting.

"Didn't you get my message?" he said, pulling up a chair and putting his arm around me firmly.

"No," I said. "I left my cell at home. When did you get in?"

He leaned back and pulled out a cigarette. "Mind?" he said in Hank's direction. Hank didn't respond. I could tell he was trying to ask me a dozen questions in a gaze, and I couldn't bring my eyes up to his. Raff lit the cigarette, and stared at Hank, marking his territory with a glare.

I looked at my watch and started talking. "Oh," I said, "Rosie. Sorry Hank, got to go," as I gathered my things. I pushed my notebook his way in the shuffle to load everything into my bag. He caught my glance and nodded, sliding it into his briefcase. "Thanks for looking at my story," he said. "I'll look forward to hearing what you think next time."

I smiled, grateful for his quick understanding. "Yes, I'll tell you everything then," I said. And then quickly followed with "about your story" and "great beginning though, keep going."

With that, Raff and I headed to my house. I knew Rosie would be at Lana's getting off the bus and busy with her cousins. It wasn't unusual for me to pick her up later if I was working, so I knew no one would miss me either. But the fact that she was safe made me feel suddenly strong.

We got to the house and Raff surveyed some new pieces of furniture, a piece of art on the wall, and a bottle of wine on the counter. "For me, sweetie?" he said, smiling.

It was strange. He seemed to be in a good mood, so I played along, waiting to see what he was up to. "How've you been feeling?" he asked as he poured two glasses." A bit better," I said. "It comes and goes."

"Well, have a drink, and sit by me," he said. "I have a lot to say to you." As he walked across the room, he took off the jacket he'd been wearing and his right wrist was bandaged. He half-smiled. I looked at him sadly and said, "I'm sorry you felt that bad, Raff."

He looked down and began to speak. "I've felt so worthless all my life. I've always thought I had to be this huge person for anyone to notice me. But I don't know how to just be. I thought you were the one who could help me be different Elaine. But all I've ever done is hurt you. I'm really sorry about that. I just came here to say goodbye for good."

I can't remember what I was feeling at that moment. I don't think I really believed him, but I'd learned long before that there wasn't much I could do in these situations. He was incredibly strong, but when he was in this kind of mood, he usually just drank till he fell asleep. But not today.

He just kept talking. Mostly he talked about the kind of life he'd wanted for us. Kids, and Rosie, and a house and all that. Everything he could never really handle if it had actually happened. Then he told me he'd gotten a job with one of his old friends back east, a schoolmate from the Catholic military boarding school in Long Island who'd gone on to a different kind of fame.

He said, "I'm going to the old country to settle a debt for him. And after that, I may not be able to come back. But it's a lot of money and it might give us the start we need."

I was so confused. What was he really saying? Goodbye for now? Or did he really expect me to follow him to Italy? I drank the second glass of wine without thinking, and forgot about the valium I'd snuck when we first got to the house. I did the one thing I'd spent years avoiding. I let myself relax. Just the tiniest bit. I remember leaning back into the corner of the couch, the autumn late afternoon light sliding through the blinds onto the space between us. I leaned my head to one side on my hand. A moment later, out of nowhere,

Raff leaned in to kiss me. "One time, Elaine. Let me be with you one more time. Then I'll leave. And I promise you I won't bother you again ever, unless you want me to."

All I knew at that moment was that I couldn't let him see the fear in me. I closed my eyes and he kissed me. He pushed me down on the couch and I didn't resist. I let it happen. I let myself remember a girl with hope, a girl who was so in love with a broken man. That girl who believed in the power of love to heal any hurt. So I gave myself to that vision of love, though I remember crying almost the whole time. Silent tears fell, till my face was wet and he felt it too. He pulled up and away and just looked at me, tears in his eyes, too. "I do love you, Elaine. More than I could ever explain. I have always loved you."

I closed my eyes and he moved away from me. I felt him walk away and then come back into the room. I pretended to be asleep, terrified that the spell would break if I so much as breathed, and that this would finally be the end of me. But instead, I felt him lay one of Rosie's blankets across my body and kiss me on the forehead. Then he turned and walked out the door.

And, as it would turn out, out of my life forever.

When I heard his footsteps fade away, I lay there for a long time till I felt sure he was really gone. Slowly I rose and locked the door and stepped into the shower. I wasn't sure what had happened, or what the future held, but I   stayed in there till I was at least awake and able to face whatever came. I knew enough to be cautious, but for some reason, I wasn't afraid.

I called Lana and asked if she could bring Rosie home, as I wasn't feeling well. She sent her oldest over with my girl and we spent the evening laughing over mac and cheese and an old favorite movie of Rosie's. And that night, I let her sleep in my bed and we both woke late Saturday morning. I felt different, but I didn't trust that feeling, or frankly, anything I felt for a long time to come.

A few days later Andrew showed up as I was working in what I pretended would someday be a garden in the back of my little apartment. He made fun of my efforts to turn the desert dust into a hospitable home for tomatoes and basil, but I kept on with it.

He said, "You know, he's really gone this time, E."

I laughed sarcastically. "Ok, Mister Mind Reader. Whatever you say."

"Fine," he said with a serious face, "but you'll see I'm right this time." He took the large watering can I kept on the stone wall I'd begun to build, and started watering the tiny seedlings along the back of the plot. I stopped and sat back on my knees and shaded my eyes as I looked up at him.

"From your mouth to God's ears," I said, "as my nana used to say." He smiled that goofy smile and said, "Yeah, I can do that."

It's late now. I'm outside on the cabin deck on a cool late May night, after one of those weird Arizona rainstorms that threatens and threatens all day, building up in piles of dark purple clouds that look full to bursting. And then it rains, like soft mist for ten minutes. But the air, the air after that feels lush and warm but with a crisp edge.

I curl up in the beat-up Adirondack chair with a blanket and April's big mutt Sam at my feet. I'm staring at the creek reflecting the last of the day's light. And I'm remembering the rest of that year.

It turned out Drew was right about Raff. I never did see him again. He went back east and then on to Italy to finish the job for his boss. But he came back to New York, and for the next three months he wandered from his old haunts in Brooklyn to Florida and back again. I guess the drink finally made him careless, and one night he picked a fight with the absolute wrong guy. Oddly enough it turned out to be an old rival from his military school days, and what started out as a bar fight ended up with a fatally fractured skull. So as it turned out, I never had to tell him what I had figured out about a month and a half after he walked out of my house that day.

Riley Francis Andrew Evans was born on the fourth of July. It was rather appropriate that this tiny infant arrived on a day that embodies every definition of the word freedom. I was unprepared for a second go at motherhood, and I'll be honest, Rosie had her doubts as well. But she came with me to the hospital and was the first person to hold him after me, and we both fell in love with the brown-eyed boy. Just like that, we knew what our family was meant to be. The rest, as they say, is history.

That's the story. I haven't left anything out, and I won't apologize for the choices I made. Aside from loving too easily, I can't think of anything I would have done differently, since I've come to realize that regret is an empty glass. Whatever time I have left I want to drink in all that life offers me. I can't make up for lost time, since it never is really lost. Every single moment has a lesson, and I'm pretty sure I paid attention. Whatever is left to learn in the moments, and days and hopefully years ahead, I think I'm ready.

43~ Waking Up

I fell asleep on the couch by the fire even though it was early afternoon, and didn't wake up until I heard the sounds of dogs and children, big and small, unloading groceries and backpacks under a full moon. Rosie walked towards me, and found me still wrapped in the blanket and sleepy-eyed, smiling as she carried groceries to the kitchen.

"Mom," she said, as she suddenly stopped and turned to me with a big grin. "Uh huh," I smiled back at her. "You finished, didn't you?"

I just kept smiling. She didn't say anything, just smiled back for a long minute, her eyes filling just a bit with tears. And then she said, "Good. Because Eli's here," and went on to put away the food.

When he walked through the door carrying a cooler stacked with board games and more groceries, I couldn't help but laugh. It was hard to find words that could make their way through my smile and still sound like words. It's hard to describe that kind of happy. That kind of relief, and release. That kind of faith in someone you've only begun to know – whether they are hundreds of miles away, or so close you can feel their pulse.

But I'm sure you know what I mean. I mean, I hope you have felt that way at least once. And if you haven't yet, well, when you do, think of me and this moment, and I know you'll smile again.

I don't remember much of that conversation, but I know we stayed up   and talked through the kids foraging for food, and building up the fire again while we drifted to the loveseat in the master suite, which had a fireplace of its own. I watched Eli light the kindling and the flames start to dance… first slowly, then building to a proper crackle and glow. It was right about then that another call came through and I saw Pally's number on the screen.

"Eli," I said, "Pal's on the line so I should probably get it. It's really late back there so I hope nothing's wrong." He said of course, and he'd   go check on the kids.

"I love you, E," he said as he got up to leave the room. And before I could actually register those words, the phone rang again.

"Hey Pal, what's up? Everything ok?" There was silence for a minute. Then she said, "Hey Elaine. Sorry to worry you. I've been up here at my dad's place helping get the house ready to sell. He's moving in with my brother Charlie, the house is just too much for him now."

I asked how they all were, how the neighborhood was, could she see my old house still from her kitchen window. She laughed. "Yep, the trees have all their leaves but that huge addition Deb made Francis build sticks way out." We laughed a bit more and then her mood shifted.

"So, Elaine. Ok, I know I'm a bad friend. You sent me those chapters of the book months ago, and I only just got around to reading them this weekend. I've been alone here since Dad went to Charlie's so I finally had the time to sit down and read them."

"Oh, no worries, I know how it is," I said, then I hesitated. "Um, what did you…" I began. But before I could finish, she said, "Oh, Elaine. It's so, I

don't know. I mean, there is so much I didn't know. I'm so sorry. I mean, why

didn't you call me, why didn't you… are you ok?"

"I am now," I said. "I finished the book this afternoon, actually.

Ironic, isn't it? I mean that you called now?"

She laughed a little, then got quiet again before responding softly, "I guess so."

I kept talking. "And it feels like I can finally move on, even though it's been so many

years. You know?"

"I can't imagine," she said, my old friend, the one who has always, always understood

me.

"I have so much to tell you, Pally. So much."

Silence again.

"I have to tell you why I'm calling so late. No, everyone is ok, nothing is

wrong. It's just, well, I finished reading the last of the chapters you sent. The   one

where you wrote about Drew's accident."

"Oh," I said. "That part."

"Yes. It brought back so many memories. I think now I finally understand

what you two meant to each other. I'm sorry I didn't see it then. I would have been

there more for you."

"It's ok, really Pal, I wasn't really 'there' for myself, if you know what I

"I get that," she said, "or at least I do now. But that's not what I called to tell   you,

really. I got so lost in all those memories that I couldn't sleep. So I came down to the

kitchen to make some tea. And the paper was on the table. When I sat down and opened it, it opened to the obituaries. Elaine, right in the center of the page was Drew's dad's photo."

My eyes filled with tears. All these years, no one had known what or where or why Drew's father had disappeared to. One day he was just gone. Drew never spoke about him, or his mom or anyone really. My mind went to him then. Did he know? Was he connected to this kind of information? Should I try to reach him? How would he feel? Pally was talking again so I tried to focus.

"It's so strange. I guess he bought back their old house a few years ago. Drew's mom stayed in the Florida place. He's been living right here. He had a bad heart, and I guess it finally broke for good. The funeral is in a week so his sister and Lucy can get into town. I'm sorry, E. I know you loved that guy, too."

I really didn't know what to say. I think the effort of finishing the book, the emotion of the last year, all of it suddenly hit me like a wave crashing down. I thanked Pally for letting me know. I told her I loved her but I needed some time to process this and I'd call her in a few days. She told me she understood and if I decided to come back for the service, of course I could stay with her at her dad's place. They'd moved him out to Charlie's, but all the furniture was still there; it would be like old times when I'd stay over in high school. My head was spinning with more memories.

"It would be so good to see you, Elaine."

"Thanks, Pally. It would be good to see you too. Let me think about it, ok?" I told her. "Oh, of course" she said. Then I hung up the phone.

I must have sat there for a while, and when I looked up, Eli was just standing in front of me, waiting. He gathered me in his arms and lifted me off the loveseat and carried me to the big four poster log bed. He laid me on top of the covers, covered me with another blanket, kicked off his boots, and laid down beside me. "Just sleep, E. Just give into it."

I wanted to fight the sleep, but it was bigger than me, so I reached out for his hand and closed my eyes. I woke up before Eli, and snuck into the shower to change and feel like a human again. Then I made strong coffee and bought it along with some bagels back to the bedroom. The kids were crashed out all over the living room and Rosie was locked away from the boys in one of the bedrooms. By the empty popcorn bowls and assorted clothes and DVD's strewn all over the room, I guessed they'd been up late, so I knew it would be a while before they were up.

On the deck outside the bedroom, it was a fresh, cool morning, and the sky was flickering with glimpses of the sunrise breaking strong through the stand of oaks in the big backyard that dropped off into the creek. A bird high above us was chattering away. I smiled and set down the tray just as Eli came up behind me, wrapping his arms around my shoulders from behind. We stood there without speaking. I handed him his coffee and motioned for him to sit.

"I've got a little story to tell you, my friend," I said. "I'm not sure coffee will be enough for this, but we can start here." And it's ok if you decide I'm crazy.

He looked at me and said, "I'm listening."

So I told him my story, in bits and pieces. I started with Drew, and since he knew about the accident, I started with the part that is the hardest. The part where he came back. I watched his face the entire time, waiting for him to shake his head and leave. Then I told him about Raff. The highlight reel. And Riley. Pretty much all of it.

I'd just spent a year writing it all down, and it turned out Drew had been right about that part.

The words just came. Just enough to let Eli know everything he needed to about this woman he'd just said he loved.

When I was done, he just looked down for the longest time. My heart was beating so hard I thought he could hear it. He looked at me then and said, "You know, I get it. I mean the Drew part. Him showing up and staying with you. I would, you know. You're pretty special. I wouldn't want to leave you, no matter what. I'd do whatever, and if he found that way, then I guess all I can say is I understand and I'm glad you weren't completely alone in all of this. I don't know how you managed to stay sane and even alive. But you did, because you're you. And I think, because you had someone to love you through it." I'm not sure what look I had on my face, but he started to grin. "Crazy. Yeah, I'm crazy about you. But I don't think you're crazy. "

I wasn't sure what to feel except relief. And so far, his words seemed sincere. I told him about Pally's call and Drew's dad dying and the funeral coming up. And he didn't even hesitate. He smiled all the way from those deep brown beautiful eyes and said, "You should go, Elaine. You should be there to say goodbye."

We spent the rest of the day with the kids, hiking the creek trail and splashing in and out of the water till everyone, including the dogs that followed us, was a muddy mess. The kids decided on a creek bath, despite the chilly water, so I went back and got them some old towels and laid a blanket with

some snacks in the backyard with instructions to stay outside until every bit of mud was gone and they were dry.

Eli and I went inside and he headed for the shower. Halfway to the door I grabbed his hand and said, "I think I should come with you."

And with that big grin I was coming to love more and more, he pulled   me inside and we took the next step.

Later that night I'm sitting on the creek steps with a glass of wine while Eli grills burgers and dogs and the kids play killer Monopoly on the picnic table in the front yard. I can hear their competition from here, all the way in the back.

Suddenly I feel Drew sit down beside me. I reach over and take his hand and he puts his head on my shoulder.

"You know," I say. He doesn't respond but I can feel his tears wet on my neck. "I'm so sorry, Drew. I know how much you loved him. And how much he loved you."

He looks at me then. "You told him," nodding back in Eli's direction, "about me." I nod. He smiles.

"Thank you," he says. I shake my head through my tears.

"I love you, Drew. Always."

He looks down and nods. "I've got to go for a while but I'll see you again. Ok?

Don't worry, I'm ok."

"You sure?"

"Yep," he says. "I'm ok. And Elaine?" I watch as he starts to walk away. "I'm happy for you. And him."

And then he's gone.

Eli is looking at me and suddenly I know by the look on his face that he's seen him. He's seen Drew, and he's seen me talking to Drew. He nods and smiles.

When the weekend was over, it was time for everyone to get back, for school, for work, for life. Rosie's lease was up so instead of renewing for another year, she had decided to move back home for what would end up being two years while she sorted out post-grad life.

I turned in the manuscript to Nora, who called me a few days later and told me I better prepare to clear my schedule for a while.

When I asked why, she said, "Well, you are going to need to do a tour to help us promote this book, but I'm guessing you can handle that, right?" I grinned and shook my head a little bit in disbelief, then took a deep breath and said, "I think I can. And thank you."

Eli headed back to California to take a few weeks away and work on the mountain

house. And I flew to Pittsburgh for Drew's father's funeral. It was a grey, rainy day

when the plane landed. I laughed to myself as I couldn't remember a time when I'd

come back to my hometown when it   wasn't that kind of weather. In my head, I

always call that cloudy color "PA   grey."

Pally was waiting outside security and we stood there holding each other for a

long time. Then we headed to her Dad's house up the hillside across from my old

neighborhood. Ron had stayed in Florida with the girls to let Pally do what she needed.

Time had mellowed him. Over the years, he'd watched so many of his buddies fool

around and lose their families. One day he realized he had the family he wanted, and he

had the only woman he ever really loved. So he changed. They were happy now, the

girls were growing up great, and Pally was once again the bright beautiful girl I had

always known.

We sat at the old kitchen table where we could look out the window and see

the house that Francis built. We talked about everything we hadn't known would

happen in our lives, all those years ago when we were full of dreams and plans. What

had let us down, what had filled us with joy. She told me how much Ron had changed.

"It's like I just met him and he's trying to get me to fall in love with him." I asked how

that was going. "It's working," she said with a grin. I told her about Eli, but not about

Drew. I thought I'd wait for the book to come out and then she could ask, or not. I mean, there is only so much you can ask of a sweet, conservative, Italian Catholic girl, even if she is your oldest and dearest friend.

The funeral was brief. There were a lot of faces I'd known from years before, changed but still familiar. The driving rain came out of nowhere so instead of moving outside under the tent for the burial, we all stayed in the church. I didn't see Drew but I wasn't sure if he wanted me too so I just closed my eyes and sent him love to get through this day. The next morning, I asked Pally if I could borrow the car and take a drive around the old neighborhood.

"Actually, that's great timing," she said. "Charlie is coming to pick me up so I can help him do some grocery shopping for Dad. He hasn't got a clue. I'll be back in a couple hours, so take your time."

I drove by our old house, but I stopped a few houses away, just to look. I didn't want to see Deb, or go inside. I didn't want to be there without Francis there. I wasn't ready then. Maybe I wouldn't ever be ready. I drove down the road to the old playground and drank in the memories. I wished the old monkey bars were still there, warm in the sun.

I knew then where I wanted to go most. My thirty years away seemed to disappear and my brain knew the way to Settler's Cabin Park, where Drew had taken me the first time he told me he loved me. I parked and wandered through the smells and sounds of spring, so different from that autumn day so long ago. I sat on the same log and sank into the sweetness of the past.

And there he was again, that boy. With the same face, the same grin, the same beautiful sea-green eyes squinting at me in the sun.

"I came to say goodbye, Elaine." He smiled. "This time, it's for good I think."

I nodded, a tear starting to form in the corner of my eye. He sat down next to me and held my hand.

"Ever since I found out about my dad, I've known that it's time. I missed so   many years with him. I'm hoping it works the same way up there as it did here.   That I can find him, and make up for that. But I don't know. I think that once I go, you know, over there… maybe I won't be able to come back."

I squeezed his hand and said, "You have to try, Drew. I love you and whatever lies ahead for both of us, I know we will be ok. Does that sound crazy?"

He turned and laughed. "Crazier than you talking to a ghost for 30-odd years?"

We hugged and laughed and cried a little. I was so glad that we were here, in   this place where our love began and where it could live forever. Somewhere I   can visit to feel just the way I do at this moment.

"Elaine, can you come with me to the cemetery? I want to go to the grave. I was afraid to go there when they buried him. I don't think I want to do this without you."

When I get to the cemetery Andrew is already there, walking towards the new grave covered with flowers under the brightest maple tree in the cemetery. As we approach, I see a stone just to the right, and I'm confused as I know it's too soon for his father's headstone to have been laid. Then I understand.

I started to shake as I read the words and understood. This was where the boy I'd loved since the day I met him was laid all those years ago. He turned to face me and blocked my vision. "This is where we have to say goodbye, E. I can't move on until you walk away."

I held onto his arms, unsure if I could really do this. He suddenly looked past me and smiled. I turned my head and couldn't really take in what I saw.

Eli was standing there, a hundred yards away. He and Drew shared a smile. I heard Eli say, "I've got her."

Drew looked back at me and said, "I had it all with you Elaine, and I'm so grateful. I'll never stop being in love with you." His face shimmered in front of me till all I could see was the stone again.

Just as I thought I couldn't stand, I felt the arms of the person who understood everything reach out to hold me up. And I realized that it's true what people say. Death isn't the end of the book, just the closing of a chapter. And the beginning of a whole new story.

The End – For Now

Acknowledgements

The experience of writing this book had been a very solitary one, until I met the incredible Jena Schwarz. This Poet, Promptress, Writing Coach and Editor extraordinaire encouraged me to take a languishing manuscript and love it back to life. Jena supported me with kindness and care every step of the way and for that there is simply not enough gratitude. To the original Inky Path Writing Group, thank you for inspiring me to share my words, by sharing yours with vulnerability, humility and humor.

To my very first reader, Courtney Wells Carter, who read as I wrote, and gave me the push I sorely needed the day she grabbed me by the shoulders, stared into my eyes and said, "It's so good. You need to finish this". I will always love you for that.

To my advance readers who encouraged me with their support and candid feedback as I worked through the kinks in telling a story that moves back and forth through time, in no particular order; Alex, Fiona, Claire, Krisann, Darshon, and Laara.

To Shirley Kirlan (my 'woosie, and my Annie) for giving me her blessing to share what I know was often hard for her to read. To Nancy, the inspiration for my 'Pally' and so much more. To Rosanne, who has always shared her heart, her home and my journey, for reading this book in one day and then telling me everything I needed to hear in one amazing hug. To the sisters of my heart – Bella and Luci – for showing me the power of unconditional love. And finally, to my children, Tessa and Jordan- who show me every day what matters most.

Thank you all- may the love and kindness you've shown me be given to you a thousand times over.

Tia Finn is an artist, life coach and storyteller, whose love of words and the infinite beauty and madness of life make it impossible to turn away without documenting the experience. She splits her time between visits to her children and family in Arizona and Florida and her home in London, which she shares with lots of art, history, and a few *very* friendly ghosts.

To learn more about Tia and her work visit
www.tiafinnauthor.com

60790443R00159

Made in the USA
Lexington, KY
18 February 2017